D1414481

CELIA'S
SONG

ALSO BY LEE MARACLE

FICTION

Sojourner's Truth and Other Stories (1990)
Sundogs (1991)
Ravensong (1993)
Daughters are Forever (2002)
Will's Garden (2002)
First Wives Club: Coast Salish Style (2010)

NON-FICTION

Bobbi Lee: Indian Rebel (1975, revised 1990)
*I am Woman: A Native Perspective on Sociology
and Feminism* (1988, 1996)
Oratory: Coming to Theory (1990)

POETRY

Bent Box (2000)

COLLABORATIONS

We Get Our Living Like Milk from the Land (1994)
Telling It: Women and Language Across Cultures (1994, with Betsy
Warland, Sky Lee, and Daphne Marlatt)
My Home As I Remember (2000)
*Reconciliation: The En'owkin Journal of
First North American Peoples Vol. 13* (2002)

CELIA'S SONG

LEE MARACLE

Cormorant Books

Canada Council for the Arts **Conseil des Arts du Canada**

 Canadian Heritage Patrimoine canadien

The publisher gratefully acknowledges the support of the Canada Council for the
Arts and the Ontario Arts Council for its publishing program. We acknowledge the
financial support of the Government of Canada through the Canada Book Fund
(CBF) for our publishing activities, and the Government of Ontario through the
Ontario Media Development Corporation, an agency of the Ontario Ministry of
Culture, and the Ontario Book Publishing Tax Credit Program.

LIBRARY AND ARCHIVES CANADA CATALOGUING IN PUBLICATION

Maracle, Lee, 1950–, author
Celia's song / Lee Maracle.

Reprint. Originally published: Toronto : Cormorant Books Inc., 2014.
ISBN 978-1-77086-451-1 (pbk.)

I. Title.

PS8576.A6175C44 2015   C813'.54   C2015-900098-X
                                         C2014-905125-5

Cover art and design: Angel Guerra/Archetype
Interior text design: Tannice Goddard, bookstopress.com
Printer: Friesens

Printed and bound in Canada.

The interior of this book is printed on 100% post-consumer waste recycled paper.

CORMORANT BOOKS INC.
10 ST. MARY STREET, SUITE 615, TORONTO, ONTARIO, M4Y 1P9
www.cormorantbooks.com

Dedicated to all those children
who were removed from our homes
and who did not survive residential school.

CELIA'S SONG

I

THERE IS SOMETHING HELPLESS in being a witness.

No one comes here anymore, just me. I can't seem to resist returning to the place where everyone died. Some insane kind of illness overtook them, burned them with its heat; the monster illness disfigured them before taking their lives. It's so quiet. The longhouse is decrepit now. I stand, transfixed. It looks as though a single shingle had blown off the roof during a storm, beginning the process of destruction, precipitating the damage inside. That single missing shingle allowed the rain to leak onto the woven mats covering the bones on every bench of the house, attacking the blankets in the southwest corner. The fire in the centre died long ago, but the wet ashes make the inside seem forlorn. A lonely feast bowl squats near where the fire had been. The damp has spread to all corners and, over the decades, storm rains invaded and reinvaded the longhouse, tearing more and more shingles in a steady rake. The wet penetrated. Summer heat spurred the blankets' decay. The bones lie naked underneath the rotted weavings. Under these the dead rot; even after all this time, the smell of them commingles with the mouldering blankets and mats. The scent is horrific: mould, flesh, and goat fibre rot fill the house. The bones of the dead loathe their own stench.

They should not be here. I worry for the dead.

Piled up in the last longhouse of this village, behind the perishing cedars just before the hill, the bones fret inside the decrepit structure. The people were here one day, then gone. Some small part of me resents their departure. They did not volunteer to leave, but I resent their departure nonetheless. Some days, I resent their absence; it creates such a desolate landscape, but today is not such a day. Still, I empathize with the petulance that simmers inside the angry bones. The intensity of their rage grows with time. The bones wait; wait for burial, for ceremony, for their final resting place. They shift and rattle their discontent.

I breathe deep. There is not much I can do but visit and witness for them.

That was before the storm broke.

Before the storm, the serpent protecting the house front hung by a thread; no one had fed or acknowledged him. I doubt that many living humans know about this village. It is not the only one, not that it matters. What matters is that the serpent had a right to be upset. The singing had stopped for the house protector before the inhabitants had died. It stopped during the prohibition laws. No singing, the newcomers had said. This seems comic to me and I want to laugh; I mean, how bad can singing be? But it had been devastating to the people and to the serpent, so I restrain myself.

The humans broke their contract with the serpent when they stopped feasting and singing for him. This breach granted permission to the serpent to slide from the house front and return to sea, but both heads did not want to leave — just one did, the restless head, the one that preferred shadowland. Current living humans did not seem worried about this breach with the serpent. I wonder if perhaps they no longer believe they need protection from the serpent. In any agreement, both parties must hold up their end in a timely manner for the deal to be secure. I guess in these days of cars and electric fire, it may not appear all that rational to restore old practices.

The bones think me a tad too generous. They lack generosity.

Creeping along the longhouse wall are bracken, wild carrots, and ill-scented weeds, some edible, some not. The plants lack lush leaves. Bent and withering, they died looking crippled before they had a chance to mature — as though the loneliness for humans had affected their ability to grow straight and strong. But still they had reached for the sun. I peek inside the house: the fleshless bones whimper songs of yearning, yearning for the sea as though they continue to miss it. They missed much more. They missed babies gurgling from their cradleboards; they missed toddlers just before they spoke words; they missed the music of song and they missed dance; they missed the sound of eagerness only youth make as they roll out the dugouts and challenge the sea for the first time; they missed the vision of the musculature of their young sons as they paddled to visit another village.

I miss all this too.

But for the crippled cedars, twisted arbutus, faltering alders, fir and spruce and the odd berry bush, nothing much lives here anymore; the old camas fields and riparian vegetation are dead. No more sea asparagus, sea cabbage, not a single sea vegetable. Coyote, bear, wolf, and deer fled after the people died. They never returned. I am the only visitor. I keep coming back to reminisce. Like the sea, the people who once lived here were by turns vivacious and steady, peaceful and vicious, consistent and variable — hardworking and lazy. I love them. I can't seem to live without them.

Before I get a chance to remember them fully as individuals, rain clouds from the west gather and form a thunderhead. It rolls toward the village. I need to seek cover. The wind storms so much that the cedars edging the lagoon in front of the village have been crippled by it, bent in half as though heading for shore. The inland trees lean away from the wind. I shiver as I imagine the sun quivering before the clouds thicken and obscure its light as they grey the sky. The noise increases.

West Wind screams now, sounds agonized. The storm hits. I take cover behind an old log to watch.

Night crawlers scatter. Eels, electric and dangerous, slither for cover, dive to the bottom of the sea, aiming for the protection of the grasses there. Cracked branches flail. Leaves flip and fly in the raging wind. Arbutus skin peels, swirls among the leaves as wind punishes the coast as for an imagined infraction. West Wind's bite scrapes the water in long furls of twisted rage and hurls it at the shore. Its rake claws at stone, sand, dirt, folds them, drags them from their moorings and dumps them in a heap at the end of the point marking the bay. The wind pushes and pulls toward the shore and away from it as though unable to decide whether to blow from land to sea or sea to land. It pecks at the soil, attacks every inch of shore, gouging loose the dirt, twirling it in small dusters, tossing it away in disgust.

Disgust is powerful.

The slim point at the end of the lagoon is reshaped by the storm; as the rain gathers dirt from the mountainside and the wind tosses dead wood debris about, the point steadily widens and thickens at one end.

I am fascinated by wind's work. This is no ordinary storm; something is up. I cringe as the wind approaches the log I am standing on and threatens to carry me away. I crouch close to the thin space between land and log, but cannot resist peeking to watch. In a moment of respite from the wind, I peek out at the land and watch as a lone cedar, ill and fragile, breaks at its base. I gasp.

I know Celia is watching this storm. She lives in Sto:lo territory, a long way from this empty Nuu'chalnulth village. Out of the blue she hears a shriek. "Who is that?" I hear her ask. She stands up in time to see cedar branches scattering in all directions until only their naked trunks face the wind, their roots clutching desperately at what little is left of the soil beneath them. Celia has no idea where the storm is taking place or why she is seeing it.

I know she is a seer. Few people actually believe in seers, but I am mink — the shape-shifter, the people's primary witness. I know things others don't.

Celia stares at the spindly trees buffeted by the wind. "Those trees may not survive." She sees me. I know what she is thinking: *I wonder what mink is doing there.* A tear escapes my eye. *I do not mean to do that.* She can see that I want to leave but can't seem to.

"Where is this?" I don't know if she means this to be said aloud, but I hear it.

My heartbeat speeds up, my legs shake. I can't stop rubbing my paws one over the other as my fear increases. *I need to witness this. There is no one else. The screaming wind, the flying debris, and the pelting rain are too much for me.* Celia hears me.

She watches as mink struggles with fear. She watches him leave his rotting log and duck behind a stone. She isn't crazy about watching the storm, but the pungent scent of decaying cedar soothes her and so she continues to watch mink as he struggles for breath and courage. She hears him say, "This is how it is to die in a war, nothing heroic about it."

"What is this all about? War? What war?" Celia wonders out loud. "Pick one," she answers herself. "These people are always at war. There are so many to choose from."

The wind swirls about me and blows toward the sea. On its

way it uproots the last of the firs at the end of the point. The few remaining crippled cedars and spruce perish shortly after. I stand upright, behind my stone. *I am a witness. I am obligated to watch the destruction.*

Celia's attention is drawn to the sunken longhouse, downhill from mink, close to the lagoon. She thinks she hears the bones in the longhouse talking; they seem to want this storm, behave as though they need it. She hears them say: "Someone has to pay for decades of neglect. Someone has to appease our need for respect." She shudders. Up until now, her delusions have centred on humans in full form; even the dead she saw had bodies. This is the first time she's heard bones talk.

I know the bones are waiting for interment, but there will be no burial for them. The living humans do not know they are here.

The bones want more than interment, they want to hear war songs that capture this drama, commit it to memory and identify the enemies for them, but the humans who could clarify these things are dead.

Inside me an abyss of fear forms. I cannot contain this emptiness, nor can I prevent the fear from sinking roots inside my body. I have been witness to so much of the old bones' mythology; the dead deserve a witness to the story unfolding, but still I do not want to stay. *I have to leave. I so want to leave, but this story cannot unfold without a witness. This story needs a witness.*

Why me? I rub my paws, one over the other.

The dead cherished myths while alive and the people gave the stories weight at one time, but now so much has changed that I am not sure of anything. I shift from one foot to the other and then focus on the storm. In a perverse and fearful way, I like the looking; but I am not so crazy about this business of shaking with fear that the unfolding story inspires in me. I have some doubt about the intelligence and safety of staying behind to witness, but some piece of me believes that doubt is somehow the best part of being alive;

I love the suspiciousness of doubt and all the angles for retelling stories that this doubt spawns.

This story deserves to be told; all stories do. Even the waves of the sea tell a story that deserves to be read. The stories that really need to be told are those that shake the very soul of you.

I prepare to be shaken.

This happened even if it didn't.

THE SCENE MAKES NO sense to Celia. In between watching, she fixes herself tea and eventually decides it all happened far away and has nothing to do with her. She lights a candle and settles into an easy chair at the head of her kitchen table and gets ready to sort her mail. She had put the easy chair there to encourage her to deal with the mundane business of sorting the mail, and although this has made her weird in the eyes of her family she leaves it there. The mail should get her mind off the ocean.

The stack of letters squats stoutly on the table, ready for inspection. She collects mail from Friday to Wednesday, but answers it on Thursday night. Although it is one a.m. she begins to sort the letters in two stacks, junk mail and bills. This is her Thursday ritual. She has taken to retiring not long after supper, fatigued by the business of living in an empty house. Tonight she resisted by watching several hours of television. It has been difficult to carry on the mundane tasks of living since her son died, in fact she can only endure the mundane in her life if she engages it as a ritual. The business of bill paying is one of her favourite rituals; it makes her feel so grown-up. She also likes the junk mail, brightly coloured and full of promising ads.

The thing about being a shape-shifter is I can alter my presence from one place to the next. One moment I am in Nuu'chalnulth territory, the next in Sto:lo territory.

By the flicker of candlelight Celia sorts her mail, bills on her left, junk mail on her right. In the eerie glow of candlelight she wrestles with a vague memory. The memory seeks to interrupt her ritual. She shrugs twice to shake off its persistence, but the memory is bent on coming. Se'ealth's words invade and the business of opening bills and writing cheques recedes. "The white man should understand that there is another way of seeing." *This is not my memory*, Celia thinks. Tiny beads of sweat form across her forehead. She does not want to lose her mind just now. The candle flickers in the direction of the window; a draft spills wisps of fresh air into the room, drawing the candleflame toward it instead of away. *How odd*. She shifts her weight. *Damn*. For some crazy reason her weight bothers her and a strange fatigue sweeps through her. She sighs just as Se'ealth's longhouse collapses and a little mink leaps away from the house front, barely escaping. Celia is jolted upright. She wonders what some old dead Suquamish chief has to do with her — logging, she supposes, but what is with the mink? She lets the question go.

LOGGING IN STO:LO TERRITORY has been dying, dying like Se'ealth's longhouse died. Its death throes affect the Sto:lo; it has brought another source of poverty. No trees in the last century had meant no nets, no hooks, no bowls, no clothing, no weirs, but now it means no means of acquiring sustenance. No one knows how to carve the hooks or the bowls or make the clothing, and weirs are still illegal to use.

Celia is apathetic about the end of logging. She has no husband working in the bush. Hunger and poverty are not strangers to her; the only people who bemoan hunger and poverty are those who never experience it.

Celia lives in one of her family's old homes, one of the ones left behind after most of her family acquired mortgages for new houses. She remembers being unable to grasp the concept of requiring a mortgage to build a house — weren't men supposed to build the things? She could not get a handle on the difference between a mortgage payment and rent. The amount was the same, but the renters had their houses fixed for free, the mortgagers had to fix their own. It didn't make any kind of economic sense to her, so she had declined the offer of a new house.

When Celia hears mink whisper "This is war" she stops opening her bills and focuses on what is happening. She does not want to carry on watching, but like mink she can't resist looking; she wants to know what is going on. Since her son's death, seeing chaos has been her only pleasure. The trees, shrubs, even the dead are locked in battle; everything struggles against the onslaught of wind and rain. The screams of the wind sound deliberate. It scares her. She hears a sound at the front of her house and runs to the window. She looks and listens, anticipating an intruder. Intruders aren't common anymore. White men used to come on to the reserve, grab a girl walking down the road, rape her, and return her. This stopped when Buddy, the chief's son, shot at them. The RCMP tried to find out who the shooter was, but no one would tell. The white boys left them alone.

What Celia sees stuns her. Her front yard is gone. In its place is the ocean.

She falls into the story.

THE MOUNTAINS ABOVE THE ocean are naked. They look as though they have been skinned bald. *There should be berry bushes,* Celia thinks. *Maybe spindly new trees. But before anything had a chance to take root the rain dragged soil and seed to sea.* I stare, catch Celia watching, and wonder how she has arrived here. The bare stones along the shore offer no buffer against the rain, and they cannot soak up the shock of wind. *Maybe she is another witness.* Celia doesn't like the direction this story is going, but now she is as captured by it as I am. But to her it doesn't matter; she thinks none of this is real; she thinks it's just another of her delusions.

Transform. My murmur comes from under the stone. I am about to turn tail and run, but some part of me freezes me to the spot. *Transform to what, an eagle, a human, anything but a four-legged?* As the wind subsides, I wrench myself free of the storm and dash up the bald mountainside. At the top my body shifts; my arms become wings, my back legs become talons, my tail becomes feathers. I fly and perch atop the last spruce so as to continue my vigil from this safe place.

Celia retreats from her window. On a rickety table made of pressboard that serves as a nightstand, an old plastic clock reads 2:13 a.m. She has not finished paying her bills. Celia puts the coffee on. When it's ready, she pours herself a cup and sits down. She has to finish the bills.

This is not the first time the blue waters of the Pacific have threatened to seduce her. She was six when she first witnessed this ocean. While her parents visited a relative, she wandered along the shore, excited by its strange fluidity. She had liked the way the sea stretched out as though it did not want to stop. It made her feel flush in a way land did not. Land and its erratic markers — tall trees, low shrubs, hills, valleys, gullies — disturbed her, but the sea flowed out to the edge of the earth and seemed to just fall off and this filled Celia with awe. The land was still, but the sea never stopped trying to get somewhere and she liked that. She had approached the tide's waves tentatively, dipped her feet in the edges of its watery skirt, squealed with delight when the waves advanced and then retreated as they caught her. She toyed with the tide. Other children were there, playing the same game. She squatted in the sand and stared at the water. Its curved flow moved outward in wider and wider arcs. Its shifting, rocking beauty mesmerized her. When Stacey came to get her, she was burnt on one side of her near-naked body.

Celia twirls her coffee cup as she gazes into the candle. She sees the falling trees scramble away from the wind. The delusion becomes a grisly scene of clearcut logs lying dead, stripped of bark, their bare flesh showing red or yellow. Old and unused logging roads wind their way through these bare mountains. It is nearly a wasteland. "Desolation Row" comes to mind and she sings the words of her favourite Dylan song. Not far away stands a grove of branchless, skinned alder; in front of them cottonwood saplings lean helter-skelter, ready to fall over. They all look as though they are waiting for a ship or truck to haul their anorexic trunks away. Clearcutting. Her great uncle Hank Pennier hated clearcutting with chainsaws; he said it was chickenshit logging. At least with an old Swede saw the tree had a fighting chance. But this scene is not about her family and she knows it.

Celia cannot connect these images to her present and although this is not unusual it always unnerves her. "I'm delusional," she complains out loud. The delusions convinced her family and her fellow villagers that she was half-crazed; even in her own mind they mark her as odd. They come more often now. Disruptive as they are, she ought to reject them. But she feels compelled to embrace them, or at least get used to them. Controlling them never seems to work. Not having them is not an option. There is no sense fighting what she can't change.

I want her to know they are not delusions, but have no way to reach her.

The sea appears and disappears as though playing a game of hide-and-seek; intermittently, old sayings and old phrases infiltrate the game. *Chaos, my life is about chaos.* The candle shrinks, nearly goes out, then bursts back into flame and the curtains shuffle reacting to the shrinking candle. Then the candlelight flips, turns, shrivels, and ignites.

Fire is a dancer. It is possessed of its own will. Celia's candleflame dances, sure of itself; its fire gives the room an odd sort of light. It glows soft blond on black, then it fires up bright as day, then like lightning it floods the room, painting it soft and pale, then dark gold. Then the room is awash with the candle's dim light breathing steady, nearly motionless, then constricted; it casts unruly shadows.

Rekindle the fire. Rekindle the fire. Celia ignores my hiss. *Maybe she can't hear.* I lick my paws.

In the space between fire-flicks, together the sea, the war, the bones, and I sway, dance forward and back, between erratic light and the dark folds of night. The fire bends and swirls, entices Celia to come forward, to slide into this waltz, to dance and slide into its shadowland.

In shadowland, you can see the frightening underbelly of continuous war, see its unrepentant violation, and see its relentless insistence on expressing wrath.

Seduced by the flicks of light Celia sways, lets the fire tease her. As it dances, her mind blurs and new images invade her reality. The waltz becomes more insane, the flames grow aggressive, large and threatening. Celia fights to extricate herself by focusing on her kitchen, the old cupboards, hand-hewn, unvarnished, with curtains in place of doors, but this doesn't help. She shifts her attention to the pile of bills, anything to end this crazy moment; but this too is futile. She is losing her battle with fire. Her emotions rise, raw and murky. She needs clarity, but there is nothing clear in this shadowland. *Fire is how we are* siem. *Fire is how we are.* I can't help sighing.

The tide unfurls destructive crisp wave after destructive crisp wave, each one seeming to have a specific goal, as though the ocean has a plan. On their retreat, the waves lay out strips of seaweed to form a dark green-black ribbon that tracks the sea's journey along the shore. The tide carries its debris, drops it shamelessly on shore. The mountains behind look almost ashamed of their nakedness.

Celia sees the tide grab bits of dead wood tangled with detritus from some party. She cannot stop looking now. She is caught in the seaweed ropes. Beer bottles, chip bags, hamburger wrappers are braided into the ribbon of seaweed. A wisp of shame crawls through Celia's gut. As the refuse whirls in the tide's folds, Celia's shame becomes a melancholy song without clear language. Some of this debris began as an insult to women; it makes Celia shudder to think about the underwear and condoms left behind on the open vista of the shore, unmindful of the owner's need for modesty. She focuses on the underwear: who was the owner, was she the intended love interest of the man who left behind the condom? She hopes so. She hopes that there had been some kind of intelligent consent between the man and woman. She gasps: the woman's panties are so small. Was she old enough to consent? Beach parties, too much beer, and the hormone rush of pubescence are a dangerous recipe for young girls with a desperate need to experience some sort of affection.

It happened a long time ago, Celia thinks, *This part of Nuu'chalnulth territory has been deserted for a long time — not to worry.*

But it does not help.

Celia shivers, sips her cold coffee and withdraws her focus from the panties. She concentrates on the waves, each linked to the next, becoming a series of snakes bent on destruction. *Waves are odd,* Celia thinks. *Even as they retreat they look as though they are rolling forward.* The shore, the snapping cedars take on a sinister desolation as the storm gains intensity. Wind, sea, and rain rage. The snake of waves, slate grey and menacing, topped by whitecaps cruel and triumphant, threatens to pull the entire shore into the belly of the ocean. The massive storm is a monster now. The weirdness of the storm acquires a strange ordinariness despite its violence.

I leave. I am fascinated by certain newcomers and so go to see them.

II

IN A LAB NOT far from the sea, a film reel whirs as four men watch. Its images are hazy. Sam Johnson, Frederick Bauer, Davis Jameson, and Thomas Friesen are mute and still, until something odd appears — a shadow that casts itself from the fifth minute to the eighth. These guys don't know their lab is smack dab in the middle of Musqueam territory. Everyone used to know that. Everyone used to respect that. But these guys are a tad thick. Now they are magical.

Frederick sits upright, hands on his knees, leans toward the screen.

Like that is going to help. Blond, tall, and forty, Frederick Bauer earned his doctorate in marine biology earlier than most. He has since worked at the university as a professor and as its lead researcher. Methodical and brilliant, he rarely lets his emotions get entangled in his work.

I always thought this was odd about the newcomers. I mean, no emotion? Go figure.

Frederick says nothing about the shadow, just raises his eyebrows. Sam is a little too new-agey for his colleagues; he cocks his head and whispers, "Something is wrong here." Davis rolls his eyes; it's just a shadow. Thomas points out the obvious. They all mumble a series of mm'mmhs ... maybes ... can't bes ... almost a miles ... mm'mmhs.

"There is something there," Sam offers. Frederick thinks maybe Sam has something, but he also knows Sam is quick to jump to conclusions. It's not that Sam neglects to test his conclusions, but Frederick mistrusts this quickness. He waits for the reaction of the others; clearly they are not so sure.

"It's bad film," Davis scoffs. Thomas nods in agreement. Frederick suspects the bias in these two men; they do not like life to upset their science. He smiles to himself, for at least their science was jostled a little.

I want to laugh, but I am witness and so I swallow it.

The shadow ends. Sam stops the film; each man looks at the others, and then looks back at the film. They are all suspicious now. Sam hits the rewind button and replays the segment. All four men barely breathe as the film replays the same shadowy image.

"What the hell, the thing must be a mile long," says Sam.

Davis doesn't think so, and he prepares to argue.

"A little like Hitchcock," Frederick quips. He hopes this will loosen the tension in the room. It does not.

None of the men can laugh about what they are seeing. Each has their own agenda, and this shadow is not on any of them. These guys struggle so hard to be objective, but can't get past their agendas. I leave them. I decide to retreat to another era.

SE'EALTH'S LONGHOUSE CRASHED AND his village became Seattle. Then the longhouse disappeared. I lick my paws, wondering what this has to do with Celia, the lab, and the storm. I blink and I am back at the lab and Celia is there watching. In one room, she catches sight of men in lab coats — white men, official looking. These men are quiet.

Me, I study illusions, hallucinations without any apparent motive.

Celia believes that environmental degradation threatens the earth.

Well, actually it threatens humans and the lifestyle of humans on this part of the earth, and a good many scientists have studied the ocean because of that. The earth has been through cataclysmic change a few times, every time a lot of humans perished, but the earth has survived.

From their conversation, Celia gathers that these men seek evidence of previous vegetation, unknown life before the coastline was manipulated by the newcomers. Celia chuckles; some old Indian could just tell them what sorts of tender sea vegetables perished on the coast, but then these guys would have to believe them. Their science is not about belief; their science is about proof.

This makes me laugh too.

THE OCEAN WAVES CONTINUE to thicken and roll forward, but the white froth that tipped the waves has disappeared. "Why are the waves so grey near the shore?" Celia's hands tremble as she watches the waves gain volume. She does not like the looks of the size of the swell nor does she like the feeling the waves inspire. She no longer feels compelled to watch. She shrugs, returns to her bills, and thinks no more about the ocean.

"HALF THE WORLD HAS stories of sea monsters, no less on this continent," Sam argues with the men in the lab as they head for Davis's office.

"Someone would have seen it before now?"

Thomas doesn't disguise his exasperation. He believes the film is defective. Sam wants the film tested for defects, but only because he believes it isn't defective at all. Although it's absurd to waste time speaking about it until the film is tested, they continue to argue. *I find them kind of funny.*

Neither Sam nor Davis challenges the notion that as scientists their own beliefs should be held suspect, nor do either of them think that making decisions based on belief without checking, researching, or verifying the evidence is odd.

"By 'someone' you mean you and me. Have we actually seen the atom split?" Sam challenges. "Someone has seen it."

Frederick is curious as to why Sam is so touchy about the stories of people disconnected from his heritage and scientific world, but he says nothing.

"Don't pull that race card on me, you know what I mean: some scientist would have seen it."

"No scientist believes there is a Sasquatch, but in the state of Washington, if you cause one to die through harassment of any sort you will be charged with murder. Look, I'm not convinced it's anything, but as scientists we are given to inquiry, so let's inquire." Sam's voice is sure and steady.

"It's a waste of time; we're marine biologists, not myth hunters." The possible reality of a sea creature challenges Thomas's sense of self; it's an affront to his education.

"Any judgment not based on inquiry is superstition," Sam snarls back as he fills another cup of coffee. He spoons three teaspoons of sugar into the cup, stirring it so hard that it spills. He curses, grabs a towel, and wipes it up. "In the forties, science held that only humans had language, but the Natives believed they could converse with orcas and whales. Every scientist laughed at them. By the nineteen-eighties, when the Natives who could speak the language of the orcas were wiped out, scientists discovered that orcas and whales do have language, they engage in conscious communication."

I want to tell him that I believe he is a sugar addict, but he would not hear me.

Frederick frowns; there's just a little too much push in Sam's voice and it makes Frederick wonder. Are his relatives Native?

"Just this past spring, you remember, three whales were stuck in Arctic ice. The Inuit offered to talk them out. The marine biologists forbade them to try. At a cost of three million, icebreakers from Russia and America were hired to clear a path. Every day the Inuit came and offered to talk them out. Two weeks and one dead whale later, they were nowhere near freeing the trapped whales and the other two were near death. They relented and let the Inuit talk them out. These old hunters drilled holes in the ice one hundred metres apart, then they went to where the whales were trapped and started humming. They walked across the ice, humming. The whales followed."

I remember that story. I'm surprised this guy does too.

"What is your point?" Clearly aggravated, Thomas is unable to stay silent.

"We aren't the only people who know things, Thomas."

I have to say something about that. People aren't the only beings who know things. I am standing right outside the window in full view, talking out loud, but these guys don't see or hear me.

"So what are you suggesting, Doctor Johnson? Should we find some old Native conjurer to shake his rattle and tell us what this shadow on our film is?" Thomas Friesen scoffs at his colleague.

"No. I think we should see a scientist who might know something about mythology," Sam answers.

"Before we do that," Frederick suggests, "we should have the film checked by the AV department." Frederick loves to be orderly, loves the proper order of things. It's why he became a scientist: first things first. Order gives him the courage to reach beyond the known.

"Splendid, some attempt at rational thought prevails," Dr. Friesen triumphs.

"Let's get a copy first," Sam cautions.

"Why?"

"In case the Audio Visual department ruins the original."

This makes Frederick laugh. "Okay," he says, and swings into his jacket.

LATER, OVER LUNCH, WHILE the film is being checked, Sam asks Thomas what he meant by "Some attempt at rational thought prevails."

Thomas is sorry he raised it. He is pretty sure Sam's question was rhetorical, so he doesn't answer.

"Not many scientists invent things, did you know that, Friesen?" Sam takes up the dead air between himself and Thomas. Thomas sips his coffee and feigns staring at the menu.

"Millions of items are invented each year," Sam continues, "some of them dangerous, some absurd, useless, some vital to human existence, but no one knows which until a scientist gets curious about it and tests it. Scientists further knowledge, we don't create it, and we don't invent. We test, we inquire, but we do so only if we possess a nagging doubt about the veracity of all beliefs. It's a pretty closed mind that dismisses testing, even of the craziest beliefs."

Some intelligence is being born here. I can't help smiling.

"And a completely open mind is also dangerous," Thomas says. "We could spend years investigating old wives' tales. To what end?"

This would not be wasted time.

"As scientists, we recognize our beliefs constitute a ball and chain," Frederick says. "Moving to test the mythology before we test the film is an unnecessary attachment to belief, just as refusing to test the myth once we have tested the film is an obsessive attachment to disbelief."

Frederick is one of the hopeless who now inhabit Turtle Island.

Sam nods. He can live with that.

III

BEFORE THE STORM, THE serpent decorating the house front hung by a thread. Both its heads watched the land for what seemed an eternity; day by day, one head grew hungry and anxious. The quiet about the house suited the restless head, because it was both death-filled and promising. The serpent could apprehend pending movement and the restless head grew excited as his sense of duty to those whom he had once protected diminished. The smell of the building was an affront to him. Even more, he was offended that the people had neglected to feed and honour him.

I came back to the hill to watch the serpent. I listen to the heads talking to each other.

"How long in human time have we been here? When will we know that the original contract is sufficiently broken to warrant our sliding out from this house front and slithering back to the sea?" Restless asks Loyal.

Something is wrong here.

"Time was not specified, only intentions," Loyal answers. "Intentions counted then, more than time ..."

Restless sighs and keeps moving in the direction he had set the conversation.

"The intentions of the humans were to honour us," Restless reminds Loyal. Loyal thinks his other head sounds pouty and this worries him.

"They will. Our obligation is to protect the house from miscreant behaviour and from doubt consuming human will."

"Protection in exchange for honour. It has been two centuries since anyone lived in the house."

"I am responsible only for holding up my obligations." Loyal think Restless sounds more pompous than pouty.

"The humans have not acted upon their intentions for so long."

Loyal concedes. This does not sound so pompous.

"A deal is a deal. Intentions must be executed or all bets are off," Restless ventures. "We are not responsible for their conduct; their intentions must be executed of their own free will." He bobs in the direction of his twin.

"That sounds childish. They behave appropriately. We should too. Next you'll say 'They started it.'"

"They did. Neglect is a kind of crime."

Creep face. But I do sympathize with Restless: neglect is a kind of crime. Perfection is so pompous.

The two heads argue and as the day wears on the argument heats up until both heads are shouting and twisting to emphasize their points of view. The shared body writhes against the constraint of the house front it occupies. Shingles and siding crack and the beams holding the house front shift dangerously.

They are both right. I back into the wetlands that surround the house almost in the way moats encircled the castles of the newcomers in their old countries. The conversation is headed for trouble, the same trouble as with other arguments I have witnessed when neither party is wrong but only have different points of view. I think arguments about right and wrong are funny creatures anyway, like whitecaps: they are visible, noisy, and so unlike their origins. The caps arise from the sea waves, but are not waves, current, or tide. Likewise, the heads articulate belief, but the argument is not about belief, not even close, and rightness and wrongness become irrelevant because each is emotionally attached to their point of view. Hunger gnaws at Restless, and Loyal is obsessed by his commitment to protect. As I listen to them, I decide the argument has started to sound more like a war strategy: both beings are bent on assuming executive power over the other's conduct. But conduct is a variable. Beliefs are the only constants and they cannot be proven, they can only be surrendered, upheld, or altered by the being carrying them. Emotions have no brains, so they cannot be won by way of reason or argument. If the heads crawl off the house front, the future will change and it may not be for the better. My hind legs quiver.

The sun drops from the skyline and the dark folds uneasily over the longhouse and its house front. The house is fragile and the serpent is strong.

No good can come of this. I shake as each head snaps and pulls against the direction of the other.

Each snap jogs the frail house. First a board cracks, then a house post loses its moorings. The heads twist their beliefs in a knot of conflict. War dominates the two heads as belief lies dying between them. The dry rot underneath the house crumbles and the mouldy beams fragment as the house loses a foundation timber, which drops the entire structure closer to the ground. Shingles split and tumble after the foundation timber drops. The molded midsection sinks to mush. Finally, the house front falls forward to touch the earth, but not before the serpent slithers out from under it.

Oh, crap!

Restless slithers onto the foreground triumphant. Loyal shrieks and fights to remain. Loyal hates change.

When two heads from the same body go to war, no one wins. I shake my head in disbelief. Earlier I was dying to leave, but this fight has ignited my curiosity and held my feet still. Between duty and curiosity, I am bound to witness. I want Celia to resume her watch, but she doesn't. Why am I the only witness? I clasp my paws together and watch as the two heads thrash away from each other, forcing their one body to tumble toward the sea.

The house behind them has separated from its roof and exposed the bones.

They are not going to like this.

Face down in the earth the house front is tragic. The art is shattered, the rotted wood lays bare the dead. What little that was left of the house implodes and the scent of death punctures the morning air. Neglected, unburied, and decayed, the bones wail. There is no excuse for their not having been properly interred, even if they did all die at once.

The dead are not responsible for their burial, another house is supposed to take care of that. The people had no business neglecting them this way.

The bones shuffle and click and ready themselves for the chaos to come. Northern lights several thousand miles away begin to sing. As the lights whirl about the skyline, like humans circling the night horizon, they sway and dance to the music of their own creation. The wind screams. The mood in the air shifts; even the earth seems angry.

Terrified, I scamper up the hill until I feel safe. Breathless, I feel shame creeping up on me. Fear has sparked it. Listless, I pace back and forth on the hill. I consider going to Celia's. She is the only seer I know. All the rest are dead. I scamper down the hill and head for the eastern side of the island. It is a long run to the ferry, but I like the ride. Stowing away on a big boat is always an exciting way to travel.

Carrion crows from Vancouver smell the rot, fly toward the house, but the bones have already lost their flesh. There is not enough meat to warrant staying to pick at them; disappointed, the crows squawk and leave. The smell of rotted flesh is a dirty trick; the birds beat their wings in outrage as they fly away. In Vancouver, they hook up with other crows, complain, and determine to gather together to form the biggest murder of crows the world has ever known.

CELIA TAKES A BREAK from her bills when she catches a glimpse of mink as he scurries across her yard. She has not seen a mink in this village ever; her hands tremble at what he is doing here.

What the hell is going on? Something is very wrong.

For a moment Celia looks into the dark, but nothing more shows itself. She returns to her bills. This is the best part, the bill paying; always do the grown-up stuff first. She takes a long pull on her coffee and reaches for her chequebook.

THE BONES LISTEN TO the serpent argue, feel it depart, and sigh with a strange and cruel joy mingled with relief. The serpent will teach the people respect. In the dark folds of the night an old woman appears at the top of the mountain, just above the longhouse. From this perch, she sees the whole of the territory. The old lady wants to see how the argument will unfold and end. The rain drips around her. Her dress rustles and flares to the rhythm of wind and rain as it pierces her scant clothing. I am dead; so lighten up, you can't fling me about.

IN THE MIDST OF writing a cheque for her phone bill, Celia stops; again she thinks she hears screams. She looks toward the window. The curtain moves without provocation. The screams gain volume. A soft impression of comforting voices, soft and muted, follow the screams; their softness seduces her to lean into her listening. I can hear better when I see, so Celia snuffs out the candle on the table and lumbers toward the sound. She pushes back a tattered curtain to peer into the black night. Her hand pokes through one of the holes in the curtain. She never replaced her gramma's curtains. *I have to fix these damn things sometime,* she thinks. The moon is just a sliver hanging by a thread from the sky. The poplars edging her yard thrash as though in pain. Between the thrashes she sees a shape twisting and fighting to move in her direction. *I don't think I want to know this.* She draws back. Her hands shake, but her curiosity gains strength and she overcomes her fear as she peers past the curtain into the dark. She thinks she catches sight of the double-headed sea serpent.

"My God," she whispers, but continues to stare. "What is he doing here?" Her voice sounds distraught, it deepens her fear. The ocean shore looms at the edges of her yard. "What the?" The poplars have disappeared. Celia goes back to writing cheques, stuffing them in envelopes, addressing and stamping them. When finished, she turns in to bed.

The serpent splashes in the water, tail dipping into the sea, his body swollen with the weight he has gained. As Restless lunges for deeper water, Loyal rears back to stop him; the tail snaps, uprooting and clearing what was left of the trees around the longhouse. Restless tries to bite the head of Loyal off. Loyal leans away and lurches inland, while Restless takes advantage of this defensive move and dives for deeper water. Loyal catches on and rears up, managing to drag the body out of the sea. Restless digs in and squirms to free himself from Loyal's grip. This makes the body carve a trough into the shore leading to the sea. Water fills it. The body grows.

Loyal cannot hang on much longer, but he dares not let go. Restless thrusts forward whenever Loyal relaxes or tires. An old lady appears and sits in front of the remains of the longhouse; she stares at them. She hurries away just as the one head tries to bite the other off. From the angle she was watching, it looked as though

Restless was successful. As she recedes down the hill, the body surges forward and back, trying to remain attached to both heads. Finally, Loyal lets go and the serpent is free to swim to the ocean.

The devastation is complete. The serpent has torn the last line of cedars from their moorings and dragged them into the sea. Debris is everywhere: sand, shell, seaweed, and bits of cedars lie helter-skelter on the shore.

In the ocean, the serpent sinks. The heads don't need oxygen. "Why are we not drowning?" one head asks the other during a moment of respite between battles. The other head does not answer. He isn't interested. His hunger is for mischief and he can't get up to mischief without appeasing the other head or beguiling it, so he is busy making plans.

Waves rise from the depths of the sea, massive and dangerous. Not far away, a boat capsizes and the bodies manning it drown without knowing what tipped them. It was a sailing ship, which neither head had seen before; while Loyal wonders about it, Restless takes advantage of his distracted musing and swallows the men in it. The serpent is huge now.

The argument takes them deeper into the sea. They plunge and, on the way down, they collide with sharks and barracuda. The sharks attack, but the heads swallow them; the sharks explode inside the serpent and fill its hungry form; the sharks are now part of the serpent's personality. A barracuda passes and the heads fight over it; each manages to swallow half of it. The smiling stealth of barracuda mingles with the shark's seductive joy at seeing blood. The desire for blood, for killing, marks the serpent.

The body spirals to the ocean floor and thrashes and crashes there. The massive tail cracks the earth and an earthquake erupts.

The story of the sea serpent has begun. After nearly drowning watching the serpent's heads fight, I shift and make ready for the earthquake I feel coming.

A brief ominous silence precedes the quake, and then both Celia and I hear a rumble like a freight truck driving straight for her house. Her fridge and stove dance as her bathroom light goes out and all but one of her candles flicker and die. She leaps for the cord in the shadowy light of the fat candle and pulls the plugs of both appliances from their sockets. She waits on the floor until her house stops quivering.

Celia can see the serpent under the sea as she rides out the earthquake. I head for shore. I cannot afford to drown.

The sea froths. Outraged, it whirls around the serpent. The sea considers swallowing it, but changes her mind. Instead, she negotiates a truce — but it is a shark's truce. Each head is to take turns satisfying its particular brand of hunger and quenching its individual desire. The sea's only condition: No killing humans. Restless smiles; the sea has said nothing of the heart, mind, or spirit of the humans; Restless only cannot kill his prey. "*Spirit food is what I need most anyway,*" he thinks. He isn't too far off. Spirit food is what the original humans promised to feed him through their songs and ceremony. He plans to consume the spirit of humans.

The bones in the broken longhouse giggle; their neglect will be avenged. Deep inside the mountain, another set of bones rattles. They want to know what the hell is going on. Why do they hear the serpent talking to itself? They wriggle and fight to get to the surface, but it is a slow and difficult process, this business of climbing through layers of rock and dirt. These bones are older. They died long before the newcomers came. They sense the anger of the younger bones; it surprises them. Getting to the younger bones is urgent, but there is no hurrying the journey to the top. This is not going to end well.

I rest on the shore for a bit as the story continues to unfold.

The sea hears the head; she knows Restless is up to no good, that the truce isn't any good. But she also knows that the humans have the answer to their discord with the serpent. The sea is confident that some human among them will come forward to resolve the dilemma. She settles back and the storm quiets down. Celia stops watching.

Not much of a rest for me, but it's something. I leave and stumble upon a logging crew on its way to the coast.

IV

A YELLOW MACBLO CREW cab trundles along, bouncing up an old logging road. Logging roads are utilitarian; they have no pavement as few cars drive them. They are not well maintained; rutted and dusty, they service the logging trucks with only minor use by the residents of isolated reserves. The dust creeps through the cab windows even when they are shut. The driver does his best to avoid the worst ruts; but, no matter what he does, the six men bounce mercilessly as he navigates his way around the ribbon of ruts and un-repaired potholes on this mountain edge road. The dust is cloying; it is dry and tastes of calcium, organic waste, and just a little iron.

Steve hates the taste. He wants to spit, but his mouth has been sucked dry by the dust. He is against logging; his conscience nags him. He has been kept awake nights, trying to think of other ways to earn his tuition. In place of dreaming he argues with himself, like the serpent, but in the end he invariably decides that this is the only way for him to pay for university.

Clearcutting is wrong.

Steve hates this feeling of guilt and helpless acquiescence. "Forget it," he tells himself. "This is my last year of university; it will all be over soon." When he opens the window to spit out the dust in his mouth, more flies in.

Steve's incessant arguing with himself is annoying. I would like to sympathize with these people, but they are so hard to like. I shut my ears to his thoughts for a time and just lie in the back of the truck, enjoying the ride.

"Shut the fuckin' window," Amos barks from the back seat. Amos sits in the back seat not caring about the dust, his conscience, or anything except working a little, getting paid, going to Vancouver, drinking a lot, and harassing Steve, the only white man in the crew. "You're letting all the dust in." Steve shuts his window. He hates Amos, but he is right. No sense spitting until the truck stops.

I am no fan of Amos, either, but I get his anger. I don't get Steve's quandary — if clearcutting is wrong, then you stop.

The truck pulls to a stop at the foot of a nameless mountain that has been primed for clearcutting. The men spill out and head up the incline as soon as the truck stops. This is Steve's sixth season. He is a choker man for Amos, a faller. The spacers have already been through, cutting everything down that isn't going to be logged; others loaded the refuse, hauled it out, and consigned it to a funeral pyre some twenty miles south. The forest is thin now; only big trees dot the hill.

Steve chokes off a tree, George tops it and marks it for Amos. Amos jerks the rope on his chainsaw. The saw's whine and whir sound decisive, mean, and tough. Amos likes the meanness of the saw's sound.

To tell the truth, I like the toughness of the whine of a chainsaw too, even though I don't like what it's for.

The first cut slows the whine to a groan and the tree leans into it like she wants to be harvested. Even through the earmuffs the husky whine hurts Steve's ears. The air is now full of the crackling and snapping of branches as the tree lunges to the ground. Branches pop and fly as she hits the dirt, two hundred feet of building timber crashed to the hill floor. The men stand still, watching for spikes flying in their direction.

One spike can kill you.

The men move on to harvest another tree while Joey and Sam whip up their saws and go into action, skinning her of her branches. Steve thinks he can hear the tree scream.

From seven in the morning to noon the crew chokes, fells, and skins. They fell a truckload's worth by morning's end.

Steve looks at the bald patch on the mountain and feels the self-loathing rising again. It isn't just the dust, the camp, the company, or the rain he hates. He hates the wasting of the hillside that their handiwork contributes to; the melancholy he feels after seeing the devastation they have inflicted gnaws at his nerves. He hates knowing that he helped strip this mountain bare. He knows the dirt will be caught by the rain and dragged to the sea to be lost in her depths. Alternating flood and drought plague the thin valley floors of clearcut mountains; drought in the rainforest poses a danger to the water table. Exposed by the absence of trees, the mammals leave, the land becomes a ludicrous desert in the middle of a rainforest, and summer temperatures rise — not just here, but everywhere. He feels like a criminal held hostage by his dreams.

Hostages first trap themselves, but Steve has no way of knowing this. He is a newcomer and they have a whole different way of seeing things. I want to sleep this story off, but I can't.

V

THE BONES IN THE longhouse are not very old. The ones under the house are older. They are the ones who fell from the sky when this world first began. The oldest bones buried deeper in the soil rattle and sing the oldest songs they know as they work their way to the surface. They call out to the other bones, hoping the younger ones will join them in the song. The newer bones answer and the echo is magnificent. The ancient dead roll over, keep wiggling and singing their way to the surface. The song gains volume and Steve thinks he hears it.

Something is going to happen here.

"There are consequences for negligence," the newer bones sigh to the old bones. Steve shakes his head, thinking he must be dehydrated, and reaches for his Thermos. As he sits on a log eating his lunch, he wonders about the things he thinks he's heard. A murder of crows lands on the trees not yet harvested and they caw. Steve jerks his head in the sound's direction. Amos laughs.

THE SERPENT CRAWLS OUT of the sea and lolls in the crevice of two mountains. Both heads stare at the men below. They are different from the people they knew before. What is that big yellow thing that squats nearby? Why are there no trees but for a thin patch next to the men? Loyal has no interest in doing them harm, but Restless is excited. He surmises that these men have murdered the trees; this means they lack a conscience, and so they are full of the kind of spirit food Restless craves. Below is a spiritual banquet just waiting to be devoured. Restless readies himself for his first meal.

"Antsy in the bush, se'manh?" Amos's fork clatters against his blue enamel camp plate.

"No, I'm just not deaf. I hear voices in the wind."

Amos glares at Steve. Hate tangles his insides. The arrogance of this se'manh twists Amos into knots. Steve's people spent a century and a half alienating him and his family from their knowledge, banning his people from using it. They took pains to lock the remnants of his culture in their museums, archives, and universities, and then barred him from entering. And this white man who has access to everything Amos has been denied flaunts it.

Of course, Steve did not know his people had done this. It was orchestrated so that no one understood what was going on. It would have been beautiful, if the result were not so ugly.

Restless curls about Amos's feet. "Bastard, kill him," Restless whispers to Amos and Amos swallows the words. They poison his guts. Restless smiles at Amos. The other head sighs, consumed by his sadness, he lies helpless; it is not his turn. Steve says nothing, just pulls his sandwich out of his lunchbox and eats. After he swallows the last bite of his sandwich, he heads for the sound.

"Don't get lost," Amos chuckles. He's trying hard to laugh away the shame he feels, to suppress the desire to kill Steve. The others join his laughter and this takes the edge off the burning rage inside Amos. After a short while, the foreman follows Steve into a clearing not far from camp; he sees the longhouse that has sunk into the ground. It is missing its roof, but the opening hole is still there, boarded up. Steve draws closer.

"Don't go any closer," the foreman warns. Steve shrinks back and turns toward the foreman, who points at the boarding. "They must have died of sickness. Who knows how long the illness survives? Who knows how long the house stood roofless or how long bacteria live inside dead bodies?"

They both retreat, but Steve stares at the house front as he backs away. Something is wrong with it and he is trying to figure out what it is. He gives up trying and he turns around, following the foreman back to camp.

I scamper after them. Don't even have to try to be quiet.

"So? What you find?" Amos asks, his mouth full of food. He is perched on an old stump. Steve stands downwind from Amos and wishes he had the nerve to tell Amos to wash once in a while. Amos has no manners, and lacks the decency to maintain any level of cleanliness. Steve resents him for it. His hair hasn't seen a comb or brush for weeks, is uncut and tied into a dark, tangled mass that hangs down the middle of his back. A dirty red rag tied across his forehead and a single elastic is all the care and attention Amos gives it. It irritates Steve, and he fights to ignore his own irritation. The derision in Amos's voice is ill-disguised, but Steve feigns apathy on hearing it. Amos is about to find out that Steve can toy with people too.

"Longhouse." He drops the word flatly and every man among them squirms and stops eating.

"You didn't go in there, did you?" Joey asks. The rest of the men stare, waiting for the answer, hoping it is one they can live with. Amos taps his feet like he wants to run. Steve doesn't answer right away.

"No," he says flatly. Relieved, they relax and resume eating.

The foreman signals lunch break is over. Steve strolls up the hill to choke off another tree. At the top, he glances back at Joey. It dawns on him: there was no sea serpent on the house front. He shudders.

Steve knows something.

SCREAMS COME AT CELIA again through the veil of sleep. They are soft, but insist upon being heard. She awakes, swings her legs off the bed, heads toward her bedroom window. The voices retreat as she approaches the windowsill. She peers outside at the poplars, which now hang limp, waiting for something to happen. Through the leaves, the same shape she had witnessed the night before twists itself up into a ball, unravels, stands up, and then thumps as it hits the ground. She is not sure what it is at first when, for the briefest moment, it stops and slithers back and forth. Then it looks as though it is trying to move but can't, as though something has a hold on it from the inside. Celia bobs side to side, like an old bear trying to get a better look.

No stars backlight the trees and it is too early for the sun. The dark is thick, too dense for her to see through. Behind the shape's movements, as though quarrelling with something within, Celia sees Steve's outline. Her breath catches and she moves her head back and forth. It doesn't help. Finally, the strain of peering into the dark becomes too much. She pulls the curtains closed and climbs back into bed.

Arms folded behind her head, Celia talks to herself. "I am thirty-eight and don't have a lover, a husband, or even prospects. I see things going bump in the night and have no one to comfort me or explain them away." She rolls over and returns to sleep.

I don't get Celia sometimes, but I am not alone. Her people don't get her either.

Much later in the morning, as she scrambles together some eggs and fried sausages, Celia dismisses the experience as a bad dream, even as she wonders why Steve was in it. He is white — Stacey's former schoolmate and now Stacey's secret lover. She laughs as she stirs the eggs and flips the sausages. There are too many sausages, but she is past the point of minding how much she eats.

"Guess he's not too big a secret, since I know about him." Stacey believes no one knows about him. Maybe that's the secret: Stacey doesn't know we all know about him. On the other hand, maybe she knows we know and are all pretending not to know, and she is pretending she doesn't while we actually don't know she knows. Celia stuffs the scrambled eggs and sausages into the oven and sets it at one-hundred-fifty degrees to keep warm while she mixes up a batch of pancakes. She flaps the last jack, wipes her hands on her apron, and serves herself a plate of eggs, sausages, and pancakes. For a brief moment, she stares at the plate of food and thinks it an awful lot considering she isn't all that active or hard-working. "Hell with it, I like eating," she says, and ignores the little voice cautioning her.

Her kitchen faces the right edge of her property on the road to town. The river saunters next to her house on the left side, after weaving back toward the reserve from the bridge. The bridge is not far from her house. Her old gramma chose this spot to build her house so that she could see the comings and goings of all the villagers. Like her gramma, Celia knows who's visiting who, who's keeping company with who, all based on who's riding with who in whose car. This amuses her: she's part of the reason people in small towns feel like they live in a fishbowl. Tony from the other end of the reserve passes by in his old car and the noisiness of it is comic. The river looks a little jerky today, like it isn't all that happy. The fork stills in her hand, she licks it, plunges it into a sausage, then a piece of flapjack, rolls it in syrup, sticks the sticky mess in her mouth. The curtains shift. Celia arches her back. "Whoever you are, you are starting to piss me off." There is no one there. The windows are closed. "Stop it! Stop it! Stop it!" Celia's gramma is now standing to her right.

"Ok, Alice." Celia stuffs her rage. Waiflike and thin, dead Alice sits down in a chair next to her. Celia serves her a plate of syrup and flapjacks.

"The house front fell forward. The heads of the serpent fought. The snake's body grew larger with each twist and turn. The heads thrashed their way from the old village to the sea. In the sea, the water roiled under it whipping, lashing, twisting and writhing and engorging the double-headed serpent."

"You saw it?"

Gramma Alice had seen the serpent and she fictioned up a story just as her ancestors would have. "The serpent has two heads, one bit the other head clean off." Celia isn't sure what to make of this, but she knows her gramma likes telling stretchers, so she decides to listen. Humans are suited for fiction, Celia decides. The earth and its children are subjects and not objects, nothing is solid, everything is space. We are all just space between imperceptibly small moving particles; molecules, electrons, protons, neutrons. *Maybe this is why we desire solidity. Solid facts, solid futures, solid relationships, solid stories.* Celia chuckles at her own joke. Alice arches her eyebrows, suspicious of what Celia is laughing at. Celia knows that the space between moving particles is actually immense, yet the eyes of humans fill in the blanks to fiction up solid shapes. It must take days after birth for this fictional point of view to develop. Newborns must feel so heavy; they must feel solid. Maybe they would die of shock if they did not see their mothers as solid powerful masses. Celia sips her tea.

"He is so much bigger than the house front portrays him. His tail extends nearly three hundred feet. He tore the sea shore up, dug a trench a mile long, before heading out to sea," says Gramma Alice. Celia listens to her gramma's story of the day the serpent fought itself. "Both heads set out toward deep water. Once near an underground volcano they tangled. The volcano fired up. The fight sparked the fire in the volcano. It pulled them toward its vortex. One head caught fire and screamed. The volcano erupted and spit the snake onto the shore. The serpent had only one head left. It was the hungry head."

"What happened after that?" Celia asks and fetches herself a glass of orange juice.

"Don't know, stopped watching, came straight here." Gramma Alice bites into her flapjack. She repeats the business of how the serpent lost its head: "The one head bit the burnt head right off. Just bit it clean off."

Celia listens to Alice quietly without investing too much belief in her story; she thinks Alice has jumped to conclusions before she saw clearly what was happening, so she doesn't fuss much over what she says. Still, the images Celia saw the night before seem to corroborate Alice's story.

"Free from its conscience and its house front duties, the serpent will slide along the shore looking for something to eat. You be careful, girl," Alice admonishes as she finishes eating. She leaves. Celia stops breathing, but just for a second. No sense being scared of your own daymares. She finishes her breakfast and sets about cleaning up her kitchen.

VI

I HEAD FOR AMOS'S *tent. I squat outside, listening and watching.*
The tent shakes. Amos shakes inside along with it. He is alone.
No one wants to share a space with him until he washes on some
kind of regular basis. Amos knows this and so deliberately declines
to wash because he does not want to share space with anyone.

Amos saw the serpent in his sleep. He screamed, but no sound
came. Like all other humans, Amos indulges in fiction, but he has
different reasons for doing so. His stories run in a different direction, toward absurd and hopeless murder. He fears sober sleep. Sober,
his dreams become nightmares of knives plunging into his own
body, blades withdrawing covered in blood, bits of flesh attached
to the blades. Drunk, his dreams are of him stabbing other humans,
mostly adults. Drunk, his dreams are sometimes of children's
screams. These render him powerful, but they strike terror into him
when he awakes. He reaches for the bottle again.

Amos is dislocated from himself. I can't change his story, so I watch.

The restless head of the serpent heads for Amos. It crawls about the camp, excited; it swallows every sound Amos makes. The hungry head of the serpent invades every corner, every second of Amos's night. It moves Amos to dream of the day the serpent fought itself.

He sees it swell, sees it try to bite off one of its own heads, watches it as it arches its back. Amos listens to it howl. The howl paralyzes his scream. The serpent's face twists. His eyes redden. Amos sits up. Sweat pours down his face, his back; his legs are soaked with sweat. He feels awake, but continues to dream. His conscience comes into view. He sees it. Bold and black typed words rail at him. The words kink, stretch, and whirl in front of his face. They rush at his face, enter his mouth, and disappear into his mind. Inside his mind, they take on a kind of spidery form. The serpent's head jerks. The insane behaviour of Amos's conscience attracts him. From inside the tent, in that old camp, Amos writhes, desperate for something he cannot name. His conscience bangs inside his head, its feathery web spins itself into knots. Every time Amos opens his mouth to scream the knot chokes off the sound. Finally the knot settles at the bottom of his belly in a ball. One powerful push of breath and it flies out his mouth.

The serpent had got inside him, swallowed his warped conscience, wrapped its wicked breath of horrific permission around it, spat it out and sent it back toward Amos's open mouth as Amos fought hard to scream out loud. Amos gulps and swallows his own scream before it makes a sound, just as the serpent returns his conscience now filled with the shark spirit, the barracuda, and the hunger of the serpent all wrapped around a perverse sense of morality and entitlement. It roots itself to the wall of his stomach, a toxic ulcer.

The serpent turns, smiles, and slides down the coastal mountains toward civilization. The last time he had been here there were three-hundred-thirty-seven longhouses in thirty-three villages, each house inset at least a mile from the ocean on the banks of the rivers. It's different now, there are no longhouses. He is stunned by what he sees. Rows of buildings, hundreds of thousands of humans, all shapes, sizes, and colours, some speaking the sparrow talk of the white ones; others, smaller, but looking almost like the original people, speaking in a stop-stop quick language; still others speaking in nasal rapid-fire rhythm, none of which the serpent understands. He hunts for the original people, but it will be a long time before he finds any.

The land surrounding one old woman's house reeks of pig dung. The serpent does not have a way of recognizing the animals living on the land next door, except that the old woman complains about them to the old man and when she does she calls them "pigs." Restless stares at them for days, watches their movements as these strange men throw slop at them. The pigs smell too. They smell of something they consumed. Restless studies them before doing anything, which is okay with Loyal. Each night, the men drink something that reeks. After a while they grow loud, fight each other, and finally beat the women who live there with them. At night they sleep with their mouths open like they are trying to catch flies, just like Amos.

Restless thinks he recognizes the mind-changer they are drinking. He lies in wait, and then enters the gaping mouth of one of them. The next night the man kills one of the women, chops her to bits, and feeds her to the pigs. Loyal is stunned at what Restless has done, but Restless sleeps a deep and satisfying sleep that night. These strangers are easy. As Restless sleeps, Loyal decides he has to find someone who can stop Restless without killing them both.

The new bones rattle happily. It is about time someone did something to wake these people up. The old bones groan, sing the oldest healing song they know, but to no avail. Mink determines to leave Nuu'chalnulth territory. After this, the story at the place where everyone died will be the one to witness.

VII

CELIA FIRES UP HER vacuum, throws her laundry into the washing machine. She pays no attention to the interruption by the serpent in the late hours of the previous night. While she has no idea why she keeps on having these crazy dreams, she has reconciled herself to them and learned not to think about them after she wakes up. She carries out the mundane task of cleaning to ready herself for another round of living.

It is the last Friday in March. From the window, Celia notices that the first crocus has unfolded, its white-and-purple petals thrusting its face toward the sun, grateful to be blooming. Damn, I missed it again; she wishes she had looked out yesterday, or earlier today. She regrets missing the first crocus bloom.

Celia has taken to going to her momma's on Friday all winter to tell the story of Ravensong to her nephew. Although she has finished telling the story by now, she cannot think of any other thing to do on Friday, so she saunters toward Momma's after supper. What began as a ritual in response to Jacob's question has now became a habit. No one sees any reason to stop after the story has ended.

Celia arrives and is disappointed. She can tell the story still hangs in the air at her mother's house and, while she does not want to witness it again, she wants to haul the story out of the air and be done with it. It has become a tired old beast that torments Celia and holds her captive. It wafts its way over her body, teasing and torturing her with its images of her dead son. It keeps repeating that Jimmy is never coming back.

Jimmy is gone. Her robust son hanged himself. Her nephew Jacob wants to know why. No one knows why, but they feel obligated to tell him something; so they gather every Friday to tell him the story of Ravensong. She had not wanted to hear it, but could not escape its telling, because she was one of the narrators. She thought she wanted it to be over, and now that it is she wants the lingering feel it leaves behind to evaporate. She thinks it would be easy to sit among her relatives and escape to her musings, her wakeful dreams, if only the story's feel would disappear.

NO ONE IN THIS *family knows it, but the entire story has not been told. I know it. No one knows that Loyal found Jimmy, shapeshifted, entered him, and tried hard to let Jimmy know that the serpent belonged on a house front west and north of their village, that he needed to be feasted. But Jimmy proved too fragile for the mission. Instead of feasting the restless head and returning him to his position of honour, Jimmy killed himself. Loyal was beside himself with grief at his error in judgment — some other gentler roadway than the original one had to be found. In the meantime, Loyal surrendered to the havoc of Restless. Each time Restless ran amok, Loyal slept for a long time; this sleep was his only relief. He could not find anyone who could help. What is wrong with the people?*

I know what is wrong. The people have no idea who they are anymore. They are sad, hurt, angry, and disconnected; some of them have gone crazy and are busy tormenting each other, not all of them, but enough of them. The ones who are trying to figure out how to heal have little of their original knowledge to work with; they are barely succeeding. It is not my job to make the serpent understand or restore peace or knowledge to the people. My only job is to witness the story and tell it. I leave the tormented head of the serpent to watch the women at Momma's house.

MOMMA ENDS THE STORY with a song that is supposed to bring closure to Celia's son's death, but it doesn't — not for Celia. The sound of the story hanging from the rafters taunts her memory without bringing any end to the mystery or the pain. During the song Celia holds her breath. The sound rises, filling the room and seeming to sink into the very wood grain of her mother's house beams, but Celia cannot feel its power and so cannot swallow it and be settled by its beauty. It is as though she cannot truly hear it. The song makes her feel like she is stuck in a blinding watery fog. Without swallowing the song, she cannot accept the way Jimmy died. Unable to benefit from the song, and tired of the story, she cannot stop reliving the moment of Jimmy's death.

Night after night, all winter, Celia had confined herself to her bedroom. Lights out, not even a candle burning, she sat at the edge of her futon and replayed Jimmy's last day alive. It became her private obsession, watching the light from his eyes over and over, trying to see the precise moment of his departure from the living. This obsession became her private torment, as his gaze told her nothing. It just stared back at her, burning her, burning her somewhere in the middle of her mind. Jimmy's eyes accuse her of some small neglect, some failure that led him to this crazy dance of death. The accusation in his eyes drove her to relive his suicide and wonder why he might do this, why her son? The why of it hid somewhere in the dead quiet of night, making her hungry. Restless thought he could hear her. He had waited by her house often on those nights, but something had stopped him from entering, some-thing gossamer thin he could not penetrate had kept him outside.

Celia had rushed Jimmy's burial. She had wanted to hasten his body's exit. She had buried him just three days after his death, which left little time for a wake or the burning. It was a fragile coffin, built with slivers of space between its cedar planks. She wanted the coffin built this way. The spaces would be an easy entrance for the small beings so they could feast on his body and destroy his flesh without much trouble. The thought of Jimmy rotting slowly and uselessly in a store-bought sealed coffin had been too much for her to bear. The small beings would need to hurry his decay in some final, useful way. She insisted her ex-husband build the coffin. Ned had helped. He burnt an old design onto the lid. The only other death that had disturbed her like this was her gramma's. She cocked her head to one side trying to recall her. She could barely remember her gramma's fading from there to absent. Now she could not stop remembering her son. Every waking moment she was not daydreaming, Celia was plagued with remembering him.

Inside the house, Celia nods to Jacob, who squats in the corner and chews a toothpick like some old man satisfied at having been fed a full feast of salmon. Momma, Rena, and Stacey talk about some non-existent school, and Ned and Judy sip tea without seri-ously listening. Everything is normal: they are talking and ignoring Celia.

She pulls the curtain down on the room full of people, turns the volume of voices off, and lets herself drift into her private world of scattered moving pictures, disconnected from current time. The warm fire inside rises as does a current of images from her past. They drift outside of a particular context, far from time, as though time were an insult to her memory. She watches them in a forgetful, insignificant way, not at all the way she might recall a list of items she needed from the grocery store or someone's birthdate, but in the mindless way she drops her keys in their habit-formed spot. Her memories have no order. They roll forward of their own volition in a series of scenes that slip and slide across the floor of her mind. They hook themselves onto her mind as though they have just stopped by for a brief visit. They slide in and out, tentative and unsure, as though they do not belong to Celia, as though they have been looking for a home and have accidentally stumbled into Celia's memory but are not sure this is the place they want to stay.

These memories don't come to her in the normal way memories do, when the rememberer knows that she is in fact remembering. They sit in her mind, independent of her voice — as though the memories have met each other on some arc of light, a place between where her voice originates and where it can be heard reciting memory and the origins of memory. They come to her, independent of her will. She watches them spring up and follows them as they spirit along bent light waves. She watches them settle themselves in her mind, each one free of the emotional encumbrances that accompany ordinary memories.

Relief comes. Celia needs relief from the summer Stacey left. She wants relief from the empty life in between that summer and Jimmy's birth. She wants relief from the emptiness of her house since he died.

I ponder the value of following Celia around; she seems stuck inside herself. Up to her elbows in her own muck. I can't help cursing, Oh, crap. But I hang about anyway. Maybe that is the point of this story.

Celia relives the day Stacey left. Momma and Stacey were walking arm in arm toward the bridge. Celia listened to the crunch of gravel under their feet, heard the murmur of their voices recede under the gentle fall wind. Their skirts flapped to the rhythm of wind and walking and their bodies grew small. Celia grabbed her gramma's hand and squeezed, Gramma turned to her, smiled, picked her up, and said, "She'll be back in no time. Not to worry, little girl." Gramma's assurance was fiction. Time flies only for the old. Celia had no way of knowing how long five years was going to be. There had been talk the night before of visits and holidays, but it had all been false.

There were no visits. Visits cost money and the family had none. Once every three months the whole family gathered to hear Stacey's letters filled with words none of them understood. Rena and Judy had taken turns reading them aloud, trying hard to explain the strange language that Stacey now used. One of the concepts they failed to understand was "Pedagogy of the Oppressed."

Celia did not return to her momma's house, she stayed with her gramma. When Gramma died, she took care of Grandpa as though she were the oldest daughter. She did Stacey's job and had to fight her own resentment over it.

SHE IS STILL IN Grandpa's house — the one with the kitchen window facing the road to town.

CELIA WAS OUTSIDE. SHE was little and she snuck in the rear door to Gramma's house. She crouched, unseen and still, under the kitchen table in view of the dressing of Gramma for her funeral. Celia faced the curtain to Gramma's bedroom, but dared not enter. No one she knew dared to sneak a peek besides Grandpa. Even he had always asked if Gramma wanted to go to bed, like he was looking for permission to enter her room every night.

Grandpa stayed quiet during the funeral deliberations. The women decided to have him lay her out in the living room. He did what they asked. They had fetched new clothes for her. The women who dressed his Alice for her burial did not want to dress her in the bedroom. He shuffled over the threshold, mumbling about would she mind if he might come in, and carried her out into the living room. The girls wanted to dress her, and did she know she was going home? After she was dressed, the keeper of the dead, the man conducting the burning, asked that her things be brought out. The women left then. Celia left too. She skulked out the back door.

CELIA SITS ON THE back porch, staring at the clearing in front of the poplars.

I watch from behind the poplars, standing upright, my hands clasped, my fur glistening. I look straight at her. Some vague memory of an old trapper's tale comes forward.

"MINK SKIN SLICES NEAT and easy." Some white man is talking to a younger man standing next to him. The yard collapses. The mink in the trap squirms under the man's knife. Celia is appalled. The nicks the man makes on all four legs are neat. Celia tries to look away, but she is caught. My one leg quivers. Nick, slice. My second leg shakes. Nick, slice. Leg three quivers. I wait. Celia wonders if anyone notices her staring at the carnage. It's coming any minute now. Any second — nick, slice, and pull. One wave of pain, one massive convulsion, and my skin is gone. Celia convulses with me. It is almost over. My eyes water. I retch. Celia gags along with me. In a second I give up and the shock nearly kills me before I scream and shape-shift out of my body to fly away as owl. Tears stream down Celia's face, but she makes no sound. Celia looks down and thanks the white man for disembowelling me before he skinned me. Sometimes they don't.

Just as he begins to remove the pelt, my body disappears. The white man, startled, throws the pelt into the bush. It lands in the stream not far from his trap. He heads back to his trapper's cabin, terrified by what he witnessed. I disappeared.

Okay, I shouldn't have played with the trapper like that, but I still felt a strange kind of smug satisfaction at freaking him out.

Celia is still quivering long after mink disappears. She forced herself to watch and wonders what happened to mink's little body. Celia still stands in the corner, near the door to the room, barely able to focus. She feels like mink, stripped clean of her skin, but she knows that isn't fair. She is not mink, she has not been skinned, she is a voyeur. Mink had to endure the process; he had no choice.

Never mind, I am not entirely dead. I try to reassure her, but she is a seer not a listener. I reappear as owl, floating above her grandpa and the women who helped him bring her gramma's things out of the bedroom.

Celia's hallucinations are crowding one another, slipping from one to the next. She wants to focus on one hallucination or the other; these split delusions scare her. She lets her wondering about mink go.

THEY BROUGHT GRAMMA'S CLOTH out a piece at a time. Every piece of cloth jarred Grandpa. He held each one in his hands. The men waited while Grandpa decided its fate, then they touched his fingers. Each time Grandpa looked up, it was as though he had just then realized why they were there. He nodded his head to the kitchen table or the fire heap outside.

The windows of the living room had been blackened for the wake. But for the candles glowing around the body, the room was dark. Celia stared at Grandpa. He was out the day Gramma died and even though he laid her out, he sat on his chair at the wake and looked about the house, like he was trying to find her, like he was not really convinced she was gone and he expected her to show up any minute.

After Gramma's wake, under the light of a sliver of moon, Grandpa faced the funeral pyre. The women gathered behind the men and the grieving song began. The men murmured words in the old language, tossed cedar on the pyre, and then lit it. Grandpa lurched forward. Two men grabbed him. They sang deeper. One of the men holding Grandpa urged him to sing. He held cedar against the middle of Grandpa's back. Grandpa's head lolled back and forth for a minute, the song jerked its way out at first, then it reached full sound and finally Grandpa was grieving, the sound of it loud, long, deep, and beautiful. That's when they began burning her things; red bits of cotton, stripped blue cloth, wool panels cut from old men's pants, bits of ribbon, and a mountain load of colourful cut-up squares and triangles preceded the larger pieces; finally the bolt of white cotton was unravelled and thrown at the pyre. Momma had very nearly clenched her teeth at the bolt of cotton.

Celia recognized the song. It was the same song Momma had sung for her Jimmy. Tears filled Celia's eyes. She tossed her head to one side; why hadn't she remembered hearing this song before? This time she let the song fill her up. She swallowed it. It tasted full, round, and hopeful. Why had it been so hard for her to sing that song last week? It was as though this was the first time she had heard it and felt it.

Celia watched the funeral fire until the last ember died, and then she returned to Gramma's house. Momma wept over the burning bolt of cotton, but Celia paid her no mind, Gramma's kitchen was filling up with the scent of blackberry pie in the oven. Over the stove a cone-shaped cheesecloth sack, plump with blackberries, dripped juice into a jar below, setting itself into jelly. Grandpa was not there. Celia scoured the house for some evidence of illness, maybe some pills with strange Latin-sounding names that would point her in the direction of the big medical text in Stacey's house, where she could solve the riddle. "We didn't go to them people then," some mocking voice told her. She turned to look to see who was talking, but no one was there. She shivered and kept looking.

No pills in the kitchen cupboard, just clean white un-matching dishes, un-matching mugs of all shapes and sizes; white bowls, there were plenty of white bowls threatening to spill out of Gramma's curtained cupboards. The cupboards strained to hold Gramma's dishes from view. She stopped looking at the details of Gramma's kitchen and looked about for the bathroom, and then she remembered: Gramma had no bathroom.

Celia faced the curtain to Gramma's bedroom. She stood at the entrance to the bedroom and waited. She waited for some sign of permission to invade this sanctuary, this room that no one had dared enter while Alice was alive and was now off limits because she was dead. Grandpa had taken to sleeping on the couch in front of the television; he could not face the room that was now so deeply empty without his wife. No voice, no permission was forthcoming. Celia shrank herself small. Small children are forgiven transgressions. She slid the curtain aside.

Gramma's room was awash with gold light. Filtered through the yellow-pink-magenta paisley curtains, the light was a fluid pink and pastel yellow. The fussy pleats and ruffles of the curtains stood like managers of *siem*, self-important. The pleats bent the light into a golden fan that hovered over the oak-and-cedar cupboards and trunks in the room. Gramma's shelves were peopled with masks, carved bowls, and spoons – some modern, some so old and black Celia wondered if they were made of argillite. She touched the black spoon nearest to her. "Haida," she heard her grandpa's voice say, "I am from Haida Gwaii." Her hand snapped back at the sound of his voice. She looked. He didn't seem to mind her being there. Haida Gwaii. The waters of the seas swirled around the word. Whalers, seafaring traders, men of song, of purpose; indomitable men. "I canoed all the way from Skidegate to here." He chuckled as though even he couldn't believe his youthful silliness. She stared at his still-lithe body and nodded. She could see Grandpa canoeing a thousand miles to be with Gramma. She smiled. It pleased her to know that he had left his pristine island home, dipped a paddle over miles of water, voyaged to this village, this place, and this woman who was her gramma. If Jimmy ... She stopped herself and continued to look.

One cupboard held communities of white porcelain geese, swans, ducks, and little white girls getting ready to waddle through whatever garden they were standing at the edge of when someone conjured them from clay, up to kiln, up to this sweetly lit golden wood reality. Where had Gramma found them? Celia turned to Grandpa. He was already gone.

Instead I was there motioning for her to follow. Finally she saw me and trundled along behind me as though following a shape-shifting mink storyteller were as normal as can be.

"She must have been young once," Celia said to me. She leaned against a tree. She landed in some other place with old Salish names and a language that sounded foreign to her ear not because she didn't recognize the words, but because they slid off the people's tongues so easy and plain. Today's speakers are either teachers or students, so the language sounds serious and strained, bereft of humour. It is painful to listen to, much less participate in.

Bush surrounded Celia.

I sat on a rock and watched as Celia waited for the sight of humans.

Laughter wafted from behind bushes of blackberries, between snippets of song and story. Celia rounded the bush. A half dozen young girls picked berries, their cone-shaped cedar baskets strapped to their foreheads and hanging down their backs to the waist, swishing with every movement. Neither song nor voice nor laughter interrupted the steady rhythm of the picking. In the distance, a young man stood watching the land in front of them, his back to the girls. He was positioned on the hillside to see what was coming.

Celia recognized her gramma's grandmother: the first Alice. The other girls called her "Alice." Every time they said "Alice" they laughed as though it were the most ridiculous and meaningless sound they had ever heard. It seemed preposterous to the girls that this sound should become this girl's name. The name "Alice" did not suit this girl who told stories of exquisite quality while they picked berries. Not this girl who could shrink time and enrich even the most ordinary moments with stories of such alacrity that the picking hardly felt like work at all. Celia's Gramma Alice must have been named for her gramma.

They were rolling around the story of Alice's name between fits of laughter. "This man Father McKilty runs about naming the world, naming himself 'Father,'" and they laughed harder, as though some man naming his world were about the funniest thing they had ever heard. Today they had all received new names. "Christian names," McKilty called them. He threw water at them, and then named them. The girls took water from their gourds, threw it at one another, and renamed themselves even more ridiculous things, like "See-yah," "Schokem," "Hoschem," and other berries. They mimicked the sound the priest made, Alice became "eh-ternal," Mary became "for-effer," and they laughed some more. Alice had to run off behind a bush and squat someplace far from where they picked, unable to hold the water from her body as the laughter shook it loose. This caused more squeals from the girls. Picking finally stopped as each emptied her water. All the while, the young man stood unmoving; with his eyes he swept the hillside, watching for any possible threat to the girls.

Alice's grandpa sat still on a bench outside his longhouse, talking to the interpreter who was standing next to the black robe. He wanted to know what the names meant before he let McKilty in the house. The priest had no idea what he was asking and the interpreter had no way to make the old man understand the priest. McKilty kept telling him the names meant the girls would be saved, they would enjoy eternal life, they would live forever in the lap of Jesus Christ. Grandpa thought McKilty quite mad. He could not picture any of his daughters living forever on some man's lap, much less all of them. He said as much to the translator. The translator told him that he thought McKilty meant the men too.

Grandpa doubted any of the men would want to sit on a man's lap at all. Well, maybe Lilt. Besides, humans have to leave. They can't stay here forever.

Maybe that's why these people had to leave their home: there was no room there. He pictured a land of useless old men and women sitting on some guy's lap — well, surely they took turns. What kind of a man wants to have women sitting on his lap forever? And what kind of men and women would want to stay on anyone's lap for all eternity? How big is this Jesus man? He can't be bigger than Sesquatch. How can he hold so many? Grandpa repeated the words to the translator to be sure he got them right. McKilty answered that they would sit on Jesus's lap in heaven, next to God. The old man looked around. Who is this God-man? He couldn't picture anyone wanting such a lazy eternity. The old man was beginning to suspect that the interpreter was not getting it right, that he could not do his job, so he carefully explained to him what he meant and asked the man to have another go at it. McKilty went into some fervent tirade about "fire and damnation," which was completely off topic in Grandpa's mind.

The translator was now red in the face. He had no way to bridge the gap between the vastly disconnected meanings each man held around the same words. Grandpa wasn't satisfied and the translator told McKilty this. Frustrated, McKilty's eyes flashed fire and his teeth clenched tighter than usual. "They mean your granddaughters will be baptized," he said. "Without baptism they cannot have medicine against our diseases." McKilty then looked oddly at Grandpa. Grandpa thought Father McKilty looked like a foolish boy who had stabbed himself while playing with his father's fish hook and lacked the courage to thread it through and remove it quietly without saying anything to anyone — and especially lacked the courage to tell his father. Grandpa couldn't figure out what such a look was doing on a grown man's face, but he recognized the word "medicine" and understood the threat.

He also knew that names committed a person to something or someone and the names being given to the children committed them to this man Jesus who was the Son of God, whoever that was, and this would change them and change their commitment to themselves. Names also meant something in and of themselves; they shaped children in some way. He was uneasy about having his daughters and granddaughters commit their lives to strange names that meant nothing to his people. He was also unsure of committing his children to this man, this arbiter of Jesus and God, who did not seem to be all that mature or sane. But he also knew that the villagers needed medicine to get them through the diseases these white men brought: baptism, names, and medicine or no baptism, no names, and no medicine. He turned all this over in his mind and failed to understand why anyone would put his people in such a position. Why would anyone bring disease and then with-hold medicine so they could rename you and then commit you to some stranger who wanted you to sit on his lap?

He stared at Father McKilty. This man was more than odd. He introduced himself as the old man's father. He talked nonsense about sitting forever in the lap of Jesus and forever-life in some place the old man did not recognize. Was he going to take the children there? Grandpa wondered at the arrogance it took to name yourself the father of someone who is clearly twice your age. He shrugged; clearly they were not speaking the same language. Grand-pa did not know enough about these people to dig up the question whose answer would settle his mind. He finally accepted that he would never understand this father and waved his hand at the priest saying, "Baptize and name who you will."

This was the beginning of their own end.

"There is power in naming," Grandpa had said to his daughter when she told him she was going to send her daughters to the priest to be named. "Names mean something. They encourage children to travel on a certain path. The sides of character are reflected in a name. If you don't know the meaning of the names, how will you know what sides having them will show? Meaningless names could reduce them to a meaningless existence."

"There is power in their names," his daughter replied. She had watched the men bury the dead. She had wrapped body after body in the crude blankets they had received in trade from even cruder white men because there was no time to weave their own. They all returned home improperly dressed. The shame of seeing her relatives going home half-naked burned her eyes dry with grief. She could not face another round of death.

"Both things are true," Celia's great-great-grandmother sighed.

THE CANDLE IN FRONT of Celia jumps at the accidental touch of her hand as she mimics Alice's Gramma throwing up her hands and sighing.

"You all right, Aunt Celia?" Jacob asks. Celia scrambles to come back to reality and find an answer.

"I was just wondering what happened to Gramma," is all she can come up with. She twirls a cedar branch between her thumb and baby finger, knowing full well the answer is inadequate.

"She died," Rena says as though she thinks Celia is stupid, but she says it with such an endearing flatness that everyone breaks up laughing.

Busted, Celia thinks to herself, as she picks up the cedar she has just put down. Celia has no clue how to respond to Rena, with her white girl, her Mac shirt, her dry wit, her dramatic performance of every story told. These are too many masks for Celia. Rena's voice jars Celia and catches her lying. Her words come out wrapped in a sharp-edged mystery, even now when she slops on the endearment. Celia still hears the sharpness. It slices up the possibility of Celia having any kind of relationship with her. It annoys Celia the way it sometimes annoyed her to see the black of the night sky get clouded with an opaque layer of plain blue paint, dimming the stars and ruining the sky's perfect black. Celia squirms, but just barely.

All eyes turn to her. She sniffs at the cedar bough in her hand. The room resumes its chatter after a moment of Celia's silence. Celia withdraws from the room and tries to remember when it was that the houses lost the scent of cedar, yesterday's pie, or Saturday's bread baking. Smells that individuated the women's recipes and defined the very sense of nourishment each woman offered her family. The devotion of the women used to be measured by the scent of their homes, as though the very smell of them marked the caring of the women, detailed the emotion they invested in their children, articulated the special esteem in which they held their men.

Momma's home was fussy the way Momma was. Momma put cardamom in her pumpkin pie, crimped the edges, and cut tiny v-shaped nicks in the surface of the pumpkin filling after it was done. While the pies cooled on the counter, Momma would hunt all over the house trying to find spare change. If she found it, she would get Jimmy to cycle to town for whipping cream. That was fussy. No one made fussy pumpkin pie like Momma used to. Now the homes smell of cleaning agents and air fresheners. The old smells seemed to end sometime after the 1970s, about when they got central heating. Celia sniffs the cedar. She closes her eyes.

"My life doesn't smell right anymore," she says as she lays the cedar out carefully on the coffee table.

Normally, when I hear something as plain and simple as this, I leave. But I got to thinking that something was going to happen, so I stayed. Sometimes it is hard for a mink to hang in there, but I am curious.

Rena thinks Celia might be on to something. Connecting with Celia is a chore for her. The woman dreams beyond her capacity to keep up. It is rare that Rena feels Celia is on ground solid enough to be engaged in conversation, but this is something she herself has been thinking about. She knows about the loss of aromas in the old kitchens. The old houses were cedar planked — some double-walled, others not, but all of them wood-faced on the inside. The walls soaked up smells, held them, and layered one smell over the next until the smells of the day before and the days after created a unique blend of the family's favourite foods.

"Central heating is lonely," Rena says.

I begin to get what the agony of their present is all about.

"That's it. It is so lonely," Celia says, with a satisfaction like she's found her shoe after looking for it all morning and still has time to go to town.

"Smells identify a home. They say something about a woman." Stacey puts her paddle in the water.

Jacob picks up the cedar his aunt put down and lets the lilt of the women's voices play with the skin on his back. He stares at this branch that had captured his aunt's attention. It had Celia turning the women down a road he knows nothing about but finds himself hungry to see more of. He feels as though they are telling him something he has always wanted to know but didn't realize till he heard it. His insides are quiet for a moment, pleasantly still, soft-forest-just-before-you-see-a-doe kind of quiet.

"It changed the way we cook. We don't cook with the sun any-more," Momma says. The glare of the uncased kitchen light bulb emphasizes Momma's eyes. The white light pushes the tired out from the skin around them and puffs them up. The light is stark and cruel; it deepens the sad lines around Momma's mouth and thins her lips so that it is hard to tell she was ever young or beautiful.

"What do you mean, Momma?" Stacey asks, trying not to look too closely at her face.

"Dinner was always early in winter, on time in fall and spring, and late or never in summer," Momma laughs. "I don't know how many times I heard, 'Go pick berries, I'm weaving today,' from my

Mom or Gramma, and I don't know how many times I said it to you. 'Go pick berries ...'"

"'... I'm sewing today.'" They chorus the finish, even German Judy and Rena sing out along with Stacey and Celia.

"Food doesn't taste right on an electric stove. I just can't bring myself to fuss over it." Momma winces as she speaks.

I cannot imagine having my food source altered, but I sympathize.

"Maybe that's why we don't fuss over cooking anymore," Celia offers. "No one will visit unless the host fusses over the food."

Rena doesn't think so. She looks at the electrified house. It's because it's only half like a white woman's house, she tells herself. The design is right: an island for cutting things stands in the middle of the kitchen, an electric stove squats left of centre, kitty-corner from the island, directly across from which sit double sinks. Apart from this, the rightness changes. None of the dishes match. The pots aren't good ones from expensive kitchen stores. Half the women here still use cast-iron or aluminum pots. No CorningWare or environmentally friendly stainless steel pots. Mixed-up plates and odd bits of silverware that is definitely not silver. Half the women have additional electrical appliances, most of which do not work. The other half do not have any at all; it was half-annoying for them.

It strikes me that it is like waking up to find your forest gone, no trees, no food. No sense of place. No opportunity for survival.

"Maybe matching plates would help. I'm going to get us matching plates, Judy," Rena says. "The kitchen has got to be an Indian kitchen with a wood stove or a white one with matching plates."

"Yeah," Madeline pipes in. "Right now it's an old half-breed."

"A Métis, a jigger," Rena says, doing a little dance.

It occurs to me I could not be any kind of a half-breed. Humans can do that, mix it up with others, adapt, but us minks can't. Maybe that's Celia's problem, she's like me. Can't mix it up and survive.

"No," Momma says, "It'd be a Métis if everything matched, because we're in it."

The laughter dissipates the tension in the room. It loosens the tongues of the women in the direction of who's up to what. Sweet gossip, the kind that rolls off the tongue and reminds you of how many loved ones fill the room you're in. Somehow the soft gossip, the joy of the women, brings the warm glow of Gramma's bedroom into this room, despite the glare of the uncovered light bulb, despite the absence of old fire flicks, and despite the moonless night. They float down the rivers of their stories, impressing themselves with the sheer numbers of people they are curious about. They laugh about Tony's old car, coo over the new babies, and chuckle about the secret romances — except for Stacey's. It makes them feel like everything is going to be all right because they still have so many folks to care to talk about.

The laughter enlivens the frond in Jacob's hand. Jacob does not see the humour in all this, but he feels the warmth in the room go up a notch. It warms him enough to cause him to ponder the unity of feeling between his hand and this frond. He thinks he hears the cedar say something. He is lost in the sensation, too lost to see the humour in the banter of the women, but not lost enough to commit to the words he is hearing from cedar. He rocks the frond.

Jacob is like Celia, like me, like those old bones, the ones that cannot be happy in their new state.

"It worries me some," Momma says. The laughter stops dead. No one knows what the "it" is that is worrying Momma. They are half-afraid to ask.

"Why is that?" Stacey asks. The women in the room make mental notes to themselves: Stacey knows what Momma is talking about. They let the story unfold between Momma and Stacey, hoping to get clued in as it does.

"Sometimes memory gets stuck in some sort of soup inside my mind and only the right scent will dislodge it. Stirring the soup can help you recall the story, the teaching that is going to solve this trouble, this terrible moment, and now those smells are gone.

The smells are gone from the roadside, the hillside, and the houses, and I just can't remember anymore. I just can't bring myself to the place where my memory sits comfortably. Sometimes I get so tired, trying to remember. Maybe if I could have remembered ..." Her voice trails off, the sentence unfinished.

Rena sits up.

She is heading straight for Jimmy's suicide.

"Don't go there," Rena whispers, just the smallest hint of threat in her voice.

"I know. But you know?" Momma slides from her chair, reaches over for a short stack of coloured cloth, pulls open a kitchen drawer, pulls out some fusible backing and a pair of scissors. She holds the scissors up, challenging them to recall what it is they all knew.

Stacey, Judy, and Rena nod. Celia wants to know what Momma was about to make, so she watches. The conversation rolls out.

"Yeah, I know. They even changed the smell of our world. Nothing like oolichan grease to spark up a long trail of salmon stories. You know, you just know that the smell is going to tell you what you need to know next."

Rena picks at the corner of the kitchen counter where the Arborite edging is loose. Momma fuses the stiffener to the cloth and begins cutting.

How in the world can you change the smells of someone else's world?

Cedar moves of its own accord in Jacob's hand. This is not good for Jacob, who has no idea what cedar is doing and no context for believing what he is seeing and feeling. Jacob fights cedar, tries to hold it still in his hand, but cedar refuses to be still. He feels panic rise in his chest.

Celia stops watching Momma and turns to Jacob and the cedar frond. She hears the panic in Jacob's mind. She listens as cedar whispers calming words: "Your song sits at the edge of the mountain. It awaits your voice." Celia sees Jacob is driving the words away from his consciousness, he is struggling to focus on the women's conversation. Celia's mind urges Jacob to be calm. "Listen, cedar wants to tell you something, listen to cedar." Jacob ignores her. Celia decides to let him figure it out for himself; she leans back in her chair and resumes watching Momma.

"Smoked fish?" Jacob blurts out, finding some piece of talk to jump in and get nosy about. Fear still has hold of him; the words come out high-pitched and strained. Celia recognizes the fear; it is the same fear she felt so long ago, behind the woodshed. When she first saw those tall ships.

The old bones grow determined when they recognize that Jacob is like his aunt; they need a young man to help restore balance to the village, mediate the rage of the young bones, and remove the threat of the serpent. They sing harder and rattle with greater will. They pray Jacob will hear them.

"Oh, Jacob, you make me tired already," Rena starts in on him as she jumps up and pours another coffee for herself and the rest of the women. "Any minute now I'm going to run out and have me a smoke."

Jacob winces, but Rena was rough around the edges.

"Ah hell, we'll smoke some fish this year so you don't have to ask us what we cannot explain." She takes a long pull on the hot coffee.

"Ah, Rena, leave him be." Every head jerks to stare at Celia. She's never been one to say "shit" even when her mouth is full of it.

Rena looks at her intently for a second, a small smile playing on her lips. She lets go a deep breath and laughs out loud. She is proud of Celia. The others chuckle, nervous and confused at the sound of command in Celia's voice and Rena's response. It unnerves them that she is still in the room, listening.

I am licking my paws, enjoying the easy banter of the women as they head for the place they need to be to figure this out. It is easy: the women need to find a way to reconcile the new life with the old story. But, at the same time, it is so complicated. Remembering is a matter of context and the context has changed. I look up. Speaking of change, the weather is about to shift. I look for a dry spot with a vantage point. The wheelbarrow will do. Off I scurry to get under it.

CLOUDS DARK, PUFFY, AND grey sometimes hang on to their rain. They are up in the sky hanging heavy. The grandfathers beyond the moon realize the clouds are not going to let go their earth tears without a push, a shove, and a boom. They rear up and their hollering rolls out, breaking the clouds. Their bellowing rattles the cloud's stillness, making them crash about. Their blue fire breath streaks the earth below with its bent light.

The women gasp, and then halloo the grandfathers. The women shut off the electric lights as they always do in a storm. Momma drops her craftwork in a drawer, opens another and pulls out candles and matches. Each woman grabs a candle and a match and sets them ablaze. The flickers of candlelight sway to the breath of the people in the room, transform the faces into orange-burnt-brown haunted cheekbones, almond eyes, and teeth — handsome shadowy works of art.

"How did it happen … the smells … the loss of them?" Jacob asks.

"We ran out of wood," Momma says flatly.

The candlelight dances on Momma's cheekbones, making them shine smooth reddish brown against her disappearing jawline, her brows, her furrowed age-lines. It catches her eyes in its flicker and paints her lips. Celia likes the way it burns away the years so she can't see the tired in her mother's eyes or the sad lines around her mouth.

Momma skips to the end of the story without answering Jacob. This annoys him. Celia knows Jacob is annoyed, but she lets the answer set in the glow of the candles, the art of the faces, and the bellowing of the thunder without explaining it to him.

Stacey, too, sees his annoyance. She knows Jacob wants a schoolteacher answer. It annoys her to think that he wants an explanation, as though he can't imagine enough to add a remark to the talk around the table. It's true, Stacey thinks, we ran out of wood to build homes and fires. The chief went to the government, the government came back with a plan, and then the government demanded a vote.

"We ran out of wood and they gave us a vote." Momma laughs at the absurdity. "Wasn't that some powerful piece of nothing?"

Celia nods. Nothing had ever been solved by the vote. Before the vote families talked to each other through their men, from men to women, from women to women, between children who overheard the women, back to the men, then back to the chief. By the time a decision was made it was clear what needed to be done, because much talk had already occurred, many sides had been seen, much had changed and much value had been added. The decision was obvious. Everyone knew what part they were going to play when the plan was finally unfurled. If every family sent someone to make the decision happen it flew. If there was a missing family, the chief turned over the dirt he stood on, shrugged, and went home. That was it. Momma had hit the nail on the head. The chatter died with the vote.

Celia thinks about the healing circle she belongs to. They talk to each other, but it was limited to disclosing hurt and trauma, or rage. That kind of talk feels narrow and tiring. She knows they need it, but now she wants it peppered between the other kinds of conversations they never seem to have anymore.

I smile. Celia is on her way. She doesn't know she has shifted direction, but there it is, she is on her way home to the old ways.

The vote was silent, ominous in its lack of community and collaboration. It stood between them and the ordinary conversations they needed to have to make decisions about their lives. The vote was powerful in its ability to silence the village and isolate each from the other. It was like the white men, all-powerful and silencing, except it was invisible.

"First came the vote, then mortgages. Now they want taxes," Stacey concludes in silence, not wanting to add more thickness to the air. It was more than just the food, the wood, the smell of their homes. When the tension was thick before, someone would throw a frond of cedar onto the stove and the smoke would gather it up and quickly carry it away. But now the tension increased in a room, it choked the collective breath of the people in it; it took cedar longer to burn it away.

"Ain't that some shit," Rena says again. She isn't sure about running out of wood. There are mountains of wood behind them. It wasn't that they ran out of wood. It was the absence of access to the wood in them mountains that was the problem, and now they are facing it. Rena remembers the last time she, her sisters, and Nora had hauled shakes out of those mountains; it must have been the early fifties. Helicopters whirled above, searching for them. Eventually the choppers found them. They were arrested for culling the wood from the forest. Nora spent thirty days in jail and Rena and her sisters were sentenced to three months to a year without their mother or their village. "Someone has to have a licence; stumpage fees have to be paid to someone," the judge had said. Nora refused to pay the fine. She had money, but she was not going to turn it over to some white man she didn't know, even if it meant jail and giving up her children.

There is enough wood. Rena turns and spits into an old can. She is pissed, pissed that the longer punishment was meted out to her and her sisters, one of whom had left the village bitter and resentful, never to return.

Judy frowns at Rena and shakes her head. Rena shoots an "I dare you to say something" kind of face at Judy, then looks away. They weren't allowed to have the wood and that damned mother of theirs wasn't about to pay them people a licence fee for the prohibition they had no right to visit upon them.

After the prohibition and the vote everything changed. Children grew up but stayed in their parents' homes as young couples with small children. Squeezed into too few rooms, the racket and lack of space made them edgy and desperate.

Decisions made by desperate humans are usually not well thought out.

Jacob stops breathing, he resents that he did not receive an answer. What does wood, the abundance or shortage of it, have to do with the loss of smells in our homes? What has any of that got to do with the vote? He isn't that concerned about the question. He had thrown it out more to keep the conversation going than out of real interest in an answer. He wants to hear the sound of the women's voices. Their voices take the sharp edge off missing his cousin Jimmy. They still his constant wondering about why Jimmy did that to himself. He wants their voices to help remove him from his sorrow, from this cedar branch, from this serious wondering. A chill wind passes through him. He snaps the cedar branch in his hands and tosses it at the table.

Celia slides across the room in the flicker of the uneven candles, one candle shining on her buxom chest, the other lighting part of her chiselled face, bringing out her cheekbone. One of her eyes disappears in shadow, the other comes alive, registers dangerous emotions.

Jacob shrinks back, picks up the cedar branch and hands it to her. She takes it. She looks as though she can see a secret inside him, a secret that even he is aware of. Jacob shudders. She gives him a sweet smile, the sort that goes with a wink. She goes to the stove, flips an element on, sets a cast iron frying pan on it, and burns the branch.

She returns with the pan, her face has changed. The tightness of her skin has loosened. She holds the frying pan steady while she bathes his face, his hair, his chest, and his hands with the smoking cedar. She utters something in their language. Momma stares at

Celia; she has no idea that Celia knew about this, nor does she know that she speaks some of the language. Jacob thinks he understands her. He feels cedar's smoke go down his throat. It settles in his belly and calms him. He gives Celia a half smile when she finishes cleansing him. He decides not to harm cedar again.

By the time Celia finishes they are staring at her, except for Ned. Ned does not understand what she is doing, but he figures that she lived with old Alice so she learned this business from her. Ned does not think of himself as a Sto:lo man. He adapts to whatever is before him, like a Sto:lo man, but would not say that was why he did so. When he lived among white men, he adapted; now he is here with the women of his wife's family, so he adapts.

Ned is in the corner not thinking about Jacob's question; Celia's Jimmy trails through his mind. Jimmy never seemed to be dissatisfied with anything specific, but there was always this tension in him. He came over every Sunday to visit Ned like a lot of the boys, sewed nets, cleaned rifles, and sharpened axes with him. As he grew older he took up smoking, but the tension hovering around him continued. Jimmy was meticulous: he sharpened his axe until he could split a hair with it; he sewed perfectly even stitches into the nets; he cleaned his rifle bore until it shone. Can you care too much for small things? Jimmy was at Ned's that last Sunday. He borrowed the rope that ended his visits. Before he took it home, he had walked over to Ned's rain barrel at the side of the house and cleaned it off. Ned had thought that odd, but then it was in keeping with the other odd quirks Jimmy had, so he had not said a word about it.

Ned thinks about how the villagers do things in clutches. He wonders who's next. He doesn't ponder this for long before he sets to work on the riddle of pushing back this new tide, this wave of suicide he is sure is coming. He looks for the moment, the place that someone's mind would have to come to before it threw them in the direction of killing themselves, but he can't find it. He doesn't spend time wondering what it was that piled up on Jimmy, became too heavy a load for him to carry. Youth doesn't have to carry anything. Nor does he wonder that a man as young as Jimmy imagined that he had to carry a load. Youth is responsible for one thing: to fill its basket with the taste for life and to experience the world. What is there to carry in that? This is not what he is looking for; he wants to untangle Jimmy's journey enough to see the exact point that took him in the direction of suicide. What direction had Jimmy's mind taken to lead him to that rope and the beam he hung himself from? Ned finds himself wandering around the same circle of words and realizes he is not up to this.

He is old enough to feel responsible, but too naïve to do much about it. Suicide is too complex and too foreign for him to understand. The only other suicide he's heard of is Stacey's friend — that young white girl, what was her name? That was long ago and she was white; in those days he didn't care enough for white youth to wonder about her suicide. Now he is sorry he hadn't been more curious. He looks around at the room full of women and decides that maybe Judy might know. Judy left the law office she worked for the same summer that Stacey left, took some courses in Vancouver, and returned to work for a doctor in town. He had heard her talk about the suicide of psych patients. Now he needs to know what she knows.

Ned looks at Judy and purses his lips. He jolts his head slightly, signalling her to come outside. She has lived in the village long enough to know not to holler "What, what is it?" Judy tiptoes around the bodies and through the blaze of candles to join Ned at the door. He heads outside, grabbing a pair of raincoats from their hooks as he leaves. Judy grabs an umbrella.

Outside the rain is coming in heavy, pelting the earth as if desperate to get away from the thunder. Judy pushes up the big umbrella. She and Ned stand under it without speaking for a moment, then he opens the door to his thoughts. Judy walks in.

"I just can't stop wondering about this here suicide business."

He pulls out a cigarette, cups his hands to fire up a match, lights it, and takes a long pull of smoke into his lungs. "I know Jimmy's gone. He's probably rolling around up there right now having a high old time with his gramma and the rest of them, but I don't like the way it sits on the women in this house."

"It's such a shock," Judy offers.

He wants to scoff. Shock? Jesus, this village has not lived without shock for a hundred and fifty years. What in the world makes her think he could be shocked into stupidity? He lets it go.

"I've sat through a lot of funerals, seen these women grieve so deep I thought they were going to keel over and die from it. But when Jimmy died the women barely looked at each other. Any other funeral they were leaning on each other, holding hands, holding each other up — not Jimmy's. After the funeral there was no laughter. No storyteller got up to ease us back into the everyday stuff. It was like some different dead breath settled over the whole village. How did we come to this?"

The storm is rolling in their direction. Both watch it while Judy answers.

"I don't know why, but it feels like maybe the women in this village are tired. Maybe we just can't take any more heartache. Maybe we are fed up with disappointment. Maybe we can't cope with the insult of living at the edge of survival." It surprises Judy to hear herself say "we." The village has never made any effort to include her as one of its own; she knows most of them regard her as Rena's white woman. Most of them barely say hello to her and only a few of them nod as she goes to and from work. But there it was, she had used "we," as though she belongs.

Ned offers her a puff of his cigarette. She takes it. She doesn't smoke but puffs without inhaling much, coughing what she does drag in. She hands the cigarette back to Ned.

"How did we get so tired of living?" A flash of blue light punctuates Ned's question. Under the cover of her big black umbrella,

Ned and Judy walk; he itemizes everything he knows about the yard. His grandsons had helped him transform the gravel stretch the house had been plunked on into the kind of yard Momma would love. The gravel was gone and in its place there was a smooth driveway and a lawn that plagued him with its constant crying out to be mowed. Along the edges of the yard were two six-inch columns of river stones set three feet apart; inside them were Momma's flowers, all kinds of them. It had taken him and his son years to collect those stones, but by the time his grandsons were born Momma was ready to make her garden. In spring the flowers burst into pink, purple, red blossoms. Momma's flowers were not just beautiful to look at — they were medicine. She, Stacey, and Rena dug up the roots in summer and Rena dried and took care of them. As small boys, Jimmy and Jacob had found such joy in helping their grandpa and uncle collect the stones, and in helping their gramma plant the flowers, weed the garden, and dig up the roots. On the ground in front of him, Ned's foot kicks a child's wooden shovel. He stares at it.

"Damn if this isn't the same shovel them little boys used to help Momma dig up roots." He picks it up and turns it in his hands for a minute. His shoulders shake. Judy stiffens; she lets the umbrella drop. She does not want to see Ned's face. A terrible sound is coming out of him. The thunder bellows louder, drowning the sound Ned makes. He clutches the little shovel so hard it snaps. "Oh, no." He lets it go.

"What the hell are all the names of those roots they used to pick anyway?" he asks as if desperate for the answer. Judy remains silent. It isn't the question that he needs the answer to and she knows it.

"Ain't this some shit," Judy says, pushing the umbrella back up.

"After the snake left, those girls of Madeline's got so quiet, then Stacey left, and Celia took to daydreaming her life away at school and at her gramma's house. Momma kept cooking and sewing, but now she sits at that machine cursing more often than chuckling to herself like she used to. Jimmy was a little odd, but sometimes I would see this thing come over his face, like, like ..." Ned trails off, moves in another direction. "Damn. He hated school." He picks up a loose stone and tosses it at the dark as though he hates whatever Jimmy couldn't love; at the same time, though, he can't understand why Jimmy hated school. He got to come home after all; what was there to hate about learning?

"Those boys that hung out at the snake's left one by one. A lot of the girls left to marry. The mothers whose daughters left stopped visiting the villagers. Divorce started marking many young women's lives. Maybe it is none of those things and maybe it's all of them."

"Maybe it's not about any of that?" Judy offers with as much humility as her Prussian origins allow.

Ned looks at her and wonders at what moment he found her acceptable. Ned's look is very nearly an intimate gesture. Wonderment about the inner life of a woman is not expected, is almost unacceptable. His duty is to accept what women present without wondering. Wondering directed at women by a man could be construed as invasive, rude, unless she was a close relative.

"Give me one of them smokes of yours," Judy says.

Ned laughs and digs around for a pair of them.

"Are you actually going to smoke this one?" he asks.

Judy pulls hard on the cigarette, holds it down and away from the rain, exhales and decides she has earned a place in this village. She blows out another cloud of smoke and suppresses a cough as she struggles to get comfortable about Ned's wondering before the next thunderclap.

Screw those who decided she was white and so didn't really count. Screw them all. I clap my hands together. I smile. About time you decide to face that she lives here and that she belongs here.

꙳

NOT LONG AFTER THE epidemic the voting business came. It was Judy who had said, "It will change you. I can't explain how, but it will, know that it will." It had felt like a warning then and it read like a warning in retrospect. Ned had voted against the government housing plan; but he was only realizing now that it was the voting itself Judy had warned them about. The vote confounded just about everything.

"Do you remember telling us this vote would change us?"

"Yes." She turns her face in the direction of the lightning and takes another pull of the cigarette.

"I think people thought you were talking about having the government building our houses for us. I voted against the housing program. I knew something was up with this voting business by the way you said it, but I didn't know enough about it to be able to ask a clear question. Now I know that I should have asked everyone to boycott the vote. We didn't have to vote to get the land, the school, or the vote. They would have given us anything to make sure we took out the mortgages to buy these homes."

"Hindsight is always twenty-twenty." Judy is dizzy and queasy. She looks at the stub of cigarette and tosses it into the rain-soaked yard.

"Taking up the vote was pure blindness." Ned drops his butt and steps on it, grinding it into the mud around the grass.

"What do you mean?"

"Well, before the vote we talked and talked and talked. Now we have the vote and, like you said, we let things happen without talking about them. If we had to talk over every aspect of our lives like we used to, Jimmy would be here right now. Maybe next year Jacob will still be here."

"Don't say that." Judy can hear Dominic saying "Be careful what you pray for" to her years earlier when she had doubted out loud that they could save anyone from the flu.

"Someone has to."

"So we give up the vote and start talking?"

"We wouldn't be able to talk anyone into giving up the vote, but we have to restore talking. We don't have to give up anything to talk, Judy. We just got to move our lips and clack our teeth. It won't solve everything, but talking will get us back to where we ought to be." Ned hesitates, starts his next sentence with an "If" and then stops.

"And the problem with that is?"

"Jacob doesn't speak our women's language, in either his English or theirs. They talk like they are stuck back in some old yesterday and Jacob talks like he is headed for tomorrow. We have to build a bridge between yesterday and tomorrow." Ned puts his leg up on a log and leans into the storm.

"Oh, well, gee. I thought you had something challenging for me, Ned." Judy doesn't really have a clue what he is talking about. Jacob and Rena and Celia all speak regular English.

The sky breaks, the clouds divorce themselves from one another, and the earth's crying stops. The moon and stars appear suddenly.

"We have to talk, Judy. And you have to be there." She feels relief upon hearing his words. It is as though she has an itch she hasn't been able to scratch and now Ned has handed her a knitting needle. She's been bothered by something for a long time and has not been able to name it. She realizes it was silence. Rena had come home every day in the summer and fall from picking this or that medicine, lain them out on the counter, tied them with cedar she had pounded, hung them. It had taken her hours. Judy liked watching her, but there had always been something odd about it and now she knows. Rena had not uttered a word during the hours of work.

"I want you to know, Judy, that from this day forward you are one of us to me. I am not sure if that is a curse or a blessing, but I can't ask you for anything without offering you a place here."

"C'MON, NED, EVEN I know that takes ceremony and witnesses."

Now they're getting somewhere. Ceremony, witnesses: the Sto:lo way of doing business.

"Yes, but I get to name the guests." The words fall flat onto the soggy ground.

They stand in the noisy rain for a while longer and Judy acquiesces to one last smoke. She cannot imagine a way for her to play a part in untangling this mess, but she knows that this old man is going to haul her into the vortex of whatever tornado he is planning to set in motion. The thought excites her and unnerves her at the same time. Her upbringing did not prepare her for change. She knows Ned does not think about it; he takes change for granted. He puffs out the last breath of his smoke. His tension seems to leave with it.

"Has this suicide got you feeling shame, Ned?" Judy lowers herself onto the wet bench near the porch. Ned sits on the old rocking chair next to it.

"It isn't about shame. It is a bitch of a world we live in. Recognizing the exit is nothing short of a miracle. Suicide is an exit. I never saw it. Some days like you say I get so tired I fear I won't remember my own name. I fear my wife will ask me what day it is because she is so tired she's forgotten. She has this feeling there is some kind of an appointment someone has to keep but can't remember if it is tomorrow or today because she doesn't know what day today is. No. It is about trust. Talking kept us trusting. Trusting one another secures our sense of hope in the future. The vote kept us from talking for a whole generation. Silence kills hope. It will take a generation of talking to break down the walls. When walls break, Judy, wood splinters fly, slivers land. Who knows who will get hurt."

"The vote is about not talking," Judy repeats and laughs as she thinks about the host of rules governing confidentiality — not talking — that are connected to the vote. There are even rules about what you must talk about. She laughs some more to herself. She prays everything is as simple as Ned has put it. In her world of origin it was not that simple, but here maybe it is.

"She's wrong, you know," Ned says simply.

"Who is wrong? About what? No, I don't know." Judy is back to her Prussian self.

"Momma," he answers the first question. "About no wood," he answers the second. "There was plenty of wood. We just weren't allowed to use it anymore. In those days, 'not allowed' had meaning. It doesn't now. The government is the one backed up in a corner unable to make their own laws work for them."

Ned laughs, stomping about in the mud, dancing in the rain. He lifts his head and drinks the rainwater. He hollers, "It doesn't matter now."

Judy, caught up in his joy, drops her umbrella and dances beside him.

They are about to go back into the house and I have to find a dry spot with a good vantage point. This part of the story is over. I spot an old birdhouse that hasn't seen birds or seed for a long time and skip up the tree and go inside. It is a good vantage point to watch from.

MOMMA STARES AT JACOB. There is no easy feeling between them. He is slippery, unlike Jimmy. She doesn't know this young man. She can't find the doorway to knowing him. She searches for some deep feeling inside herself for him. It is there. She loves him. She just isn't sure she likes him. Something stands between her loving him and her liking him. She wants to know what exactly it is that stands between them. In place of her liking is this gaping hole. How did it get there? Was it pages of story, was it language, was it the absence of language, or was it a different being? Jacob's life has been an electrified, television-filled life. Is this electrified life the beast that wedges its way between them?

Momma recalls scraping the bottoms of barrels, looking for what she did not have. She realizes there has been so much no in her life: No eggs to make pancakes, no television to relax to, no radio to sing along with, no newspaper to keep up with the world, no books to escape into, no battery-charged beasts to ease whatever drudgery life dares to present, no quiet moments in which to contemplate anything. It was just get up in the morning, sew, preserve, can, catch, hunt, gather, scrape, pretend you are not without, give up that dress, give up those boots, give up that shirt, give up that new car, give up that notepad, that journal, that reading time, that bath time. Give up. Her life was about giving up. It was easy when them people came and asked them to give up their old way of making decisions in exchange for houses she would not have to work her fingers to the bleeding bone to build. She would not have to truck halfway up the Coquihalla, a baby on her back, dragging a wagon full of food provisions to hunt down some cedar stump, split shakes, bundle them up, put the baby in the empty wagon and the shakes on her back, then take the shakes and child down the mountain to be delivered to a relative to build some substandard house. She would not have to dodge the white man's helicopters patrolling the hillsides for poachers stealing shingles. Her grandchildren, whom she loved more than she ever remembered loving her own children, would have decent homes without their parents risking arrest for stealing wood from their own mountains.

She grabs her knees; a wave of pain goes through them. Memory can be nasty. The pain returns like a bill collector. She may as well be climbing down that mountain with those shakes on her back, the pain is so real. She makes a feeble attempt to stop thinking about it. It's no use. Her mind keeps seeing herself, legs wobbling, the shakes swaying back and forth. They knew, she decides, the shakes knew they were not going to houses like the ones in white town. They knew they were going to get hammered onto some silly shed some woman's relatives will call a house because they will be too polite to call it a shed. The shakes had jumped back and forth on her back, scraping her elbows and threatening her balance, as though determined to force her to drop them. They did not want to come with her. They did not want to leave the comfort of their mountain home.

"We are not who we used to be, Jacob," she says to no one as she rocks back and forth in her chair. Jacob had sat in front of every children's television show. He had listened to some Indian lady with beautiful long black hair and dancing eyes sing to him. Momma never had that and she could not give it to her children. White people had so much more to give. How did they take these mountains and turn them into all the things they gave to her grandchildren? She wants to know. She can't know. The question sucks the strength from her muscle, weakens her knees, and makes her so dizzy she wants to puke. How did they do that? She swims around the question like a salmon that by some piece of craziness has gone up the wrong river. She is about to sink into a relieving faint.

"Ned," she hollers.

He comes running from outside, soaking wet, dripping all over the floor.

"You better take me somewhere, because I can't bear the question anymore. It is much too big for me."

She faints dead away.

Ned picks her up and carries her to her bedroom. This ends her night with her family.

Celia is right behind Ned, following him into her momma's room. No one in the room thinks this is a good idea, but they shrug and ignore the trio. Jacob's eyes widen. His hands twitch. He is terrified that he has killed his gramma. In the middle of their talk about the times they grew up in, Rena turns to Jacob, sees his consternation, and says flatly, "She always faints when there is some question that is too much for her. Don't you worry, she will dream on it and be answering you by tomorrow. Your gramma is a dreamer, Jacob."

RESTLESS HAS BECOME OBSESSED with conquering Celia. He thinks about how to. Loyal knows this. He is anxious that Restless might be successful, and grows determined to protect her.

NED PAUSES AT THE bedroom door, turns to look at Celia; he catches her determined look. She is too old for him to restrain. He leaves the two women in the bedroom and returns to the fireless living room.

MOMMA'S MEMORY SLIPS INTO fragments, stringing together bits of story about the newcomers that she had heard from her gramma. She was in her gramma's kitchen listening to her talk about the canoes. There were hundreds of them, loaded and ready to roll down the river to the city. Celia could see them bobbing gently at the river's edge. White people, mostly women with strange languages, scurried about, talking to anyone who would listen. They chattered at different men one by one, their voices anxious in foreign languages. The frantic blond and redheaded women ran about showing boatman after boatman bits of paper marked with destinations like Vancouver, Victoria, and Sardis, but the boatmen could not read them. Undaunted, the women continued to ask questions of them in languages the boatmen did not know, some even fought for the English words that would clarify their questions, the answers to which would quell their fears. None of the would-be listeners knew much English, nor did they care about the women — none of them were relatives or clanswomen.

The strange silence of the boatmen who had brought them here pumped up the women's fear. They would never make their destination. Before traversing the country, the women had spent months on a dirty ship that rocked mercilessly even when there were no storms. They had vomited so much that they thought they were going to die. Some of them did. Those who made it to shore had to spend months on a wagon train crossing an enormous territory of oaks, maples, and wild rice lakes before crossing a thousand miles of prairie. Just before the mountains they stumbled onto an encampment of tall and emaciated brown-skinned people with forlorn eyes who stared at them but said nothing. They scaled mountain after mountain on foot until they reached the boatmen. They had spent the past ten days walking across rocky terrain with terrifying canyons, steep hills, and sharp twists. They had canoed with these boatmen down this crazy river to this place, where the boatmen emptied them out like cargo.

The entire trip had been bereft of common language between them and their guides. They had been expected to feed themselves and had packed food, but most had run out days into the trip. The hunger, the loneliness, and the hardship of the last length of the journey boiled inside the women. Now these boatmen who had carried their loads through the treacherous Yale gorge and had inspired a feeling of safety and confidence in the women, something like closeness, like comfort, like respect, were packing up to leave. The women wanted more from these men and could not believe that they would just abandon them here.

They pleaded and begged. The boatmen left anyway, left them crying, squawking, feeling betrayed. The women scurried the landing, asking strangers about their destinations. No one answered. Their abandonment spawned fear, then rage, then isolation, and finally surrender before the night was out. Some of them were found by their future husbands, quaking and quivering with cold and hunger, humiliated into submission. Others were never claimed. They floated from man to man for liquor, food, dance, and sex until, diseased and cast off, they died.

In the beginning of the world, these mountains rose out of the sea, hundreds of them, thousands, pushing up through water that churned with such force it murdered everything inside its wet folds. The water still has the power to rise up angry, to rage at the landscape and suck back villages, slapping the humans' audacity, filling their lungs with salt death, drowning the remnants of their lives. Every now and then it does. Once the raging water destroyed most of the people here; it drowned their baskets, their canoes, their treasured shells, their homes, their burial grounds. It buried what they were and what they might have become. But they began again, despite the flood waters and the massive death of plants and animals and humans — but not before the serpent rose up from the receding waters to swallow their babies.

In one village, a woman stood on the shore pleading with the two heads for her child's life. Screaming women tried to hold her back against the serpent's threats. The bulge in its upper body terrified them. This serpent did not like being ignored. He rose from the sea, rampant on his tail, and bent both heads as he roared at the women on shore. His heads birthed screams that rang out. The screams from the women grew louder as the small spears that flew from their hands bounced off the beast. The men harpooned him, but the harpoons bounced off too. The men moved closer and one of the serpent's heads darted out and swallowed one of them.

The newer bones remember this story; they remember their sacrifices on behalf of their descendants. They resent the absence of courage or loyalty in them.

I know why they are terrified. It wasn't the monster that terrified them, it was something intangible, steady, and perverse — an unspeakable horror. I remind myself that I am here to bear witness, not to try to find remedies or to remind them.

"There is another village downriver. Don't go there. People die in the streets and they just step over you. The women die alone in that village and no one cares. It is as though the breath of the serpent has been swallowed by everyone." Momma was sitting on her grandfather's lap, toying with the pouch around his neck and the big knuckles of his fingers. She asked the village's name. "Vancouver," he said. She never wanted to go there.

THREE WOMEN ARE GATHERED around Gramma Alice and the things they are supposed to burn, but Momma keeps fainting. She does not feel grown-up enough to do this. If she burns her mother's things, her mother will hurry to the other world. Momma isn't ready for this.

She is awake. Rena is looking at her. Momma's Jim is straddling a log playing with a branch of cedar; every now and then he gives her one of those deep looks that says, "It's okay; faint away; it's okay; we don't really have to do anything; it's okay; we do not have to do this burning today." It calms her to look at him. The calm invigorates her and so she doesn't want to see him. She doesn't want to be strong enough to do this.

"We'll finish this, Momma."

This jars her.

"Oh, no. I can't. I don't want to do this."

"What do you want to do?"

"What I want, no one can give me now."

"What do you want?"

Momma nearly fainted during Jimmy's funeral. She can't afford to faint now. She is near to gone when she finally lets out what she thinks is a scream.

"Rena?" The word barely makes it out into the room. Momma begins to sway.

"Yes." Rena turns in her direction, bannock dough dripping from her fingers.

Momma's blood pumps, her lungs shrink, her strength leaks from her legs, her head swims. "I got to sit." Rena catches her. "Paper bag," she hollers. Judy throws her one.

"What's that?" Momma hears herself say, and cannot now remember what she saw or heard to spark the question. She tucks her head between her legs and yells, "Rena!" Her voice is louder now.

"Yes." Rena's hand grabs Momma's neck and holds her head

down. Rena's voice barks, "Breathe out. Out, out." It works. It saves her from fainting.

After that, through the feast, funeral, and burning preparations, Momma would just say "Rena" and Rena would grab a paper bag, curl its edges, hand it to Momma, push her head down between her legs, and bark, "Breathe out. Out, out," and Momma would be all right.

VIII

INSIDE, THE CANDLELIGHT CURLS about the faces of the women, painting blotches of honey brown where the light dances and black in the spaces where it does not.

Loyal is becoming more and more disheartened the longer Restless wreaks havoc. He is failing to find someone to honour the serpent and allay Restless's anger.

The new bones have stopped singing. The old bones are getting closer. Soon they will meet. This meeting of the bones has never happened.

I can't say whether their meeting will be good or bad.

The people are in such a state of disarray that Loyal has no idea how to reverse it. It is more than the sickness that has destroyed them, more than poverty. If he could find the key to what malaise holds them, he would choose the right person to bring them back to upholding the original agreement between the serpent and the people.

The old bones rattle louder as they get closer to the new bones. They sing and pray, pushing for the surface as they grow more concerned about the influence of the enraged younger bones. The old bones have no idea what has happened, but they are certain they have the song to fix it.

THE NEWER BONES HAVE begun to surface. This has sparked excitement among anthropologists, because some of these new bones are only a few hundred years old, epidemic survivors, another field of study. It surprises the anthropologists that these bones so far west suffered epidemic loss more than two hundred years earlier, but it does not surprise Celia. She knows about the deaths. She knows about the travellers, the indigenous traders who preceded the newcomers, who brought with them the diseases of the east. What surprises Celia is the interest of the indigenous people in anthropology. She worries for them. She is right to worry. The bones have no good intentions for their handlers.

I AM IN THE *tree house. I look down. My paws flutter with fright — the serpent is out of control. I am weary of witnessing his crazed hunger. I try to get Celia's attention, thinking she might witness with me, but getting her attention proves more difficult than I imagine. I consider shape-shifting back to owl, but this is difficult to do and I want a rest, not more work. Then I hear the bones, the new and the old rattling together, at odds with one another. Shivering, I pray to the bones. The young ones are the first to respond and the response is not promising. "The serpent will teach them a lesson," they sing. They are stuck on vengeance. These words come overtop the deep, gentle prayers of the old bones and my prayers for reason.*

I fear a quarrel between the bones. Any quarrel can become war, and the bones could inspire humans to go to war over which way to turn and that means violence from within. I do not want to witness that.

MOMMA WINCES AS SHE comes to and realizes that she is in her bedroom. It is dark, but she knows Celia is there. The others are still in the kitchen. She tries to remember what they are doing there. It isn't Sunday. Momma almost says something about why Celia has come into her room without permission, then decides this child hasn't had much of her.

"I think I ought to grow up," Momma says to Celia, as she starts to rise.

"Are you okay, Momma?"

"No. I am not, but I will be." She laughs and swings her legs out onto the floor.

The candlelight catches Celia's face at an odd angle.

"You look like your gramma in my first memory of her face. I was five, that would have made her forty — and you are thirty-eight. That would be about right." She reaches out and puts her hand on Celia's cheek, careful not to change the angle of her perception.

Celia remains motionless, hoping to stretch the moment. It seems like forever since her mother last touched her face, appreciated its lines, its cut. Celia has never as an adult woman heard her mother comment on the nature of her looks. They sit in the quiet, each looking intently at the other. Some wisp of something lingers in Momma's touch. It pulses in the air surrounding them. It teases the sensibility of both women. What is it?

"We had so little time, you and I," Momma begins.

Celia feels the backwater of years' worth of longing for her momma and Stacey start to rise like a flood in her belly, threatening to destroy the sweetness of this moment. She swallows her tears and holds back the floodwater rather than close the door to this first communion as a woman with her mother.

"I missed you, girl. I missed mothering you. You know what I mean, Celia?"

"Yes," she lies. Celia knows she has missed being mothered, but she did not know her mother had missed being a mother. They are sitting so close that Celia feels the warm current of Momma's breath. Momma's hands move through Celia's hair as though to render it familiar.

Momma chuckles and this makes Celia smile.

"Can we just sit for a bit, Celia?"

Celia assents wordlessly.

Now Celia is going to get all fuzzy and that will end her witnessing. Don't have a chance of getting out of this.

Two languages run along parallel tracks in Momma's mind, neither of which ever crosses over; she shifts between them as though she is one person in one language and another in the other. She has never felt sure of who she is in either, because the words of both have never come together to speak her memories to her. Her mind preserves her memories in moving pictures unanchored to word-posts that could frame what these memories mean to her. Her emotional being is hungry to have memories translated into words and thoughts before they are transformed into actions. She wants words that will deliver the significance of this child's memory to her.

After the 1954 flu epidemic, their world changed. Automobiles and traffic arrived. Televisions arrived; people would gather at the house of the person in their family who owned one. Momma liked the news. No one talked about race then. No one said "white man" out loud. Then something shifted. Though no one in the village suspected it, the flu reminded them of how little others cared for their survival. The shift began with Rosa Parks and it turned into a movement for civil rights. It finally came to the villages as Aboriginal rights.

That was not the only thing that changed. A half dozen years later highways, sidewalks, and shopping malls began to dominate their lives. If there was no mall, people wished for one. By the end of that decade, nearly every city and town had one. The malls were full of mothers and children. The crowds picked stuff out, some casually fingering this garment or that, some testing toiletries and scents, some languidly sitting on benches examining new purchases. Town folk stared at the Indians who came from the other side of the river. Some stared with interest, some looked with hard blank eyes, and some stared as though they couldn't believe there were still any Indians left.

Momma watches the endless canning kettles boiling on her stove. She watches herself shooing Celia out of the kitchen with a go-play-in-the-living-room instruction as though it were one word. She sees Celia trying to catch her attention by saying, "Look Momma, look," as she shows her a picture she has drawn. The picture has written words on it. Momma knows they are words, but cannot read them. She cannot tell if they are spelled correctly, so she just grunts at Celia. This picture wants to anchor itself to words and a date.

In the summer of 1954 Stacey had taught Madeline and Momma to read, so it was before then. Celia was seven during the epidemic, so Celia must have been five or six when she learned to read and print. Momma sniffs at her memory to recall what they had been canning. Peaches. Just before fishing, just before learning to read.

"Celia. I like the sound of that name. Wish I knew what it meant." She stretches the sound of each syllable out, careful not to push too hard on the breath delivering the sound, while she plays with Celia's hair. "You were showing me a picture a long time ago. You kept saying, 'Look.' I kept saying, 'I see.' You kept repeating 'Look' and I kept answering, 'I am, Celia, now move out the way. These peaches are hot.' You ran out of the house and you never showed me anything after that. Now we don't can together the way my momma and I did with Stacey and your brother Jim. Stacey and I and your brother still can together, but not you. I know I never really looked at your picture then. You knew it, too. Is that why you don't can with us, Celia? Because I never really looked?"

Celia roots about the cellar of her mind, hunting for the same moment, fighting to drag it along.

The steam in the air from the canning kettle is almost drinkable. The smell of peaches consumes every space in the room. The heat is almost unbearable. Momma is busy moving back and forth, hauling jars, emptying them out, washing them. Jim moves the big canning kettle when the peaches are done. When he isn't sitting, waiting for the processing to be done, he is cutting peaches next to Stacey. Every now and then the air is split with their laughter. Celia wishes she was a jar so she could be carefully cradled in her momma's hands and set carefully on the counter or in the water and finally be set in the cupboard. She draws a picture of the canning kettle, her momma standing over it holding a jar up to the light leaking into the kitchen from the little window. Celia trots after Momma with her picture. She has it in her mind that maybe this picture will make her part of them somehow, but it will not. It will separate her more completely. Momma tells her she saw it, but Celia knows she did not really look because she did not recognize herself in it. Celia goes outside, behind the shed, to watch. She rarely draws any pictures to show anybody.

"Mostly I stopped drawing," she says now, as if this were responsible for the distance between her and her mother.

"I remember the picture," Momma continues, as though Celia has not really intervened with her terrible guilt. "It was me, holding a jar to the window, to the light, trying to see if it was overcooked. Sometimes with peaches you can't tell how ripe they are — an extra minute can spoil the texture. There was the canning kettle, the stove, my backside, and this jar of peaches. Even the little peaches inside were coloured orange and pink, magenta and almost-yellow. The water was a see-through pale yellow, just like how the water turns colour in the finished jar. The sunlight spot on the glass was there. My faded old apron strings hanging down the middle of my back, even. So many details of colour were in that picture. That picture gave me the idea for my garden."

Celia stares, incredulous, at her mother. Her mother's memory is detailed, flawless. It humbles her to know that her mother had cupped this picture in her mind for years in all its detail. Even more humbling was that it had inspired her mother's garden. Tears trickle down Celia's face and onto her knotted hands. She stares at her hands, wondering why her hands had to stop drawing — as though her hands had lost their connection to her mind. Not drawing and not canning with Momma go together like a truck and its load, but Celia cannot explain this to Momma. She has no idea why they go together. She had gone on drawing for a short time after that, but with less and less frequency until finally she stopped. She had kept her drawings secret. She cannot figure out how to tell this to her mother. She decides to talk to Stacey. Stacey will know how to tell Momma.

"Doesn't matter, Momma. I'd like to can with you now."

Momma reaches over and wraps her arms around her daughter.

Momma watches the tears roll down Celia's face, the face that was Gramma Alice's face. It is heartbreaking to know that she hurt the only child that looks like Gramma Alice. She does not know this woman. She remembers sending her away to Alice's house. This was an extraordinary act on her part. Children ought not to witness dying.

Momma had volunteered to be the caregiver of the village and had battled the flu. Stacey had to help her. Celia did not return. This didn't surprise Momma or strike her as unusual; Gramma wanted to keep her. Celia seemed content to stay with her, so she just let it be. When Celia grew up, she set up housekeeping in her gramma's house after Gramma died. Momma has no way of connecting her sending this child away with Celia's ambivalence toward her family. She has no way to connect her unfamiliarity with Celia to her sending her away, either, so she searches for something else to hang it on.

In 1954 the death toll would not stop rising. The flu would not stop taking their babies, their old, and their fragile. It kept coming for the villagers like some vengeful beast, forcing person after person to vomit, cough, and burn away their lives. Momma fought for the strength, the tenacity, and the caring to go on in the face of the beast. Every day she woke up and prayed for the will to take the beast on, until finally her caring thinned. She braced herself and rose anyway out of duty; when all else failed, there was duty. Each death thinned the caring out until she didn't seem to have any left.

It was as though caring for the old and the very young in 1954 took what love she had to give. No, it wasn't love that they took; it was the liking, the everyday appreciation for the nonsense of being, of growing, of nodding her head and chuckling at ordinary things. She had grieved at every funeral, but each life that slipped through her fingers took a chunk of her already smaller, less intense emotions with it. Grieving was enough. Saying goodbye had not been enough.

After 1954, Momma cooked. She cleaned. She fed her children, but she never played with them like the moms across the river. Like her mother before her, work became her life. Water had to be hauled from the well; wood had to be hauled off the mountain, bucked up into fire logs, shakes, and kindling; water had to be heated in gigantic tubs every day for all sorts of washing.

Tuberculosis dogged the villagers then. It seemed like every week they were headed to some relative's to bring the children of the sick home to be tended while their mothers tried to rest and recover. When they did not recover, the children were divided up among relatives. Momma's mother raised two of Momma's cousins.

Momma and her mother had always done things together: sewing, weaving, knitting, berry picking, fishing, canning, feasting, laughing, sharing stories of caring, of fighting, of sharing; but not playing. From the cradle to the grave, Momma was handy underfoot and completely understandable to her mother. Stacey and Jim showed Momma the work they did at school. Gramma, Momma, Stacey, and Jim had become a unit. Even though Gramma brought

Celia over to Momma's almost daily, Celia never became part of that family unit. Momma remembers that she had been a little jealous that her children had the privilege of learning about these people and their chicken tracks that lit up memories. She had wondered how they managed to carve their little tracks onto paper that was so smooth you could barely feel the letters. Her childhood had been filled with the same old same old that had still consumed her life up to then. Maybe when Stacey taught her to read it closed the gap for them. Jim had helped Stacey with that summer reading business, but Celia had been too young to help.

Celia went to school, like her brothers and sisters, but she didn't live with Momma after Stacey left. She stayed with Gramma until she died.

Momma chuckles at the pettiness that jammed a wedge between herself and Celia; she decides she ought to grow up. Maybe then Celia will share her life more freely. It doesn't dawn on Momma that Celia didn't want to be sent away, that she might harbour resentment over it.

Momma jumps up, lights a candle, and rummages around in the top right-hand drawer of the dresser she reserves for important papers. There, carefully wrapped in see-through sticky shelf paper, is the picture.

"Ooh," Celia sighs, as though she is looking at someone's fine art. It is beautiful. The picture's colours are carefully shadowed. Even the window is three-dimensional. Momma still has her youthful shape. The shaded colours give her face and body definition and depth. The jar has a pale yellow halo around it that bleeds into the ordinary sunlight of the room. Each peach slice stands alone in its colour and character. Celia has more of her pictures at home in an old box with a carved lid.

"I have more," she says.

"Yeah?" Momma is surprised at the secret life this child has maintained.

"At home. Old ones. No recent ones." Celia grins sheepishly. "Not many."

"Let's look at them on Monday. At your house."

Celia stares at her mother for a second before answering, "Okay." She is surprised at her mother's sudden curiosity about her paintings. And it is the first time Momma has asked to come over to her house.

"You sure you don't want to add some work to that, maybe do some of my dishes while you're there?" They chuckle.

"C'mon. I got to grow up," Momma says, and they head for the living room.

When they enter, Momma puts her hands on her hips, scans the room, and then spots Rena. "Rena, why the hell didn't someone tell me to grow up years ago?"

"You obviously don't know yourself well. No one who cares about themselves dares to tell you anything quite that stern, Momma."

"I swear you're both sides of that sea serpent," Stacey offers with a wink.

"I don't remember you handing out this kind of an invitation before now, but if you are I would be happy to rasp a little on your skin occasionally," Ned offers, taking advantage of his wife's magnanimity.

"I am almost sixty years old and I still want to be rocked by my mom." She urges it out into the amber-tinted room. The jagged edges in the room smooth themselves out. The candles flicker less violently; no one speaks for a moment.

"Do you girls ever want that?" she asks. No one answers.

"Whose momma are you talking about — not mine for sure," Rena says. "No use trying to get blood from a stone. The only rocking my momma did was rocking the logs she was hauling. They would sometimes get stuck up in the trees after they were cut. Widowmakers. She would grit her teeth, then she would tie a rope to them and we would all be at the other end rocking the upright trees until that cut log fell between the trees holding them captive."

Rena lets this go with a rich dose of cynicism. The information falls with a thud. It lands on the shoulders of the women and makes them bend their shoulders toward the floor. Jacob tosses his cedar sprig in an abalone shell. He lights the cedar and the crackles of its pitch send its aroma twisting through the room as if it was the sweet side of that old snake.

"Maybe we have had too many reasons to need rocking. Maybe there is too much death and not enough reasons to go on living."

Jacob might as well have thrown a hot poker into the middle of the room and made a bunch of logs stand up next to it. The words shoot through the room; they stun the women, making them sit up straight.

"There is plenty to live for."

"What are you talking about?"

"You better not be thinking ..."

"Jacob! You have family."

"You have ..."

"Shut up. Shut up." Momma cracks it out like a whip.

"Momma, is that you talking?" Ned asks, feigning innocence.

"Yes it is. I am sick of hearing people say, 'You got family.' Where is my family? Auntie Nora was up there in the bush hauling logs. When she wasn't sawing logs she was sawing at your insides, and now she's gone. Instead of rocking her children, she was rocking trees. That was my great gramma's first daughter. Where is her brother's son? Dead. Where is my family? Brother Ben hauled his crazy ass ten thousand miles across the ocean to kill people he didn't know for a thing called 'freedom' that we didn't have. Where are his children? The old snake terrorized Madeline and her children. Nora's husband was my only uncle. He died before I was eight years old. Only two of Rena's sister's daughters survived and no one here has any idea where the one who left to marry whoever she married is. We don't even know if she did get married. My sister Anne's daughter was beat to death by someone who called himself a man and a husband. He was less than an old snake. Where is my family? My grandson killed himself last fall. What the hell is going on?"

Celia knows what has happened; but, unlike with Stacey, her mother has never taught her anything. Celia wants to say something, but dares not; she twirls her fingers, prays for escape into her dream world.

But I block her entry. Not now, Celia, you cannot escape now. The escape won't come. It is the first time her dream world has failed her.

"We're here. Dis is all dere is left. We need to begin all over again, jist like after da epidemics, but we're scared." Madeline's hands drop into her lap with a plop sound. The last faint boom of thunder had ended the storm just as Momma had opened the door to a whirlwind of rage. They were all of afraid of its size; it was so big, so justified, and so terrible that they stared in paralyzed silence, except for Madeline who had looked at it, faced it, and pointed out the obvious. They were scared. But the whirlwind would have its way. It channelled itself into a force unto itself, and pulled them all to its hungry edges; one at a time they were drawn into the tunnel. They barrelled down through its confusion, fatigue, and loneliness. Madeline meant for them to face their fear. She had given them something to look at, some terrible side of this jewel called family, this crazy ball of wax that they all thought so perfect, and forced them to face its dark underbelly, its wrinkles, its sharp edges. Maybe Momma meant them to face it too, but no one wished to face anything that required that they face themselves. Facing the world had fatigued them. Facing the world had thrown mountains of water on their fire and there was hardly an ember of courage left for them to face themselves. They intended to stand silent for a moment, and then change the subject once Momma had calmed down. Madeline robbed them of this privilege by jumping into the maw of Momma's tornado.

"That's it," Momma says.

"What's it?" Ned nearly growls. Neither he nor Jacob know how to be around women whose emotional bearings have been uprooted and whose threads to the ordinary have been severed.

"We didn't begin again."

IX

MAYBE IT IS A *full moon, maybe it is not. Maybe it is a moment of craziness, maybe it is not. Maybe the stars are peopled by strange beings, maybe they are not. None of it matters. What matters is this moment, this burning candle silhouetting this young man in front me who is feeling this sadness and wondering about the wasted life of his cousin. I am resting at the edge of Celia's yard, lying in the line of poplars, wondering where all this is going to end up. What matters to Celia? This moment, this candle, and this young man. I feel it in her feet. Her feet want to follow her gramma's life, and the life before her gramma.*

Celia wants to know what happened to her village, so she may tell this young man, his cheeks appearing burnished gold in the flicker of light, his hair purple, his hands twisting a different cedar branch.

He looks at her in hope she might be able to solve his riddle for him. Jacob feels as though he knows something; he remembers his grandpa saying that everything begins with knowing something. But he only has a feeling; the knowledge seems to elude him.

I shape-shift into owl so I can call Celia. She failed to notice me squatting in the line of cottonwoods at the entrance to the village. I hoot, but she ignores me. She does not wish to engage me in any kind of conversation. This is disappointing. Not all messages are about death, I sigh. I am a messenger, but not all messages are disastrous. Sometimes they are no more dangerous than a phone call.

IN THIS VILLAGE, SATURDAYS are full of the mundane acts of living. Grass is cut; in the old houses, wood is chopped; in the newer ones, gardens are weeded; everyone is busy with laundry and going to town to shop. The air is filled with the sort of chatter that accompanies the business of readying oneself for another week's go at life. Everyone's guard is down on Saturday.

Celia hears the crackle of Stacey's car on her gravel drive and slips into her jacket before the car stops. On her way out the door, she takes a look around; it strikes her that a year ago she would have been hollering at a half-sleeping Jimmy as she ran out the door: "Breakfast is in the fridge. Don't forget to mow the lawn. I'll be back around noon." Today, she slips into her jacket and out the door in silence.

Celia flumps into her seat and asks Stacey to stop, so she can tell Jacob to mow her lawn once he's done with Stacey's. Stacey raises her brow. Celia's smile looks mischievous and her voice has changed. There is a determined sound in it. Even her body seems to move with more deliberation.

"Where are you getting this piss and vinegar, girl? I want me some." Momma turns to admire her second daughter. "Let's go, Stacey. Kmart awaits." They open their windows as soon as they leave the gravel road of the reservation and cross the bridge to white town.

"Got to pave this damn road sometime," Momma mumbles. "I can't stand the fucking feel or sound of it anymore."

Stacey raises her eyebrows again; this is the second time in a week her mother has cursed, and the curse word was deeper in the gutter, where Momma had always cautioned her children not to go.

"That's what white folks collect taxes for, Momma," Celia scolds. "Want a road, got to pay taxes."

"That's why we should be charging those people from across the bridge some kind of rent," Momma says. "So we can tax each other."

Stacey stifles a laugh.

Under the bridge the serpent coils, stretches, lolls, and sets to waking himself up for a good crawl through the village.

Bones emptied of their living flesh are stones. They hold sound. They carry the dreams, the joy, the rage of their forebears. Some bones carry sweet old songs, others songs of torment and agony. The old bones feel responsible for stopping the serpent that is encouraged by the young bones. The young bones argue back. The old bones realize the argument is driven by anger and grief, no amount of reason will persuade. And so they sing a low, grieving song to the new bones.

The restless head of the serpent hears the old bones and ignores them. He crawls toward a bedraggled section of town, wanting repair and a good cleaning, looking for another victim. A group of boys hangs on the edges of life, despairing and needing excitement, something to help them feel alive. The serpent surrounds them, steals their breath, squeezes their hearts, empties their bodies of empathy, until only war will fulfill them. Some of the boys begin organizing themselves into gangs; others join their nation's army and go halfway across the earth to kill people they do not know.

Momma is antsy and nervous. Something is wrong and she cannot put her finger on it. She wants so much to rage at something or someone, but has no idea what in the world is making her so angry.

Kmart is in the middle of white town, and going to white town is a challenge for Momma. As a young woman, the people in white town assumed she was stupid because she was Indian. Now they assume she's stupid because she's old. Loyal breathes courage into Momma, hoping this will ease her anxiety and mediate her growing rage.

"I would just for one time like to walk around the world as though everyone thought I was a smart human being. No race, no age; just smart. Have someone take my money without any questions and give me my change."

"PARDON ME?" the cashier says, speaking slowly and so loudly that she is nearly yelling at Momma.

"Never mind. You have a nice day, dear." Momma leans toward the girl and feigns an old woman's voice. As soon as she is out of earshot she repeats the exchange to her daughters, only she tells Stacey and Celia what she could not say to the cashier:

"'THAT WILL BE FORTY-TWO DOLLARS AND FIFTY-FOUR CENTS. THAT IS A LOT OF MONEY. ARE YOU SURE YOU CAN AFFORD THIS?' the cashier hollered at me. Yeah, bitch, and I plan to rob another bank as soon as I've blown this wad, so just give me my goddamned change." Momma's outburst produces a warm feeling; it feels good to imagine saying this to a shocked young cashier.

"Momma," Stacey manages to say before both girls squeal with laughter.

"Stinky witch," Momma grumbles as she heads for the car. "Don't you just want to give it to them sometimes?"

Her daughters are laughing too hard to answer, but they know exactly what she means. Somehow just saying these words out loud relieves Momma of some of her fatigue, and the laughter relieves the two girls of some unnameable melancholy. Momma likes the fact that they are laughing together, and that she has set it in motion. She is laughing at something completely different than the girls, but does not intend to share her joke. Her devilishness enlivens her.

Nice. I like that.

Momma stands a little straighter and her walk is a little peppier. Celia and Stacey recognize that they have not laughed together like this for a long time. They find it difficult to stop.

This is not exactly the reaction Loyal wanted. Humans are so variable about righteousness, he sighs. Restless laughs; he knows righteousness is so much more complex and difficult than his aims.

X

CELIA HEARS A STRANGE hum. It comes up on her, sudden and sure
of itself.

She lets it come and watches the tall ship that arrives in the wake
of the scold her mother has handed out to the people in the room.

CELIA IS SMALL AGAIN, her tiny little body crouches behind the
woodshed as she watches the ship. Men gather logs for the newcomers. They trade them for the ill-fated blanket death that will
follow. As these men lie dying they scream and moan, unable to
urinate. Some of them take to the mountains and never come back;
others take to the sea to try and quiet the fire coming from their
manhood; others waste away, screaming as they exit. Two men find
the hill runners, their bodies decayed beyond recognition. One of
the men is washed ashore, bloated and unrecognizable but for the
amulet he wears around his neck. Those who die at home harry

their families with their screaming. Their hysteria sparks the kind of helplessness that goes with watching a fire burn down your house and knowing there is nothing to be done.

The black robe comes, offering medicine in exchange for baptism. The old men refuse. With every scream, the women are worn nearer to insanity. With every death, their resolve to begin again is sandpapered down. Finally, the village's governor relents and they go in droves to the black robe. The black robe has a tornado of his own buzzing around in his head. Inside its vortex are shame, fear, and repentance. It has not been holy water he has bathed the people in. It has been the words of the devil. The incessant *mea culpa* poured like water on the fire that moved them to speak, to play, to rock their babies, to enjoy their lives.

"The worst part was it did not help us to live." Celia ends her dream-walk out loud, wringing her skirt in her tense little fingers.

"What?" Momma, Stacey, and Rena blurt out at the same time.

"The epidemics, the conversions, the medicine. They didn't stop us from dying."

"That's enough," Ned says. "This is too long a story to be told here tonight. Maybe we do need to start again. Anyone who is up to continuing this conversation can come on over next Friday and we'll have another go at it." He turns on the lights and blows out the candles, one at a time. The cloying smoke of dying wax that still wants to be fire bites their noses. It bites them in the same way that the smouldering breath of humans fighting to fire up the soul bites the lungs. It stills their hearts.

The humming inside Celia stops. Celia's body has gained weight. She feels it. It isn't from her overeating, and it isn't the sort of heaviness she feels when the load she is carrying is too dense; this weight gain comes from her breath failing to get inside her bones. Her breath has been used up. Her brain cells are dragging the air from her muscles. The tightness makes her feel like her muscles are being strangled. Her muscles panic at not having enough air to push her body around. Her bones chill from want of fire.

Jacob sees this strange fatigue wash over his aunt Celia. He saunters over and offers up his arm. Celia acquiesces.

Night settles on Momma's house uneasily, jumping from dark to light and light to dark as though confused about the direction time is moving. Momma settles into Ned's arms and wonders about the village, her children, and her family. Ned murmurs words of comfort and rests his hand on her forehead. Her eyes fog up enough to erase the night with its horrific sack of alone. She settles into sleep, leaving night to pout alone in the sky.

The fragments drift away and settle into a corner of her mind. She awakes. She is curled up in a ball on the floor. She wonders where everyone has gone, then she remembers. It's Saturday night. They were at a ball tournament after shopping. She hadn't been feeling well, so she had not gone. She had fallen into a fitful sleep. Now she is awake, Ned is still sleeping. Embarrassed, she jumps back into bed, careful not to disturb Ned.

"MEN ARE ANCHORS," CELIA tells Jacob on the way home from the ball game. "Sometimes a woman feels rootless, like she is some crazy maple leaf shifting in the wind, looking for a place to land, but all the other leaves have eaten up the space on the ground and she just keeps getting caught in the updraft, unable to find a place. Sometimes, though, the drifting, the updraft play is full of magic, of seeing, of pending clarity, so eagle-like that you really don't want to settle anywhere. A man comes round, and plunk: you land."

Jacob murmurs assent as if he understands. "You are so courteous," Celia chuckles. She slips her arm through his and points at the moon. It is dropping out of sight behind new clouds — a huge yellow balloon sliding behind a barely visible cloud. The moon doesn't seem to want to share its brilliant hue. It slides its way behind the cloud without letting any halo of light brighten the mood.

"I love you, Auntie," Jacob says, the way men say it when they have a feeling that their woman is standing on the edge of something dangerous they don't understand and they want them to walk away from it. It was a "don't jump" kind of "I love you."

Sometimes to really know something you have to dive deep.

This time Celia hears my whisper. Celia needs to know something. This is an old edge. She has been do-si-do-ing back and forth before it for a long time. She breathes slow and deep, puffs up her lungs, pumps her blood, shores up her muscles and kicks up her agility. She understands Jacob's "I love you," but she means to leap anyway.

The weight leaves. All that remains is a faint feeling of trepidation. Celia knows this trepidation and doesn't really mind it. It is the sort of fear she felt the first time she was asked to prepare someone's feast food. She wondered, "Do I know these plump berries well enough to turn them to feast soup? Am I familiar enough with salmon to urge him to rise to the feast house all still and dead like that? Do I really remember how to dig the roots, season everything with the sort of medicine that will open the throats of every human and inspire them to dig inside their spirit for words, for song, for the sacred?" It is not unlike the hesitation she felt the first time her body responded to a lover's looks, the skin, the touch; she had no words with which to speak to herself about it. She just wanted to be next to that skin, that body.

The trepidation anchors itself to the kind of confidence she has acquired from knowing she's crossed this bridge before. She is up to the journey, up to the flight, up to the silk-soft landing, up to the unfamiliar, because she has mastered the unknown before. Her people swallowed the serpent generations ago — one head was courage, the other fear. They had found a way to anchor the fear to courage; the courage underpinned and softened fear. Fear helps her to look twice before leaping, to exercise caution. Fear does not stand alone inside her body, so it can never consume her.

"Let me pop by Alice's place," she says to Jacob. "She was something else at Nora's funeral."

"It's late, Auntie."

"Alice writes poetry. She doesn't sleep on nights like this."

The word "poetry" scrapes its way down Jacob's throat, sharp and full of the ridiculous smells of musty odour and sterile-coloured classrooms. The sound of boys and girls mimicking rhymed couplets carefully memorized for no reason at all returns to him. Why anyone in this village would drag that old dead cat home and participate in its foolishness is beyond him, but he swings alongside his aunt into his cousin's drive. Her living room light shouts out a welcome to visitors.

"Ha-ay," Alice sings out. "I was just heating up some water for tea. Come on in."

While the ginseng steeps, the women cluck on about the storm, the dark, the gathering at Momma's house. Momma's stunning fine rage, the way she shut everyone but Madeline up. Neither woman mentions that Madeline is part of their healing circle because Jacob is there, but it clearly cheers the women the way they are cheered when female blackberry vines droop low with the weight of children and the male vines are stiff, jutting out straight and strong, disconnected from the females, making the picking so easy. Alice pours the tea.

"Read me some of them words, Alice. The kind that make a body feel big and strong." Celia nestles into a chair, half-leaning forward. Jacob looks for something to distract his mind. There are photos on the wall: photos of Alice, of her small children by themselves, and some of her with her children. He focuses on Alice's son, Mike. In this photo he is hardly older than Jacob is now. There he is with a pair of toddlers and a woman Jacob does not really know. He thinks this must be Mike's wife.

"I swear, Celia, with this one I must be losing my mind. I have no idea what got into me, but here it is ..."

Jacob barely hears over his musing about Mike marrying and having children so young. He couldn't have been but eighteen ...

"*I want to walk along with eyes/Wide open and see the world.*"

Alice's voice grabs Jacob. It is lyrical and soft, with that slight accent and wee rasp that Salish men find sexy in their women. Alice is his cousin, so he tries not to think about that. But it is the words; the words hold him. *Me too, me too* runs through his mind. The poem settles into the room. Jacob imagines it breathing life into the candle that burns in the centre of the table. It creeps under his skin and smokes its way to his bones, his flesh, his mind, and opens doors to sky, to being, to home and sound. He follows Alice's words as they play about the room. The words land easily on the flickering candle-tip, jump onto his skin and somersault their way through his chest, filling his lungs with purposeful breath. Alice's words engage his thighs and set his feet to tapping the rhythm of the song which hums beneath their meaning.

"I want to see," Celia moans at the end of Alice's recitation. She swallows the last bit of her tea, and bids Alice goodbye. Jacob cannot be so casual about what he has just heard. He rises in stunned silence. He wants to say something, to engage Celia in some kind of discourse. Celia has been as familiar as an old shoe and now she is as a stranger. He nearly trips going out the door, stubbing his sock feet on the carpet where his shoes lie waiting for him.

Outside the clouds have disappeared and the moon brightens Celia and Jacob's path. It sprinkles bits of light among the trees lining the road and makes it easy for them to find their way. The stars wink an old hello and Jacob slips his arm in Celia's, more to anchor himself than to help her find her way.

"That's poetry?" he says with some surprise.

"That's what she calls it. To me, those words are personal power songs. Jewels. Carved word-paintings and woven rugs all rolled into one."

"She do that often?"

"No. No woman gets to do anything fun very often. Not here, anyway. No. Sometimes I go there and she has a new one. Most times I just get her to read some of my favourite old ones."

"She has more?"

"Oh yeah, Alice has been writing poetries since she first learned to read. You know, to read in a serious way."

Jacob restrains his desire to correct his aunt's reference to "poetries," and instead asks, "Anyone else know she does this?"

"I don't know. I don't talk to anyone about it. I don't know if she ever does. I just remember her sitting there, candle burning, light on late one night. I was turning in and asked her what she was doing so late with a single small lamp going and a candle on the table burning when she clearly had electricity. She offered me tea. Told me that the candle lit a fire inside and the words came from that fire. 'What words?' I asked. 'Poetry,' she said. 'Read some,' I said, and she did."

A stone from the gravel road jumps into Celia's shoe. She wiggles her foot, sends it off to one side, leans over, removes it, and carries on without stopping.

Don't throw that stone away. I am tripping along in the bush next to the road, following Celia home. Truth be known, going to Alice's to hear poetry is my favourite part of being a witness. Then Celia picks up the stone and stuffs it in her pocket. We are getting along now. I have to stop myself from laughing.

"Do you visit her much?"

Celia doesn't want to talk just yet. She wants Alice's words to roll around in her mind for a while. Talking stops this from happening.

"Jacob, you quit skirting and jumping around like a square dance team and get to your real point or I will get over the feeling Alice just filled me with."

"I just want to hear more."

"Next time I go, I will swing by and get you."

"You could phone ahead."

"No," she says. "Feels better if I don't touch anything electrical before I go."

XI

SALMON DON'T DANCE ON *their way upstream. Their dancing is done in their ocean playground with its infinite breast of salt water, coloured green, slate grey, silver, white, and blue, depending on the mood of the sun. Sometimes the ocean's water is warm, sometimes it is chilly, but the fish play, discover, dance, and flirt their way to strength, to knowing, to preparing for the journey upstream. In this place of dance and play their language is born. This language has reference posts that head them up the right stream to the river the fish-women know well. The men dance themselves to a mating pair and learn the language of these women who are the only ones who know where the spawning grounds are. The dance and the play get them ready for their silent war with the current. This swim will carry them to death whether or not they experience the ecstasy of procreation.*

It was winter. After the blankets. After smallpox tore through the village. After the forest had been set ablaze. After the vicious hunger that followed the fires. After the foreigners settled on the lands that grew their precious camas. After the sod had been rolled over and the original food had been buried deep under the soil.

It was before cars, before radio, before gramophones, before television, before English swallowed their tongue. It was just before the songs and dances of the village became lawless things.

The first Alice lined up with the children of her family and stood ready to enter the smokehouse. They were going to come out with their own song, the one that would be their personal road to power. Alice's gramma was dead, but her mother had done her best in the language to prepare her for this moment. Alice sensed her mother's wavering commitment to this ceremony; it was in the hesitation she heard in her voice and the nervous movement of her body. This wavering pushed itself onto the words her mother spoke and it wrapped a thin wire of fear around Alice. Alice quietly prayed that her song would melt this wire of fear.

Language needs a post, like dogs need stumps to piss on, or wolves need to turn around and look at the tracks they have made. It needs a reference marker to remind, to tell the rememberer they are hooked to some moment, some familiar place where bearings can be found. The rememberer need only clear the underbrush with old familiar tools and locate the starting point. All people have to do is identify who is the one that can remember. Alice stood in her kitchen musing over these her last words as her spirit left. She tried hard to say them to someone as she slid down the wall of her kitchen, but there was no one there. She died but she could not really leave. She floated about the space between the stars and earth, hoping to find someone to say it to.

No one hears, but Jacob feels something. This is a different kind of see. I smile; he will get it eventually. I set to witnessing again.

JACOB FEELS AS IF he does not have reference posts to understand Rena, Momma, Stacey, or any of the women. He doesn't know there is any other life but the one that they live; he sometimes thinks they are mean. He imagines them throwing dirt on his tracks, stopping him from pissing and marking his own territory. Celia eases the scrape somewhat, but even the cloth of her voice seems to dampen his sense of belonging. At times it stops him from being part of her. He needs to know he is part of something. It rankles. It rankles the way blackberry vines can rankle a run down the hill along the edge of a forest, a forest so young it makes you want to run, seduces you into it, and then sends up these vines to shred your skin and betray your very desire.

Rena shreds Jacob. He is convinced that she sets out to shred him. After Rena starts in on him, each woman by turns shreds his perception. They shred his linguistic markers, rendering useless as slugs the words he so carefully learned at school at their behest. These women, who paid such close attention to the marks the instructors handed out to him at the end of each term, speak in a language that contravenes everything those marks stood for. Damn, he thinks. Damn. And he vows he will never again ask why his cousin killed himself. The trouble with ending the question is that Jacob stops looking for answers. He closes his own door to wondering, but he has no way of knowing this. He decides he wants to hear more of the "poetries" his aunt loves. He laughs secretly at his aunt Celia, who behaves as though she can make this language behave, moving subjects into objects, making them plural by adding an *s* to them.

"Plump berries sometimes fall where the ground has not been stirred by light-stepping feet; these babies then wither and die before they sink root. Sometimes children hear them weeping, fighting to be born, to be fed, to be. Pick the berries; they like it." The first Alice says this to him, but Jacob doesn't hear her. Jacob doesn't wander through the bush much anymore. He doesn't like it. He doesn't wonder about why he doesn't like the bush. He just knows he doesn't like it.

THERE IS AN OLD shack in the common, down past the end of the village. Folks tell the boys some old snake used to live there, but no one can remember his name. It isn't that they've forgotten. The "can" in this case is about permission: no one is allowed to think of the dead man's name. He is what the old folks called "forever dead" — meaning dead to memory, dead to speakers, dead to story-tellers, and dead to mythmakers. The boys who used to hang about with him and might have talked about him have never said a word about him. Most of them left and drifted their way to death in broken-down hotel rooms, or drowned in their own vomit in some place called "Blood Alley" in Vancouver. Rumour has it one of them was crushed in a dumpster. It doesn't matter; the mythmakers have had a fine time drumming out tales about the three young men who used to hang at the snake's because they were not dead and they were fascinating in the terrible cruelty they had inherited from the one who was dead.

THIS MORNING GRINDS OUT sunshine in fits and starts, clouds jerk back and forth across the sun. Jacob finds it annoying. In the west the mountains and the ocean's gentle wind-warmed water don't spark much more heat than a sweet taste of sun on the skin, quickly followed by a breeze to cool it. Summer days like this make Jacob's body restless. He is still a teenager; the natural restlessness of adolescence on days like this turn his youthful restlessness into a cat's claw of anxiety.

The ball tournament has been neither exciting nor emotionally satisfying. He is antsy all day. After leaving Celia at her door, he takes to wandering around his village.

Don't go there, I warned, but I was too late.

Jacob is on his way to the old snake's cabin.

My timing does not matter. Jacob cannot communicate with animals; he cannot hear me.

Jacob has always been curious about the old snake's cabin.

Momma and Stacey warned him against going there in case he swallowed whatever poison the snake ate to make him so evil. Jacob does not believe this, and it perplexes him that Stacey does because as a teacher she ought to know better. None of the teachers at his school believe a person can swallow what has poisoned someone else's mind. They refer to the beliefs of the old people in this village as superstitions or old wives' tales. Until his cousin killed himself it hadn't crossed his mind to go down to the old snake's, but now the desire to peel back on the taboo is burning him up. His foot taps senselessly and the tapping unnerves Stacey who tells him to get on outside and do something besides wear a hole in the floor and tear at her mind. It is just the kind of scolding he needs to abrogate the caution not to go to the old snake's cabin.

The road ends before the patch of dirt in front of the old snake's cabin that once served as a yard. The villagers had built the road to bypass the snake's place. The patch between the road and the cabin is overgrown with dense brush and small trees. It is creepy, this thick little stretch to the snake's. The brush scrapes at Jacob's arms; Jacob whacks himself, thinking he is being bitten by some bug. It is cold inside the brush; there shouldn't be any bugs out. Still, he feels like he is being bitten steadily. He is beginning to feel like turning back when he hears voices. The sound of a little girl whimpering and begging nips at Jacob's ear and freezes his feet. A man's voice punctuates the pauses between her whimpers and the pleading phrases.

"No. Please. No."

The interplay of snarling and wicked laughter behind the pleas and whimpers weakens Jacob's legs. He stops, steps, stops, then steps again; each time he stops he listens to make sure the man hasn't heard him. Before taking another step Jacob hesitates for a second, and then carries on. It can't be the old snake. Who then? Who would dare to live here in this place of the forever dead? Jacob listens as the sun sets.

How can Jacob listen to this and not curse? And then my very soul grows terrified. Jacob should be a lot more offended than he is. I roll from side to side, praying this boy will be horrified by what he is witnessing.

The moon comes out and the clouds drift away. The stars paint the sky cold cobalt blue, but their light does not make it through the brush. He barely sees who's there, but he figures it must be the old snake. But how can it be? He's banned. Who is it then? Even in this barely lit underbrush, Jacob makes out the body of a man and a child, but it is too dark to identify them. It must be the old snake; who else could it be? Jacob decides it is him. No one knows the old snake is back now except him. He shudders to think he is the only one who knows the snake is here, up to his old tricks again. The child looks like she is tied up. He thinks he can see the man poking her with something.

The shack is a shambles. The yard is worse. On the right side of the house a hide is stretched out, covered with maggots. At first the hide doesn't interest Jacob; but, as he watches the man torment the girl, he is drawn to it again and again. He decides to have a closer look. He inches his way forward. Then he sees it.

He vomits.

This relieves me; whatever he swallowed is up and out.

His belly heaves. He looks up between heaves to make sure the snake hasn't seen him. No one in the house seems to hear his heaving guts. The hide was a dog. He knows it. He has no idea how he knows it. He has never seen a skinned animal, but he is as sure of it as if he had seen hundreds of skinned animals of all shapes and sizes. This was a dog. He can't get the image of the dog out of his mind, even as he hears the whimpers from the little girl, and wonders what the man tormenting her is doing. Then he sees clearly what the old snake is doing to the child and he gets sick all over again.

His stomach has already been emptied, but he can't stop heaving. He sidles closer to the shack.

There are two men with the child. Each holds a bottle. It looks like cheap wine. They take turns torturing the child. They poke her with a rod, heat it up in the fire they have going, then poke her again. She stops whimpering. Her eyes roll back. Her body goes limp. Jacob can see that they have shoved the poker up between her legs. He very nearly screams. He wants to run, but can't tear his eyes from the grisly scene.

I want to heave up my food too, but dare not. Jacob cannot see me here with him.

Someone is passed out on the floor. It looks like a woman, but Jacob cannot tell who she is. Her soiled dress is up over her hips; she has no underwear on. After the child faints or dies — Jacob cannot be sure which — both men help themselves first to the child's vagina and then they help themselves to the woman's.

Jacob heaves. Some bile rolls into his mouth and burns his throat. He is too close. One of the men hears him and comes charging at the brush. Jacob swallows his bile and breaks into a run. The man sees him running. As Jacob's distance increases, the man decides not to give chase. He shrugs and returns to the cabin, where he grabs his things. Both he and the other man leave.

With each pounding step, Jacob persuades himself that he could not possibly have seen what he knows he saw. He tells himself he imagined it, and he grows terrified of his imagination. He stops running near his gramma's house. Panting, he leans up against a stump and wonders if he had seen the old snake. "I couldn't have seen him," he argues. "He must be dead by now. Those kids are grown-ups. Maybe it is one of those young guys. I saw a man. I saw a child. I know what I saw. I just don't know who I saw." He needs to talk to someone, but he cannot see telling his grandmother. She does not deserve to hear this story. He has no idea who else he can talk to. Not any of the women or the men who told him not to go to the snake's shack. They had made so sure he knew their caution was meant to be honoured. "I have to tell. Maybe Aunt Celia will listen."

He finds his way home and straddles the bed, but he cannot sleep. He fights hard to focus on Alice's poetry, but to no avail. In the end, he lets the pictures come and go. He replays the sound of the child until his ears hurt.

XII

IT WAS SUNDAY MORNING and while half the village was at church the other half lazed about wondering what they should be doing. Stacey and Celia were at Momma's and Momma was fixing Sunday brunch. Celia leaned against the back of her chair, sticking her belly out trying to get some relief. Any day now her baby would come. She watched Jacob. He was in the centre of the living room, just off the kitchen, playing with some blocks Ned had made for him. He left his blocks and wandered over to the kitchen. "Here, Gemma." His awkward little tongue had uttered his first words. They slipped from his mouth into this circle of women and spawned the purest kind of excitement. The giant women gathered him up. They accoladed him for these his first recognizable sounds. He didn't seem to know he was being adored or that these words were his doorway to communion with them.

He has no memory of that moment, not that this matters because

Celia remembers it. She clings to Jacob's first words and fights to remember Jimmy's, his first communion with the women of his house. Those first words elude her. All she can think about now is Jacob. He has found his second doorway. Celia has witnessed it.

SOME DAYS ARE SO ordinary they make you feel grateful. Everyone needs ordinariness to settle the dust kicked up the night before. Momma is getting ready to go to Celia's to look at her paintings. Ned thinks this odd. Momma does not like visiting her daughters, she prefers they visit her. He says nothing. He has his own restlessness to deal with, which means heading to the river to fish. He walks with Momma a bit, and then swings into Stacey's to see if Jacob wants to join him. Jacob is anxious to get out of the house; he wants to be busy at something that might erase the horror of the night before and relieve some of the guilt he feels at what he might have seen. Fishing will do, he decides. He needs to be lost in some place a long way from this memory. Dipping a net in and out of a fast-moving river will keep his mind in the moment and a good distance from memory.

Stacey sallies onto the porch and hands Jacob a backpack filled with bannock, coffee, and the odd sweet. She sees Momma's back sauntering down the road toward Celia's and is about to ask Ned about it when a car pulls into her yard.

"Say. Jim!" Stacey runs toward the car. It is full of little people. Jim and his wife, Esther, are laughing before they get out of the car. The kids hit the dirt running, jumping and squealing with delight the moment the doors open. Stacey twirls the children one by one until they've all been whirled around. Jacob and Ned look at one another. They still want to fish, but they have missed Jim. He doesn't come by as much as they would like. They look at their gear, then each other with the same expression.

Jim hugs his sister, sticks both his hands in his pockets, looks at the fishing gear. He pulls his hands out, lights a smoke, and tosses his head toward Ned and Jacob in a "let's go" gesture. Ned's walk looks less tired, Stacey thinks as she watches them disappear into the tall grass to be swallowed by the cottonwoods that edge the river. They will be gone all day. Stacey decides to call on Rena and the rest of the women. She doesn't want to spend all day alone with some woman who is not quite a relative and is completely devoted to a religion this family does not subscribe to.

The river looks outraged today. It scrambles the logs at its centre, bangs their ends together; splinters fly and the sides of the banks are slowly scraped away, muddying up the blue, the grey, or the green, or whatever colour the water wants to be. In a few quiet parts the river looks like she wants to be blue, but where the mud is thickest she is khaki green. Jacob's mind lacks the language to interpret what he sometimes sees. He likes playing with the colour of things and imagining the character attached to a shade or hue, the way he attaches mood to light and sound. From the colour of the river, Jacob decides she is angry. The shades of rage change, whirl, and jump from khaki to steel grey to near black. It sends shivers up his spine. He prays she isn't mad at his silence. The spot on the river he is staring at settles into a sheer blue swirl and he decides it isn't him she is mad at. It settles him to think this.

"What you been up to, Jim?" Ned asks his son.

"Having too many kids is what."

"You know how to stop that," Jacob teases his young uncle as he saunters in the direction of a rock jutting out into the river, his net in his hand. "Put a jacket on that soldier." Jacob stops to shift his hips a little to sharpen his point and makes them laugh in that bragging kind of satisfied-man way. Jacob teases his uncle a little more, telling him about the kind of jackets they make to cover that little man of his.

"You obviously don't know my Catholic wife. You ought to let me introduce her to you sometime." This makes them all laugh more.

Jacob is ready to dip a net into the river. He takes off his shoes so his toes can get a good grip on the slippery rock he will stand on. Bending slightly at the knees he plants his feet apart, and breathes nice and deep.

"Wait," Ned says, and ties him off. The two other men carry on talking while they hold the rope. Jacob knows that the rope will not save him if he slides off, but it will give them a body to bury if the river takes his life away. This is satisfying to the two men on shore and all right with Jacob. Jacob does not give falling into the river a moment's worry. He does not intend to slip. He turns to give his uncle and grandpa a smile, as he remembers Uncle and Grandpa having done before challenging this river, then he dips the net in a wide arc against the current. The dip and swing wake his arms up and anchor his feet to the stone he's standing on. He looks across the river, with its sun-dappled surface changing colour, and his memory melts. All that is left is the peaceful quiet of the dip and the swing of his net.

"I was coming up here last week, and the heel fell off one of the baby's shoes. I don't even know which one, there are so many. There goes gas money, I thought. I swear, Ned, how do other men manage?"

"Most of them don't," Jacob says. Jacob's words almost get a rise out of the other men, but the net starts jumping in his hands. He tosses its contents onto the bank. Ned and Jim give each fish one good blow. The fish flip-flop a couple of times, make a kind of screaming sound, and die.

This is the hard part of witnessing. Seeing the fish and not being able to eat the carrion left behind right away.

Jacob hands the net to Jim, pulls his knife out, and kneels next to his grandpa, who has already severed the gills from the head of one of the fish. Ned jerks on the gills and guts and pulls out a neat string of eggs. He pulls the eggs off the string and looks at Jacob, hoping like hell that Jacob has brought something to pack them in.

Jacob winks, cups his hands, and shakes them up and down. This gets a rise out of Ned. They laugh as Jacob pulls a freezer bag from his jacket. Ned feigns a punch at Jacob, and they both crack up again. Jacob nods in the direction of his backpack and begins gutting the second fish. After the fish are cleaned, the men eat a little bannock and drink some coffee.

From Jacob's backpack Ned pulls out an old gym bag filled with several small plastic bags and a large green garbage bag. He puts the bag of eggs in one of the smaller bags. Jacob cuts both fish in half. Ned sticks them in another of the small bags and puts the works in the big green one. He shoves these into the gym bag. He hands some food to Jacob, and adds, "Although you don't deserve it."

"Two with eggs, three without," Jim says. "What you think, Jacob? We get the whole damn family?"

They had not caught the whole damned family and I know so. The salmon with eggs were not partner to the ones without. That's the problem with open fishing. When the people used weirs, they could choose couples. Now it's random. The partners will die without progeny. Ten sets of family lines dead. What a waste.

"You always were disgusting, Uncle." The notion of catching and eating the whole family makes Jacob squeamish. Jim likes seeing it.

"They wouldn't be any more related than your gramma and I," Ned assures Jacob. "Fish aren't as stupid as some people."

Jacob is startled by this remark. Jim makes a note of it and commits himself to remembering Jacob's response. They smoke. Jacob wants to set again, but Ned shakes his head. "There aren't so many fish left in this river." They will have to let most of them go. It makes Jacob sad that he can't just take what they need as he mentally sorts out which ones to keep and which ones to let go. The sadness passes through him, leaving as quickly as it came. He selects three more and puts them back into the river. Jacob wants to stay by the river, half-afraid the snake memory will come back.

He tries pushing conversation, but the other men just sit quiet. He shifts from one foot to the other, and looks at the river, hoping for something from it. He looks back at the men and then over to the net.

"I swear, boy, you got some wild hair up your ass. What's eating you?" Ned drops his question almost like an accusation. Is Jacob withholding information that they need? It's a test, Jacob thinks. Can I pull this past my grandpa?

"I don't know," he answers.

"Who the hell does know then? I have me here a quarter. You tell me who would know and I am going to call them right god-damned now," Ned bellows. He does not like being told "I don't know." It unnerves him that a grown man could feel something he is not able to name. He suspects such men are powerless. He especially does not like the suspicion of powerlessness when it arises from one of his boys.

"I think you know," Jim says to Jacob, helping his father out. "Fact: you are the only one who knows."

"Oh yeah, tell you right here with my back to the river and no witnesses, just go ahead and drop on your furious cranky-ass selves the story of the worst thing I've ever done." Jacob bites his lip.

"What did you do." Ned turns the question into a near-threat by dropping the usual inflection at the end.

Time and Jacob freeze. He considers saying that he does not feel like sharing with them. He heard one of the women say that, and it had killed the men's curiosity. They would respect him for it, but then again, maybe they would not. He has never heard a man tell another man he didn't want to talk about something. It is tearing him up to hang on to this thing. Ever since he went to the old snake's he's found it difficult to stay focused on things. The images return to haunt him, making him restless, so he decides he'd better let it drop.

The restless head of the serpent lies in wait, hoping Jacob will retreat from telling his grandpa the story of the snake. He had lured Jacob there and tried to seduce him with the images of Amos tormenting the child. Amos was an outsider, but Jacob lived inside the village. It would be a victory to create this terror inside, but it is Loyal's turn and Loyal breathes desire on Jacob, the desire to speak, to tell, to let go the nightmare he has witnessed.

"I went to the snake's house."

Ned is about to bellow, when Jim holds his hand up to stop him. Jacob closes his eyes so he won't see their faces or the blow he is sure is coming.

"What did you see?" Jim asks gently. Jacob starts and looks at his grandpa, who glares back at him.

"Do you see things that aren't there? Does anybody? Is it possible? I swear I saw him, the old snake, at his house. In a corner of the yard there was this dog, skinned and stretched. There was this little girl tied up. That old guy was doing things to her with that hot poker. What the hell was wrong with him, Grandpa?"

The sickness comes again.

Jacob wants to know the journey of these men to the horror they had visited on this child so he can be sure he might travel it himself. His cowardice at not trying to rescue the child makes him feel that he is capable of going there. He feels like the difference between him and these men is a matter of them having taken the wrong path when faced with a fork in their journey. He is repulsed that the snake's behaviour is just a matter of a fork in the road. What he saw was sick. Could he do terrible things but never face that they were terrible? His mind flips pages back in time to a hillside, to a child, a small child, tied up. He is poking the child with a stick, making him whimper. Some beast inside him is laughing. It wasn't Jacob. It can't be Jacob. Jacob is nice. Jacob would never do such a thing.

Now he faces his uncle and his grandfather with the truth of his looking upon the unspeakable, wondering if they see how close he was to the snake's pit. What is he more afraid of? Them knowing what he is thinking about, or them not knowing?

"What scares you, Jacob?"

"Wondering if I saw it."

"Wondering if you saw it, or wondering if you made it up?" Jim queries. Ned is starting to see what Jim is getting at. His line of questioning unnerves Ned. Not one of us. Can Jim be thinking that Jacob might be like the snake? Ned is accustomed to giving his son a lot of rope, unnerving as it sometimes is, so he just lets him be.

"I guess I am wondering if I made it up. And I am wondering about me."

Jim has him. He knows that Jacob will answer any question he asks now. All he has to do is make sure he asks the right ones.

"Did you make it up?"

"I must have."

"Have you done this before? Made stuff up?"

Jacob squirms.

"It's okay, Jacob, it's just us here. You've made stuff up before?"

"Yes."

"You want to tell us about it?"

"I was small." He wants his smallness to excuse him, but he knows it doesn't. It won't in the minds of these men, either. He bulldozes his way forward. "I made stuff up about the smaller kids, and then I did them. Tied them up, poked at them with sticks — but not like the snake, not in places like he did, in those private places. Just in their bellies. When they cried, I laughed."

Jacob throws up, shoulders heaving. No food comes up, just the sound of his heaving. Jim put his hand on Jacob's shoulder.

CELIA JERKS UP FROM the painting she is showing Momma. She cocks her head to one side and half closes one eye. She's caught sight of Jacob for a split second, but now she is back in the room with Momma.

"What's the matter?" Momma asks.

"Nothing," Celia answers. Now she sees Jacob heaving but chooses not to tell her mother. "You see," she explains, "This one is about the river, how she wanders to the sea, bent on travelling in the same direction but unable to do so." The river's rapids roil pale blue and mud grey. The banks are inundated with black lines, shifting its course. Momma sighs.

"THROW IT OUT. DON'T swallow, breathe out. Out."

Jim bends Jacob's head in the direction of the ground so it will be difficult for him to re-swallow his shame. The sun wraps itself around Jacob. Jim points out the traces of Jacob's illness on his shirt. Jacob takes his shirt off and swishes it in the river, feeling the water as he has never felt it before. It is crisp, clean, and cold; it shines a pastel blue at him. He returns to sit down and Ned finishes the moment off.

"Men sometimes have thoughts they aren't supposed to have. We are supposed to take them to our fathers, who will tell us where they come from and how to get rid of them."

"You don't have a father, so you kept this secret, and then you acted on it," Jim says. "Now you are afraid you might turn into the old snake. You could, if you don't go see your old grandpa here every time you have them thoughts. You got that?"

Jacob feels a lump in his throat. He remembers fantasizing about his father as a small boy in his dark room at night. He would lie in bed pretending his dad had played ball with him or taken him fishing. He was swinging outside on a swing he had made himself when he decided not to make up stuff about his dad anymore. "No use thinking about it," he said as he swung back and forth. That summer he was nine and his meanness had come forward. He feels ashamed now. He looks at his uncle, amazed at the connection

Jim has made for him between his meanness and his not having a father.

"What's the difference between having them thoughts and the snake doing them?"

"Plenty and hardly anything at all," Ned answers. "Men don't act on their thoughts when they take that kind of a turn." He tries to keep it simple, but he knows it isn't that simple. Men don't have thoughts like that after they become men. Boys don't act on their thoughts when they take that kind of a turn if they are raised right. Very few boys he knows had such thoughts. Jacob had acted on his thoughts. Now Ned wants to be sick. He shares an apprehensive look with his son.

Jim takes some tobacco out of a pouch and says, "Go talk to that river. There is a woman in that river. Ask her to watch over you." When Jacob is out of earshot Jim says, "We better talk, Ned. Don't you go telling Momma or any of the women about this." Ned nods; he does not want to keep this sickening secret to himself, but he knows his wife is overloaded, full up. One more shovel and she might cave in.

"Tonight," is all Jim says.

THE LAST PICTURE IS a sunset. No objects, just the sun setting on a thin line of black. Behind the sun, the light is nearly white; emanating from this ball of yellow is every possible hue of red, orange, pink, and pale yellow. The colours fill the page. Celia is about light, her mother thinks. She is about light and colour, and these colours shaped her somehow. Momma closes the book.

"Let's go by Stacey's," she says. "We'll all go to my house and I'll make some pie." Celia smiles. All her paintings add up to some pie. Somehow she doesn't feel so strange. She might not know her mother well, but they share the same odd sense of logic and that makes her one of them.

THE MEN PACK UP their fish and saunter home. All the way there, Jim keeps the three of them laughing with stories of cow shit, bear shit, and any other tale he can drum up that might help them forget about the scene by the river. By the time they arrive home, they are like any old clutch of men who have just had a very successful fishing trip.

XIII

THE WOMEN ARE IN the kitchen making pie by the time the men return. The kids are running about the house, raising a ruckus; their laughter cuts the air into bouncing little pieces that seem to massage Ned's bones. Jacob has gone home to put his share of the catch in his mother's freezer. Jim is ready to talk. Ned and Jim go outside for a smoke.

"Spider is a storyteller. She weaves soft silk threads across human pathways. Be careful to unhook the web on the far side and clear the path. Her threads may otherwise get tangled up on you. In the fight to clear the thread you might swallow the spider. She is a predator too. You don't know what her story is about until after she has spun the tale inside, twisted you in all kinds of crazed directions." Ned isn't sure why Jim has begun the conversation this way, so he lights a smoke and waits for him to explain.

Celia hears the story as she sorts through the wild cherries they are turning into pies. Her brother's voice comes at her, sifted through the words young Alice gave her the night before, the ones she has been turning over in her mind. They disturb her. Stacey watches her sister; Celia looks distracted and Stacey feels suspicious about her because she knows she is daydreaming again. Stacey understands why children daydream, but Celia is too old. The lines of her face show her age. She joins Celia and sorts the cherries as quickly as she can, stewing over how in the world to approach her younger sister about her neurotic daydreaming. Momma rattles on about Celia's paintings. Rena jokes about who knows what. The kids are antsy by the time the pies are done and the men have gotten back.

Jacob returns in time to join them in eating the pies.

Celia sits in her momma's kitchen, wishing she were in her easy chair, the black night hanging over her, so she could smile at the memory of her gramma while reliving the lines of her cousin's poem. The candle in the kitchen dances. The room softens. Celia thinks she might get through another night without her son if she can just escape this kitchen.

Mink is merciless. Celia does not need escape, she needs to be part of this story. Mink is determined to prepare her for it. Nothing happens after this moment, no dreams, no fear, no suspicions — just a family eating pie, telling stories, and sharing laughter. Celia is relieved by the time she leaves for home.

AT HOME, BY CANDLELIGHT, she retreats to her bedroom to recite her cousin's poetry. She fought all day against resenting the intrusion of family that kept her from her musing. The only way she managed to get through the day was to promise herself that tonight she would sit in the dark tasting Alice's words no matter who came. She has barely begun to roll Alice's words around in her mind when the knock comes. The last line Alice read drops into her mouth and she feels herself swallow it. She savours the texture, the sound, and the taste of the words. Whoever is knocking is persistent. She ignores it. The tap becomes a rap then a bang. She clutches the arm of her chair. "Don't answer that door," she tells herself. The banging persists and finally she gives in and gets up to answer. Her aunt Martha stands there, mouth agape, looking at her. What in the world has driven Martha out of bed this late?

"What is it, Martha?" Celia steps back to let Martha enter, but she doesn't.

"Celia, can you help me? I have to get my granddaughter."

"How come? Where's her mom?"

Martha's face is ash white. Celia doubts she can solve whatever problem has turned Martha's face this ash white.

"I don't know."

"You don't know?" This agitates Celia. She is not in the mood for riddles. "At home, I hope. Don't be pestering me with riddles without answers, Martha."

"Celia, will you help me? My granddaughter called. All she could say was 'Help me, Gramma.'" Martha is sweating. She is looking out over her shoulder at something — or maybe it is away from something.

Celia runs for her coat, wondering what in the world has made Martha think she could be helpful with anything that has got Martha this upset. Alice's words have taken such a beating, first last night and now tonight. Celia's ritual of listening to them, then going home to the pleasantness of the dark to play with the words until sleep comes, has been interrupted by Jacob, then by the humming, then by her momma's paint viewing, then by the pie eating, and now by Martha. This means Celia will have to go Alice's again; she chuckles as she slips her bloated feet into a pair of worn-out shoes.

The gravel in front of Celia's yard crunches under their feet as she tries to keep up with Martha.

"C'mon, Martha, you know I gave up men so I could get fat. I can't run. Slow down."

"We have to hurry. Shelley called me. She was barely whisper-ing, saying, 'Help me, Gramma, help me.' That girl would not dare phone unless something terrible happened. I can't face it alone, so I stopped to get you." Martha keeps right on flying down the road. Celia finds the strength to heave her nearly two hundred pounds after her.

"Shelley called. She's only five years old. She knows to call." Celia pauses. "I didn't know that girl of yours had a phone." She tries to consider the shack Martha's daughter lives in and can't imagine it having a phone. A phone seems absurdly extravagant given the conditions of that shack.

"I got the phone for her," Martha says.

Celia can't decide if this is funny or insane. Living in an old shack with barely any electricity and no running water doesn't jive with a owning a phone.

"Slow down," Celia urges. Until this moment, she had not thought her two hundred pounds were an inconvenience. In fact, she'd thought she deserved every tasty chocolate-filled ounce of them, but now she wishes she weren't so heavy.

"We have to hurry. I am afraid of what Stella might have done to her. I've always been afraid. I got her the cell phone just in case."

Celia is fighting to keep up. Halfway down the road, the impact of what Martha has said dawns on Celia. Something terrible has happened to give that child the cheek to use her mother's phone. Shelley is a furtive and timid child. She doesn't misbehave. Panic settles in Celia's body as she catches a glimpse of what might have happened. Her legs move faster. She passes Martha. Something is so wrong in there. Martha struggles to catch up. Both women find it difficult to breathe.

Shelley lives with her mom and some guy down at one end of the reserve, not far from the old snake's shack, in an old house that had been deserted until someone desperate for something to call her own moved in. Celia fights for breath; she fights her legs for agility, for speed, for something to move herself along. Nausea teases at her stomach. She is about to tell Martha to go on ahead when she sees the house. There are no lights on. She wants to tell herself that this is not unusual this late at night, but she knows that if Shelley were awake there would be a light on.

"Children don't sit willingly in the dark," she says out loud.

Celia reaches the shack and pushes open the door. The blast of chill air that meets them indicates the wood stove is out. The child must be cold. Celia flips the only light switch in the cabin. The light does not go on. Celia goes back to open the door wide so that the moonlight might help them to see. They stand for a moment, letting their eyes adjust. They can see the child lying there; even in the dark her eyes are vacant as they stare into the black. She moans so softly, so gently, so quietly. It sounds like a muffled hum. "That hum," Celia mutters to herself. Is this who she heard screaming the other night? Celia feels her blood chill as the picture of the limp child staring at nothing with the phone still in her tiny hands comes into focus. Off in the corner is a woman, her legs spread open, a bottle of beer in her hand, her lids half-closed, her mouth open, and an unlit cigarette hanging from her mouth. Celia fails to recognize Stella.

They move toward the child's body like two people carrying a coffin, slow and reverent. Both women pray the child is still breathing. Martha fishes in her pocket for a match and lights it. It bathes the room in pale light for a moment; when its fire shrinks Celia can see that Shelley's forearms have small, round purpled-red burns. There are bruises just about everywhere her skin is showing. Celia sees a small pool of blood near Shelley's private parts.

"Oh, no." Martha drops the match. She hunts for a wad of paper, twists it up, lights another match, and sets fire to the paper.

"Oh, Martha." Celia reaches for the phone.

"Who are you going to call?" Martha's voice has the quality of a threat.

"Nine-one-one."

Martha grabs Celia's arm and stops her.

"They take so long. She'll die. Or they'll take her away and I'll never see her again," Martha pleads with Celia as she reaches to take the phone away from her.

"We can't just leave her like this." Celia snaps her hand back, clinging to the phone. "She looks like she's already dying. I'll call Momma. She saved that awful snake. Maybe she can save this child."

Martha remembers the snake, that beast Momma so carefully tended. When she was young, she had hated her aunt for her devotion to reviving that old snake. Now she hates her daughter, who cannot tend to her grandchild, this sweet child who is much too obedient, much too grown-up to be just five, and now is much too innocent and much too small to be this tortured. The hate catches fire, hooks itself to Martha's voice, floods her arms with the need for revenge, and brings the worst sort of foulness from the bottom of some well of decadence she had swallowed a long time ago. She screams the foulness out at Stella. "Wake up, you fucking bitch. Wake up!" She shakes Stella by the hair.

Her daughter comes to, mumbling, "What's up? Fuck off."

Martha's arms pummel Stella's drunken body. Celia grabs her cousin as soon as she gets off the phone.

"Martha! What are you doing? The child, the child, she is still alive. Momma says we have to do things for her." Stella tries to rise from her corner, remembers her cigarette, looks for a light. She catches sight of her daughter. She eases herself toward her; then, like a rabbit that has caught sight of a fox, she hunches, stands still, and collapses. Her eyelids, loaded with defeat, fall shut.

XIV

"NED. WAKE UP." MOMMA squeezes the words out between tense lips. Ned wakes up, sits up, takes one look at his wife's determined and frightened face, and scrambles to the floor. He jumps into his pants, grabs a shirt from the closet, and, putting it on, heads for the door. Momma throws a wet sheet into the freezer. Ned pays no attention to what she does and asks no questions. He heads to the car, where he waits for her. He knows he will find out soon enough what the horror behind Momma's face is all about.

Momma swings into the passenger seat and instructs Ned to stop by Judy's. Momma runs in and comes out with Judy, who is still tying her scarf around her neck and buttoning up her jacket. Rena is standing on the porch, watching. She is going to Momma's house. "This is going to be a long one," Rena murmurs as she picks up the phone to call Stacey.

After hearing Stacey's sleep-filled grunt, Rena says, "Get your shoes on, Stacey."

"Whassup?" Stacey drawls, still half asleep.

"I don't know, but your momma came and got Judy. You know she wouldn't wake Judy up unless it was critical. You get ready and pick me up on the way to Momma's." Rena declines to tell her how horrified Momma had looked.

Momma is aghast. How could this happen? Even in her unconscious state, the child is murmuring, calling out to her mother in whimpers. Martha paces, wanting Momma to work magic.

"Do something." She wants Momma to relieve her grandchild of the hell she is living. She stops pacing and attacks Stella. Celia separates them, reminding Martha of her grandchild. Momma understands Martha's rage. She feels the same in her own bones; she wants to shout at the child, "Who did this to you?" At Stella, "How could you let this happen?" At the world, "What has happened to my family?" At anyone who will listen, "Are we less than animals?"

Ned stands in front of Momma, terrified by the scene. His shoulders sag, his body almost unable to hold his weight. He has fallen into old age and lost decades all in one moment. When he begins to move he drags himself about the room, doing whatever the women instruct him with no enthusiasm. He hunts his memory for someone to hate, to blame, to help him understand how this could possibly happen. As he hunts his memory, the fire in him begins to drown in the guilt that is being born.

As a young man, Ned had left this village and headed out on the open road. He learned things on that journey, things about electricity, about positive and negative, about grounding and shorting out. He thinks about it now. It tells him something about humans. Humans are charged or they are not. They are grounded or they are not. They are transmitting or receiving, or they are shorting out. The dust, the gravel, the hard work, the mountain climbing, the fishing, the berry picking, all this keeps the villagers grounded. The hard work and the mountain climbing wore out the charge. Someone had lost connection to his ground wire; two positives had collided, shorted out, and aimed the force of the charge at this child. Ned finds a comfort in seeing all of this in the light of the metaphor of electricity, as he cannot contemplate the level of meanness, the depth of Stella's uncaring numbness, or the intensity of hate that are required to commit this act.

He feels his own charge waning as he looks for water.

"We have to move her," Celia says. "This place is too filthy."

"We can't," Judy argues, her hands and legs shaking violently so that her words jerk. "She needs a doctor."

"They'll take her away. We will never see her again," Momma says, wondering if they deserve to ever see this child again.

Martha starts after Stella again. Celia catches her before she gets close enough to haul on any more of her daughter's hair, pummel her, or tear her clothes.

"Momma," Shelley mutters as she awakes and looks at the face closest to her. Momma finds some kind of confidence in this girl's waking up and recognizing her. If she can wake up and discern one face from another and call out her name, maybe she has the strength to fight for her life.

"Help me," Momma says to Celia. "Get me plywood," she directs Ned. She turns to Judy, "You don't have to do this. I know your people have rules. They mean something to you, but they don't mean anything to me."

"O God, please help me and forgive me, but I do have to do this," Judy says.

The women talk about how to move Shelley. When Ned returns, they lay her out on the plywood.

Momma grabs hold of Martha's face. "You listen to me, now, Martha. If this child is going to make it, she is going to because someone talks her through it, someone encourages her every second in a golden-throated Gramma voice — a voice free of rage and hate. You forget about your anger at that girl over there and you make sure this child makes it or you will never be able to live with yourself. You hear me?"

Judy shivers at the depth of cold in Momma's voice. Martha shakes, but agrees. She closes her eyes and blocks the picture of her daughter out of her mind. She reaches for the memory of her own Gramma's voice and calls out to Shelley, "You hang in there, baby. Gramma's here. You just hold on." Martha feels forever rising inside. She tells herself that she can do this; she will find a million different ways to say, "Hang in there, sweet girl. Clutch that thread of life. Cling to it. Don't let it go. Stay with your gramma. I got you. I have you."

STACEY PREPARES FOR WHATEVER emergency might have caused Rena to be awakened at two a.m. Sickness, birth, or injury are the only emergencies that would get her mother out of bed this early. She tries to think of any illnesses. There don't seem to be any. She looks at the store of medicines in her cupboard. Some have been there a long time. They are still good. She decides to take a little of just about everything. She shovels them into her bag. She grabs sheets from the closet. Clean white cotton. Maybe it's a birth ... but who is pregnant that won't go to the hospital? "Just about anyone," she answers herself. Birth is a hope. She thinks that any- one with a two a.m. emergency on a Saturday isn't full of hope. She braces herself for shock. Maybe a drunken relative shot another one? She backs away from the closet and steps on Jacob's shoe. The clatter of nearly hitting the deck as she trips, and cursing Jacob as she dances herself upright, wake him up.

"Where are you going?"

"To Momma's. Celia called Momma, and Rena told me to get over. Something has happened."

"I'm going too," Jacob says. Stacey does not think this is a good idea. Men are only in the way during medical emergencies.

They're so fragile when they are as young as Jacob; but she is too tired to argue with him.

"You drive," she says and hands him her keys. She clutches her bundle and remembers she has a pinch of tobacco. "Wait," she says. "Swing by the river."

Jacob drives by the river, though he thinks this is an odd request. There is an old cedar there that has escaped logging. It is big and round, and Stacey has taken to talking to it. Jacob stops the car and Stacey gets out. She lays a pinch of tobacco down, mumbling, "We could use some help" to the cedar. Jacob thinks speaking to the tree is even odder than the tobacco stuff; he stares at his mother when she gets back into the passenger seat.

"You do that a lot?" he asks, heaping on the sarcasm.

"No. Not enough, apparently," she answers.

"Does it help?" This question sounds much more genuine.

"I don't know. It makes me feel … like … well, like I can get through anything. I have a feeling the anything I need to get through tonight is going to be awful. Let's go pick up Rena."

On the way to Rena's, Jacob prays for Celia.

"Hey," Rena hollers as they pull up next to where she's standing in the driveway. "Thanks for the ride." She throws her things in the back seat. She looks at them for a moment, while considering mentioning how horrified Momma had looked. Then, with a "Gawdammit," she jumps into the car, complaining to Stacey and Jacob, "If I knew what the hell was going on it would help."

Jacob swings the car out onto the road.

"If you knew what was going on, it wouldn't be so exciting." A half laugh escapes Jacob. The women let go a quick half laugh too. They need to laugh, but the rest of the laughter won't come. Jacob pulls the car into his gramma's driveway. It is one of three paved driveways on the reserve. He wonders why no one else has bothered to pave over the gravel leading to their homes. He decides it's no use thinking about. He stops the car and the women get out. They enter the house without noticing that Jacob is staying in the car. He reaches into his shirt pocket, unravels a cigarette, and prays Celia is all right. He gets out of the car and drops the tobacco by a tree.

In the living room, Jacob sees his grandpa sitting in the dark. The air surrounding Ned has a dangerous texture to it. It is thick with things Jacob dares not consider. He can barely move through it. He sits next to his grandfather. The women are in the kitchen.

"What happened?" Jacob asks.

Ned knows that Jacob wants a simple answer, but he also knows that there are too many threads to this web that a simple answer is impossible. What happened? How does anything like this ever come to his village, to his family? How could anyone let something this terrible visit someone as heroic and as lovely and as sweet as his wife? What crazy train of thoughts, of madness, travels in the mind of the man who did this to a child? What happened? What happened to drive someone to this kind of deep, hate-filled sense of lust? Ned fights for the simple explanation his grandson hungers for, but he can't find it.

"I don't know. But what you thought you imagined? What we talked about by the river? You saw it. It happened, not when you thought it did, but it happened."

Jacob's shoulders pull in, then down. He wraps his arms around his upper body. He wants his body to be small. He wants to go back in time, to undo this thing he saw, to un-see it. He wants his cousin Jimmy to rise from death, he wants to trot him off in some innocent direction, free of this grisly memory. Jacob hears the sound of defeat in his grandpa's voice. He shakes with fright. He knows his grandpa is courageous, decisive, and terrible in his determination; but now when he looks at him he sees none of this. He wants more from him, but his grandpa dismisses him with a wave, then covers his face with the same hand. Jacob moves away before the disgust at his grandpa's weakness can rise up in him. He walks to the periphery of the kitchen, where he can see and listen to the women.

Jacob hears Momma and Judy arguing about getting a doctor. He begins to glean a picture of the emergency from the bits of their argument he can make out.

"One of you has to stop arguing long enough to tell me what to do with this child." Celia's voice is tight and full of command. This is the second time Jacob has heard her talk like this. Something strange is going on, the world is being upended. Celia is finding the strength to stay in the real world. Momma is arguing, which he has never seen or heard before, and Celia is taking charge, something else he has never seen before. The child he imagined he had seen is real. Jacob wants to escape, but his feet feel nailed to the floor.

The women stop arguing and Celia tells them to get a sheet from the freezer. How did Celia become the centre of solving this mess? He is accustomed to everyone relying on Rena, Stacey, or Momma for help. Celia is a flake. Jacob loves her, but if he were in any kind of trouble she would be the last person in this family he would call upon to get him out of it. He hears Martha's voice, speaking soft and sweet to the child. It must have been Martha who had called Celia.

They talk about Shelley's burns. "What kind of a thing did that crazy man use?" The question sears Jacob's throat. This must be the same girl. What if he had seen it before it happened? What if he was not some madman, but had been shown something? What if he had seen it in the flesh, the drama unfolding as it happened, and he had done nothing? If any of this is true, he is no better off than if he had imagined it himself out of some perverse hidden desire. His silence may have helped to kill her. If it does, then Ned and Jim are complicit.

"It's too late," Judy says. "She's not going to make it."

They might have been able to save her if he had run straight to Momma's with the tale. What if no one had interpreted it that way?

What if they thought like Ned did, that he had made it up? He would have a clear conscience now. His body feels drained of all energy. He leans against the wall and hopes it will hold him up until he recovers. He isn't sure that it's the same girl. He needs to look. He dares not.

Celia curses the indecision of the women who might have a clue as to what this child needs, and runs for the door. Celia comes through the door too fast for Jacob to move and pretend he's doing anything but eavesdropping.

"Jacob," she clips out as she hustles past.

The door is open. The heat rises. The air lightens. Jacob floats to the entrance; the child's face is aimed at him. It's her. He imagines that she recognizes him and that her eyes accuse him of cowardice. He wonders why he did nothing when he saw her. The accusation he sees in her eyes stills his blood. Jacob shakes. He can't seem to keep his feet on the ground. He hears "Move" and he slides to the left and stumbles as Celia passes him carrying a cold sheet. Jacob sees her covering the child in a cold wet clean sheet.

Celia goes in and comes out again, stops at the maw of the room holding the accusing eyes of the child. She hands Jacob a sheet and says, "Wet it, get it good and wet, then freeze it in this bag. Don't touch it with anything but these here two bags. Here, put your hands in the bags. Don't breathe on it. Put it in the freezer. You got that, Jacob? Do you understand me? Tell me you understand." He hears her voice coming at him, strident and sharp as it punches its way through the thick darkness of the hall.

Jacob lets a "Yes" slide out from his constricted throat.

Her nephew is in a conundrum. He looks like he's seen the dead rise from the grave. Why in the world is he looking in on this grisly scene, if he doesn't have the strength to accept what he sees?

The sheet has weight. It helps him feel real. He focuses on its weight; its reality grounds him as he heads for the kitchen. He breathes out, away from the sheet, when he can't hold his breath anymore. The sink is clean. It smells of alcohol. These women are not taking any chances. He puts the sheet in the sink, soaks it, rinses it, then drops it in the bag and stuffs it into the freezer without touching it. There's too much food in the way. He puts the sheet back in the water, adds more alcohol. He rearranges the food, clearing the basket. He wets a rag with the alcohol and cleans the basket, then stuffs the sheet back in a new bag, and places it carefully in the freezer.

Ned watches him. Jacob is moving about in the kitchen like he's in the middle of a nightmare, not at all like he is awake and trying to save a child's life. Something is up with that boy, Ned thinks, forgetting that he knows what is up with him.

Jacob doesn't want to feel this guilty. He fetches a chair. Maybe if he does not permit himself to sleep until the little girl is better, the guilt will ease its grip on him. Maybe he could tell her that, and her eyes would not accuse him anymore. She might not survive, Judy had said. Jacob decides that she will. He places a stool very carefully just outside the door. He does not want to disturb the women in case they come out and he sees the little girl aiming her eyes at him again.

Not long after he sits, Stacey opens the door and tells him to fetch another sheet. He does. All night long he boils sheets, then freezes and fetches them.

EVERY NOW AND THEN, Celia feels a wave of nausea pass through her. She wants to beat herself up for threatening to be sick, but it isn't her who keeps conjuring the desire to vomit. It is her body, operating independently of her need to stay well. There is nothing to be done about it. Her guts can't accept that this could happen to a child whose grandmother is there with her. Her stomach cannot allow that this has happened to a child whose mother is connected to her, to her mother, to their grandmother. Shelley is thin, half-starved. They must not have fed her. Celia's weight grows unbearable; every ounce of once-comfortable fat is tormented by the emaciated body of the little girl. Her bones ache. She shifts, hoping this will relieve her of the pain. She had liked the presence her fat gave her, but now the weight sours inside, shrinks her large presence to a withered worm that wanders loose in her belly, teasing her stomach's nerves. She glances at Stacey, who is focused on cleaning each wound with hydrogen peroxide. Celia marvels at how focused Stacey is. She imagines that Stacey does not think of how many wounds there are to clean, how hopeless it is to bother because this child is likely not going to make it. No. Stacey has been asked to clean the wounds and, with delicacy and precision, that is exactly what she will do all night and all day if need be. She will dab each wound in its turn without doubting the sanity of what she is doing. Not for a second. Stacey is stalwart and Celia loves her for it.

Every now and then Momma looks at Rena, raises an eyebrow, and signals Rena to give the child a breath through a mask she is wearing on her face.

Rena can barely stand to tend this child, Celia can see it. She looks like she wants to bring up her last meal. Rena is tough, not as sentimental as Celia. It frightens Celia to see her frail.

Judy does not think that anything they do will work; and so, between ministrations, she says this to the women: "Burn victims this bad need to be put in a germ-free tent, chilled, undergo skin grafts, and given oxygen in very controlled doses. This room is not sanitary, cleaning it out with juniper is not enough. If this child survives tonight, and if she gets through the pain, she will likely die of infection." Every second they spend trying to save her will be damned in the eyes of the law as proof of negligence, criminal negligence, because it was obvious the child had been raped, burned, and beaten. The law requires that they report this. Even if she survives, the scars will be there forever, and they will still be required by law to report it. Judy tries every which way to convince the women to take Shelley to a hospital, but Momma is stubborn. She keeps asking, "What next, Judy? What next?" Judy is exhausted and cannot think of anything more to do.

The sheets they are using are being boiled in juniper berries and washed in alcohol, but Judy does not believe this is enough. "Germs can get through the cloth," she explains. Celia wonders what kind of world this woman comes from that she cannot see that the women are not going to do anything but try to nurse Shelley back to health.

"Shut up. Shut the fuck up. If you are going to do this, then do it. Or go home."

Rena hears Celia swear and take on an angry tone for the first time and she laughs. Stacey, Momma, and Judy stare at Celia as if they have just seen their kitchen table do a jig. Martha doesn't seem to notice that this is the first time anyone has heard Celia swear.

Celia touches her mouth and says, "How did all that gravel find its way in there?" Stacey, Momma, Judy, and Rena laugh the kind of relieving laugh that jiggles away the hours of tension.

When they stop laughing, Celia asks Judy if the sheets they used to make the tents were made of plastic or cloth. Plastic is her answer. "Doesn't Ned have a roll in his garage left over from when he did the roof on the addition?" Celia asks.

Judy gets excited. "Ned has a roll of plastic?" They send Ned out to the garage to get it. Judy cuts off the first six feet, throws it aside, then cuts more, holding it away from her face. She shapes it and engineers the overlapping flap. Ned busies himself constructing the four poles for the tent. They cut four holes in the first layer of plastic so that they can keep an eye on Shelley or reach in when they need to, then they cover the plastic with another layer.

Jacob helps Ned erect the structure and attaches it to the bed. Both men work without looking at one another, without speaking. Words make breath and they dare not breathe on the child. Judy reminds them not to breathe on Shelley and Celia tells them it's best that they don't even look at her, but Jacob does not need this last instruction. Together, Ned and Jacob finish the structure.

The child's grandmother continues to urge Shelley to hang in there, to keep fighting. "We are making you a tent," Momma soothes. "Do you like your little tent? Shelley, you're on a camping trip in Momma's kitchen." Celia is not entirely sure what the child has to hang in there for, but she hangs in there all night long anyway. Rena drips Pedialyte into the child's mouth, drop by tiny drop, every swallow of the fluid making the child convulse. Rena begins to feel like a kind of cruel taskmaster, but she does not stop. Celia believes Judy. She believes the child needs glucose, a sanitary room, and surgical instruments, but she also believes that those sterile things alone will not be enough.

Later into the night, Celia and Judy have found their way, plodding on next to the women who are praying for forgiveness and continuing to minister to the child. Just about the time Celia and Judy have reconciled to doing what they have to do, Shelley's frail body begins to quiver.

"She is in pain, Judy. Terrible pain." Momma's voice cracks when she says this. It crackles like dead leaves on a drought-ridden autumn day. It rakes the room and crunches on the ears of the women with its desperation. Celia does not remember her mother sounding this vulnerable or desperate.

"Oh, God. She needs …" Judy starts in with her doctor, hospital, and the law sermon.

"No lectures, Judy," Momma says. Celia can see her mother's intense rage boiling to the surface. Judy hears the warning in Momma's voice and backs down.

"I have painkillers. Can she swallow them? Will she choke?" Stacey's voice is textured with the same desperation as her mother's. The women in the room want to scream at someone. They are standing at the edge of the same desperation. Thick desperation swims through the room and into their bodies; one more doubt threatens to swallow them.

"We can crush the pill and jell it, then slide it on the end of a tongue depressor to open her throat. The gelatin will dissolve. Won't it, Rena?"

"Yes, it should. It's worth a try." Only it is Celia who answers. Judy crushes the painkiller and brings it to Stacey who has been busily preparing the gelatin on the stove. Stacey has put some distance between the absurdity of what they are doing and the possibility of it working. She knows Judy cannot do this.

"We aren't as barbaric as you believe, Judy."

"I don't …"

"Yeah, you do. And right now that's okay. We just have a different slant on how this business of healing works. That's all." Celia speaks without the slightest hint of accusation in her tone.

Judy sighs. These women could well be right; she thinks about the hanging herbs, the all-night vigils, the talking to the child, all these things are part of what modern medicine's proponents refer to as magic, witchcraft, voodoo. Judy has seen them work in less serious circumstances. Every now and then she thinks these things are missing in Western society's healing practices, but when push comes to shove she wants to see surgical steel and antibiotics, not juniper-drenched cold cotton sheets and jellied painkillers. She wants to hear "scalpel," not "fight for yourself, child, Gramma is here." She wants to see clean pastel walls, not moonlight flooding a jerry-rigged tent for a wounded child. The picture of Rena breathing for the child every time her breath gets too shallow or her pulse too slow horrifies Judy, but she isn't exactly sure in what the horror lies. How can Rena watch the quivering little body with all its burns, then shrug, lean down, breathe, drip Pedialyte, watch, shrug again, lean down, breathe again? How can Rena do this all night and look so ordinary, like she is doing nothing more than tying the child's shoelaces and getting ready to pick berries?

"How do you do it, Stacey? We went to the same schools. How do you reconcile the science we were taught to this?"

"I went to our school with several pounds of doubt. Tons of it, in fact. You did not. We need to have some doubt right now. Look at what we're doing, not how we're doing it. We are patching a child who has been tortured by one of our own. Someone of us birthed the child who became the beast who did this. We didn't see it coming. We didn't watch that child, didn't see the twists inside the boy who became this hateful man. We need to have some grave doubts, not about what we are doing now, but what we have been doing. We need to doubt who we have become, because Shelley needs to be healed. And we need you, Judy."

The gelatin is cool and ready. They combine it with the painkiller carefully in the bowl of a spoon.

They return to the tent with the jellied painkiller. Judy reaches into her bag and takes out a sterilized tongue depressor. She looks at it before she tears open its wrapping. She nearly laughs. This will be the first sterilized instrument used on Shelley tonight. Her hands are out of control, they shake so badly she cannot feed it to the child, so she hands it to Momma. Gramma Martha instructs the little girl to open her mouth. Shelley's lips part enough to let Momma place a bit of the jelly mix at the back of her throat. The child convulses. With another tongue depressor, Rena pokes the little jelly farther back into her throat. Shelley's throat reflexively swallows. Momma and Rena continue until Shelley has swallowed all the pain-killing jelly prepared for her. Throughout the procedure, Martha has kept talking to her granddaughter. Shelley smiles a Madonna smirk, but quickly drifts off to sleep.

"We need help," Momma says. She explains her plan for a twenty-four-hour watch on the child. "Judy, you go to sleep now."

"We can ask the women who belong to that healing circle to help," Celia offers.

"We need help, not a bunch of holy rollers screaming rage at their mothers," Momma answers.

"They do stick together," Stacey offers, trying to soften her mother's bias.

"Alice goes there," Celia murmurs defensively. She is not in the mood for her mother's unfairness to Alice and the healing circle. She wants to argue with Momma, but to do so she would have to admit that she has gone there too. She knows that the circle is not about disclaiming anyone's mother, but this is not a good time for Celia to bring up her participation in the group.

"They might call the cops," Martha warns.

The women turn, surprised to hear Martha say anything but encouraging words to her grandchild. Celia knows this is also untrue. As a self-help group they are not bound to report anyone. She can't think of any way to promote engaging their help without telling Momma she belongs to the group. Celia lets the suggestion fall flat, and the women order the vigil among themselves without further chatter.

"Wake me as soon as the drugstore opens. We will need some more things." Stacey goes into the living room, where she falls asleep on the couch fully dressed. Rena and Judy crawl into bed in Stacey's old room. No one will wake them until they are needed. Jacob still sits on the chair. Celia cannot sleep. Momma can't, either.

DAWN COMES FUNNILY OUT *here in front of the mountains that face the sea. The mountains look like they are a skirt shaking the sun loose from its mooring until it reshapes itself into a smooth blanket lighting up the day. The day wakes up the same way a photo develops. It kind of wobbles its way from dark, to shades of almost clarity, until everything comes into focus.*

Celia and Momma watch the blurry image of their village outside come to light without speaking.

"I really think we should kill the man who did this," Momma offers with such calm sincerity that it startles Celia. Celia is not upset by the words; Momma might just as well have said, "Pick the berries; they like it." She is more surprised her momma is able to say anything.

"Yeah," Celia agrees. This, too, comes out easily. The icy blood that pumped cold into their veins all night has warmed. It flushes both women's cheeks a sweet, deep red-brown to say that they want him dead. The flush relaxes them.

Momma stares at the mountains and, as she does, she flips through page after page of memory searching for a word in her language to describe this man's behaviour. If she could say it in her language, the word for it would lead her to name the kind of death she should make sure he gets. She would know how to kill him. White people would arrest him. They would charge him. They would find him guilty only if Stella helped. They would stick him in a small room and feed, house, and clothe him. It irks her that they would give him good food, a warm house, and a clean room after what he has done. Taking care of him after what he did is unthinkable.

White people's laws are crazy; they starve the innocent and feed the guilty. She knows the law functions to help you know what to do in a moral crisis, so she doesn't hold it against them. She just wants to know the law of her grandmothers, the law that will tell her what to do. She has never tried to cross the two languages in her mind before. They don't fit. She accepts the lack of a fit as a child would and keeps them separate. She needs them now to come together in some way that will tell her what obligation she has to undertake in order to kill him and still be able to return home to her spirit world.

"Do they hang people for killing someone like that?" Celia asks.

"No. They put him in a nice warm room, in a nice jail, with clean sheets. They feed him and take care no one hurts him for the rest of his life." She laughs at the absurdity of it.

"I could handle that," Celia says, because she can think of no reason to fear jail. Her son is gone.

"Celia. There is no word to describe this in our language — at least none I know. There is a word for a man who takes his daughter as his wife, but the word implies the daughter is a grown woman and this father loves her in a perverse way. When that happens he is branded and ostracized, and this kills him. There is a word for battering a wife. When that happens, the husband is ostracized and taken to the mountains and left there to die. He dies of starvation or some grizzly or cougar gets him. There is a word for battering a child, and the women take the culprit into the bush and kill him. But there is no word for what that man did to this child."

Celia wonders what Momma is trying to get at.

"Either I don't know what I believe I knew, or we need a new word, a new law, a new response," Momma says.

"Well, if a man batters or rapes some woman, he destroys her life and so he is destroyed by those who cherish her. If a man tortures some child, he should face torture."

"Mm," Momma responds. "That's the word. Torture. There is no word for torture." She accepts Celia's words. It makes sense, torture for torture. She is quiet for a moment, then says, "Do you think we could actually do that?"

"And get away with it? No."

"I just mean could we?"

"I think I could." Celia lights up a cigarette, feeling satisfied that she thinks she could.

JACOB SITS IN THE hall, watching the clock's hands tick by the hours as he listens to the child. He hears the women talk and sees pictures of a parched man so fatigued he can hardly stand. The men he does not recognize sing songs he has never heard. In the background there is the sound of the child struggling for even, slow breaths.

The parched man is dragging himself through a crazy dance, surrounded by clacking deer hooves that seem to be driving him to dance to his last, waterless breath. The hooves seem not to be attached to anything.

Loyal breathes inside the house, hoping his breath reaches Jacob. Jacob looks as though he feels something; he straightens up, like he has had a renewal of energy. He no longer feels sleepy.

THE CHILD STOPS CONVULSING after sunrise. Momma checks her; she breathes still. Her little pulse is weak, but her steady breath is relief for Momma. She leaves the room to tell Jacob to go to bed. He shakes his head. She decides something is up with that boy, but this is not a good time to go sniffing around in someone else's backyard; this yard here has trouble enough to keep her busy.

When the clock strikes seven, Jacob awakes and phones Jim. Thank God; Jim answers and not his wife. Jacob doesn't want to tell Jim's wife what he's calling about.

"Whassup?" Jim asks his nephew, who has never phoned him before.

"Remember what I told you I saw?"

"Yeah."

"It happened. It was Martha's girl, Stella, her daughter, Shelley, that I saw. Grandpa is asleep, Uncle. You better come. We have to find the guy." Jacob hears the half whistle that escapes his uncle's mouth.

Jacob must have seen. Does Aunt Celia know that he saw this happen? Jim decides she would have to know. He prays that she cares enough to still want to help him, because she is the only one who can help Jacob sort out what he saw from what he imagined and keep the two pathways clear. Jim and Ned had already talked about it, now here it is. Ned's just too tired to deal with it. "I'll be right there," Jim says, and hangs up.

Jim's wife wants to go to church. He tells her she can go on ahead if she wants, but he's going to his mother's. She complains that it is impious and unvirtuous to miss the Sunday sermon, and she begins to get the children ready to go to their gramma's. "No. You had better go to your church and pray for my sorry-ass village, because the kids can't come to Mom's today."

"What happened?" she asks. He tells her that he will tell her tonight, out of earshot of the children. She shudders, makes the sign of the cross, and says, "God bless" as he walks out the door. He holds the door a moment before shutting it. He loves this woman, but some days her Catholic devotion annoys him. When it does, he holds her and reminds himself of how much he loves her otherwise.

XV

SUICIDE IS A FIRE *underneath a peat bog burning airless and slow. It needs a fissure to open up the bog and oxidize the fire. Suicide's fire is a beast. It has its own character, a sense of determination; its hunger rips open the soil that it feeds from.*

Jimmy's suicide is not the only one Stella has endured. After her husband threw her out and kept those first two babies, she took to wandering the streets, hopping from bar to bar, looking for any kind of love — lowlife sex, accompanied with meanness and disease — it didn't matter, just so she didn't have to go home and sleep alone. She discovered that men paid for sex, and took to making her living this way. She holed up in a hotel room on the seedier side of Vancouver, selling herself to any trash that would come along. Sometime after, she got friendly with the guy next door to her hotel room and they made a mating pair.

He flipped out when he discovered how she made her living. He said he would get work. He did. She quit turning tricks. He got fired. She went back to turning tricks and everything was fine until someone offered her a lot of money for an all-nighter, and she accepted. She came home the next morning and there was Frank, hanging in her room. There was crap everywhere.

She called the cops. They came and took him away, but not before harassing her about how it had happened. They searched the tiny room for a note, some indication of his unhappiness, some reason for his choking the life from his own throat — all the time carefully avoiding Frank's crap. Every now and then they glanced at Stella as if she was a beast that had jumped off the moon and landed in their midst, and they couldn't for the life of them figure out what to call her. It had taken hours for Frank to die, they said, because his neck wasn't broken. Later that night, over a few drinks with a trick, Stella pictured him squirming, shitting his pants, trying to die or get off the noose. She laughed and the trick laughed with her. They staggered back to her room, thinking the cops must have cleaned it up by now. They would have cleaned it up, she was sure. When she came down the hallway, the night clerk hollered at her.

"Man says you have to clean up that mess Frank made or move on out."

"The cops didn't clean it up?"

"It ain't their room, honey."

"Shit."

"That be what it is all right," the john cracked up.

"Well, honey. Unless you're into cleaning up crap, you best be moseying on home," she said to him. He beat her, helped himself to her womanhood, and left. After, she cleaned Frank's mess. Whatever dignity she had left skipped down the hallway without her chasing the john. It went out to the street and disappeared into the city.

Whatever caring she had in her flipped from one head of the serpent and was swallowed by the terrible hunger of the other.

Her dignity took with it her ambition, her inspiration to dream of a different life. The serpent's restless head crawled around the room, pouring his hunger down her throat. The hunger consumed every good feeling she was capable of and she slid through life trying to feed that hunger — but the hunger was insatiable. As long as she was awake it gnawed at her insides. She swallowed violence; she swallowed pills, alcohol, her own blood, semen, the dirt of every man who crossed her path. The hunger was a sign, glowing blood red on her forehead, saying, "I eat shit." Every piece of trash that came her way saw the sign and conjured new ways to demean and humiliate her. They left unsatisfied. She swallowed what they gave her. She sometimes swallowed pieces of them. She sometimes scared them she was beaten so low. Nothing seemed too terrible for her. She only felt alive when she was in pain.

Sometime between one crazed man and the next, she became pregnant. She sat alone in the dark, praying for the blood between her legs to come. It didn't. She could not take care of this child and she couldn't get up enough concern to consider an abortion or enough effort to adopt it out. She sat in the dark trying hard to have some kind of thought, some kind of something, a response to the blood that refused to come. She wanted something sensible to happen to her.

An inkling of a memory of some other life came to her in the fifth month of her pregnant state. Blurred images of purple berries hanging from hard-leafed vines, smooth salal bushes on hillsides just made for climbing. Sun kisses, cool winds, and the golden glow of lamplight on stormy nights danced about her beat-up face. She wanted to go home. The memory left. She stayed. The baby came one night after some man had left her.

For a while, the baby amused her. Between bouts of alcohol consumption and turning tricks she would clean and feed her.

Sometimes she came close to playing with her. She talked to her all the time. Her brain didn't seem to be connected to real thoughts, so she drivelled out her day-to-day speaking words that were disconnected from any kind of deep meaning. "I'm going to the bathroom now. Stella needs to pee. Let's turn on the light. I am making soup now. Stella is hungry. Let's eat. Stella feels so lonely and she's nearly broke. I've got to find a john, baby."

Stella didn't let the baby cry. She held a hand over her mouth every time she tried. The baby got the idea pretty quickly. She was quiet, strangely so. The hotel manager didn't like Stella having a baby there, but the kid seemed to be a quiet one, so he never bothered them. None of the johns paid attention to the child lying on the floor in a cupboard drawer not far from the bed. She never seemed to awaken when they were busy getting what they wanted from Stella. The little girl learned to walk and talk, but soon discovered that Stella only liked to hear the sound of her own voice. She wasn't interested in the prattle of the small being; every time the child tried to invade the space with her own sound a few backhands quieted her chatter.

Rob picked Stella up from a bar. He was weary of the city, weary of his life, but did not have the courage to hang himself. He latched on to Stella. For a while he worked, but he resented his money going to feed a child that Stella did not have the good sense to care for or give away. All the child did was stare at him. He would stare back at her, but she didn't answer him when he spoke. It annoyed him. He kept telling Stella there was something wrong with that girl. She never talked. He would try playing with her, but the child went limp in his grasp. He couldn't figure it out. Stella began to hate the way he attended to the child. She hated hearing him say he wanted to leave the city, go home, back to the rez. She wanted to go back to her tricks, to her johns, but he wouldn't let her. She started sneaking out during the day, while he was at work, until he left his job and nagged Stella until she agreed to go home to his village. They were to leave on Tuesday. On Monday night, Stella packed up a garbage bag and headed home to her reservation without him. She hitchhiked.

The man who picked her up was the man who did this to her daughter.

She never meant to stay. There was no place for her on this reserve except this broken-down old shack. She took it. She had no ambition to clean it up and start over. But the guy who brought her here kept coming back. He liked her being here in this old shack whenever he returned from hauling a load. He didn't give her money like the others. She might take off; he wasn't stupid. Without money she couldn't leave, but he left her enough food and booze. She decided to wait until he let his guard down, then she would steal his money, drop the child off at Martha's, and head out on the road again.

In the meantime, she floated from one drunken moment to the next. If she ran out of booze before the man returned, she would try to remember what women did all day. The effort made her head hurt. She sat on the broken porch for hours, waiting for her truck driver and another load of booze. Sometimes she ate food, the kind that takes no real effort to prepare. Days flipped into nights and she sat, rarely leaving her porch. Her mother came by every now and then and would tell her she should help her clean this place up. Stella stared dumbly at her until Martha started to clean and Stella would join her. She frustrated Martha with her "What for?" attitude. She knew it was just going to get dirty again. The child would help. She took to talking to her gramma. There was something different about her gramma that made her want to talk. She would say things in her soft voice to Gramma and Gramma would always answer.

The man was mean. He subjected Stella and the child to all sorts of indignities. But Stella always got excited when he returned. It wasn't love or lust or loneliness that propelled her to invite him in. It was more that his face broke the monotony of the ugly land-scape of her home, her life, and the future that yawned before her. He always brought groceries and beer. The child took to crying when he came. She was such a noisemaker. Stella couldn't remem-ber hearing such a racket coming from one of them things. Her mother had had so many. She complained to her mom who gave stupid advice to stop the child from crying. Pack her, her mom said; like I got nothing better to do but pack this thing and feed her, like strength and money falls from the sky or grows on trees, Stella said. Soon she quit saying anything to Martha. The useless man brought food for her, not this child. Feed her what? She tried packing her; put her on her back in a blanket. The child still cried. She was five years old and cried like a baby.

The man built a hammock on the porch and she put the child in it. That seemed to settle her. He brought food enough for all of them and she fed her and that seemed to work some too. He almost seemed nice in some vague way, but it never quite registered anywhere inside Stella. Martha was frustrated with her daughter. Stella took to bringing the child to Martha's on weekends. Martha wanted to keep her. She was too small, too obedient, and altogether too quiet, and that place of Stella's was no place to raise a child. But Martha could not keep her. She was Stella's after all, and Martha worked.

Pretty soon the little girl was walking about, naming things as they were, and getting cheekier by the day. "This place needs a good clean," she would say and Stella would beat her. That intrigued the man. He joined her. Eventually, the child became a source of enter-tainment for the man. This almost woke the woman up. A crazy kind of fascination was sparked inside as she watched the man diddle the child. The little girl seemed to like the tickle game and the sex with the man afterward was great for Stella. His appetite increased over time. Not satisfied with Stella he made a wife of the child. Stella got jealous. It was the first emotion Stella had felt in a long time. Her jealousy made her meaner.

Stella tormented the child. She and the man would get drunk, so drunk, and before Stella would pass out she would beat the girl. In their drunken stupor they would sleep, leaving the child out in the cold, whimpering. Soon he began to participate in tormenting the child to see if she would still respond with her little giggles. She didn't, but he started to like the little whimpers from the girl better than her giggles. Stella would wake up and reach for the beer he always brought, drink herself into a stupor, pass out, and begin drinking again before either of them was fully awake. The process repeated itself.

He used them for his entertainment, then he left. He was sometimes back soon, sometimes he was back later. While he was gone, Stella's memories fought to be heard. She took to blanking out — staring off into space, emptying her mind of all thought so the memories sank to the bottom of some well of self-induced stupidity, impotent and unheard. He had been gone for a particularly long time this time — months. The little girl seemed almost happy at her mother's deprivation. This chilled whatever feeling Stella had left for this child. When the man returned, he was terrible to Stella's little girl. Even in her blurred state, she knew he was doing terrible things to her. She finally said something about how he was going to kill her and she would have to clean up the mess; he beat her, beat her unconscious.

Suicide is a permit; a licence to kill that hangs in the air like a stench. This stench covers everything. It calls up the murderous spirit in everyone who sniffs the scent of it.

He could smell it. He smelled her too. What difference does it make if you murder yourself or someone else? Only fools kill themselves. If you're going to check out, take someone with you. She watched him burning the life from the child and planned his murder, then her own.

Memory has its own journey. It possesses a strange insistence. It will not be ignored. Quiet, it freezes the spirit. Alive, it binds us to time, to eternity, in strange ways.

Stella was fascinated by the slow murderous dance between the man and the child. Some image stubbornly appeared through the fog of her dying mind. She was rolling down the hill and laughing with another girl child. The laughter ended quickly. The old snake appeared and took both girls. There was a dense silence that started in her feet and rolled its way up through her legs, her hips, her belly, her chest, and finally settled in her mind. That's when the words dropped: "You going to kill her, you keep that up. Don't expect me to clean up your fuckin' mess." That's when the beating came with that hot poker. That's all she remembered. Someone woke her up. At first she thought it was her mother, but it wasn't. Someone else woke her up. Who was it?

It didn't matter. She was awake, wide awake. She paced, hunting around the shack for something to put her to sleep. This awake was so strange and unfamiliar, it seemed to hang outside her, in the air, on her skin, then it was in her mouth; at some point she swallowed it. She didn't like it. Awake she saw things differently; she felt things she did not want to feel. Awake she remembered things in crazy fits and starts; she remembered the hillsides before she was tormented by that old snake. She remembered her mom's words, "Fucking bitch, what have you done?" She remembered Celia and some other blurs and some crazy kind of unnameable feeling they brought with them.

Memory forced her to know things.

She was wrong. She knew she was wrong. She didn't know if she was mis-wired or something, but she was definitely wrong. This shack, this life, this dirt, this child, this torture, this hunger — it was all wrong. Everything about it was wrong. This blur was wrong. She sat in her filthy chair and slept again, musing on her wrongness.

Memory moved her to dream.

Gramma was sitting at the edge of the river, her tiny feet dangling in the swift water, angling her legs out from her knees. Stella sat next to her. She told her gramma her legs looked funny. Gramma did not share the same definition of funny with her granddaughter because she had laughed as though Stella had told a joke when she had meant her legs looked odd. It didn't matter though, it felt good to be sitting there, feet being pulled by the river's current, the soft west coast sun kissing her skin and the warmth rolling around in her mind slow and sure. Gramma pointed upward to the top of the mountain at the edge of sky and Stella saw a goat with big horns. That goat crawled up that mountain sweet and easy. Stella wanted to be him for just a moment. He was balanced at the edge of a stone face, fearless about climbing, sure he was going to make it; he skittered toward the top of the mountain.

"Where is he going?" the child asked, still squinting into the bright sunlight to follow the goat picking its way up the mountain's face.

"Home," her gramma said.

"Where has he been?"

"Why, he came down to leave his hair on the thorn bushes, devil's club, so we could pick it and spin it up."

"What's spin?"

"That's when you twist up the fur of the goat so it makes a yarn like wool." Gramma pointed at her sweater.

"Do you know how to do that?"

"Sure do."

"Do you use his hair to make wool?"

"No, not anymore."

"How come you don't go get his hair and spin it?"

"I spin sheep hair now. We aren't supposed to spin that goat without dog hair. The white man killed our dogs, but he never told the goat, so the goat still comes on down anyway to leave it behind."

"How come we don't just spin it anyway?"

"Because it would be wrong, we made a deal and it would be wrong to break it."

"Why does he still do it then?"

"Because he loves us, child, he is like us. When we love we scale mountains for our loved ones. When we don't love, we wallow in the shit on the valley floor." With that, Gramma had laughed long and hard.

Stella woke up in a sweat. She did not like her dream. She tried to forget it, to bury it, but the damn thing just sat there squarely in the centre of her mind and nagged. She stumbled around, looking for something to help her forget, then remembered she didn't have anything. She lay down again, tried to sleep, but it wouldn't come. The sheets on the bed she was lying in smelled of stale beer and sour soap and it bothered her so much it kept her from sleeping. She tried to convince herself she had not been bothered by it before and so she should not let it bother her now, but the smell kept reminding her of her dream. When she thought of the dream, the aroma of the river and the plants edging it sneaked up behind her; they competed with the smell of her bed. Her body started to feel something she did not want it to feel. She got up with a string of curses and tore the sheets off the bed and threw them onto the floor. She lay down on the bare mattress. This didn't help; the mattress smelled worse than the sheets.

"Shit." She grabbed the sheets and looked around the room. Her hands shook. The DTs were coming. "Shit, not now. Not now." She sank into a rickety chair next to the bed. The floor moved with the hallucinations. Remnants of her filthy past came back to life. Her shoes bounced off her feet and onto the floor by themselves. They did a little jig; the tops looked like faces that were laughing at her. She threw the sheet at them and hollered for her child. Silence. Where was the damn little shit? Stella crawled on the floor toward where she had last seen the child tied up. She finally found her thongs where they lay on the floor and, like the shoes, they grinned at her, teased her. This made her body shake; she was near to convulsions.

"I'll kill you when I find you, you little bitch." She shook so violently she could no longer crawl. Her skin burned, itched, strained to get loose of her shaking flesh. The room continued to move; it swayed stupidly. She swore at it, grabbed objects and threw them at the walls, cursing and shaking by turns. "I need a fucking drink." That was when the door opened. She saw three men. She lifted up her skirt, spread her legs and whimpered, "Please, a drink."

One of them handed her the lip of a bottle. They looked so familiar, but the blur was too thick and she shook so violently she could not get a bead on their faces and so could not determine who they were. Another of the men pulled her to a sitting position while he rearranged her skirt. The bottle pulled away from her mouth with a popping sound, its froth bubbling up as it left her lips. She reached for it. "Not yet, you let that settle a minute first." She went to lift her skirt. The one on the left said, "No way," and she thought he wanted it the other way so she flipped herself onto all fours and offered them her backside, holding her skirt around her waist. One of them slapped her behind and told her to sit up right. "You want it rough, hon. I don't mind. Just give me another drink." The shaking grew more intense.

She sat on the floor legs wide open, hair matted and hanging in front of her face, lips drooling, last night's madness interrupting today, while she waited for the roughness these men had in mind. They gave her another drink. The shakes subsided.

"Another one," she whimpered. "Don't be cruel." She started to sing some old song the young man did not recognize. The old one told him what it was. Stella felt the familiarity in the tones and the rhythm of the voices, but she couldn't drag hard enough on her memory to identify them. One of them offered her a hand. She got up on her knees and started to fiddle with his belt buckle saying, "This you want. Give me another drink." He smacked her hands. She sat back down and whimpered.

"Get those lamps going?" This was such a foreign request for her usual company. Stella grew afraid. These men did not want anything she offered and they meant to watch her and hold on to their beer. What were they here for? Who were they?

"This is Ned, Stella." It came out hard and sharp. It sliced at her stupor cutting away the blurry veil, leaving only the pain of her skin again. The shakes that had almost settled down returned after he finished telling her why he was there. "You are going to sober up, Stella. We are going to watch every painful minute while you do that. Then, when you are good and sober and not shaking, you are going to tell us just exactly what happened to your child." She looked around. Where was that child? Then she passed out.

JACOB DOES NOT WANT to watch the child back at the house. He wants to be here when they talk about it with Momma. He asks to come. Now, seeing Stella vibrate in the haunting backlight of the bright lamps that fail to fill the room with light, he isn't sure he can watch this. This relieves him. He had been afraid he was mean, like the old snake, but now he feels that he was on some other trail. He looks out on the mountain her window faces and sees trails of berries hanging plump and ripe and he wants, for some strange reason, to leave this woman and go pick them. He does not want to watch.

Jim motions his nephew outside. "Those are our mountains," he says, pointing. He lights a smoke. They stare at the mountains wordlessly. Jim tells Jacob that he had climbed these mountains and stayed up there in their dark for four days as a teenager. Jacob wants to know why. This surprises Jim, but he tells him. "So I could know what I was about." He wonders if the other nephew, the one who killed himself, had climbed the same mountains.

"How come everyone who has ever done anything Indigenous talks in riddles?" Jacob asks. He throws his cigarette to the ground, crushing it out almost at the moment the butt lands. Jim laughs and waits a minute before he answers. "You can only know what our stuff is all about if you do it, that's why." He turns to go inside. Jacob tells Jim he doesn't think he can watch after all. Jim says he would be able to, if he had climbed Cheam Mountain. Jim leaves Jacob sitting on the half-rotted-out stoop, pouting. He rejoins his father inside.

Ned's anger is a hot rock rolling relentlessly; it sears everything he thinks about. This is his clanswoman. She has no right to be this way. It outrages him to see what she let happen to her child — his blood, his great-niece. He is determined to will his rage along a path to sober Stella up, exactly as the women in his house instructed him. Every indignant thought diminishes his empathy for Stella and every time he feels a soft feeling for her coming up, he stokes the fire of his rage and sends it flying in the direction of his spirit. This cools his empathy. He is not ready to empathize with her.

Jim watches his father, making sure he is successful at keeping the woman on the path to sobriety. He is not the conductor of this ceremony, so he can let his sympathy rise. He locks it to his voice. His uncle seethes at Stella when she tries to throw fits, but Jim calms and soothes her when she cries. When she quits crying, she appeals to Jim, who gently tells her that she is talking to the wrong man. Ned is in charge. This sends her into a frenzy, crawling around in half circles for minutes, letting go curse words some of which Jim has never heard. When she settles, she lies down and shakes. If the shaking becomes too severe, Ned will give her another pull on a beer.

Jacob sits on the stoop, stewing over what he saw or did not see. When he was down at the old shack he had thought he was seeing what was happening and not imagining it. But when he went to tell his uncle and his grandfather, he wasn't sure. If he'd actually seen it, then was he not as perverse as he had originally feared? If he imagined it, then is he no different than the men who did this? He stares at the skirt edges of their mountains. Cheam is at the end of the valley; her seven peaks jut higher than the rest. The old folks talk about a screaming woman inside the hills. Between what Jim said and Jacob's curiosity over the screaming woman, he is driven from the stoop and toward the base of the tallest mountain.

XVI

STELLA CURSES, SWEARS, WEEPS, crawls, shakes her way to some semblance of sobriety. It takes two and a half days, during which time Jim makes tea, cooks, and cleans what will need to be clean for him to feed her, but not a dish or pot more. There are two boxes of Kraft Dinner. They will do. Jim eats a bite directly out of the pot, offers Stella some. She takes a bite, heaves it up. Jim cleans it up with ashes from her stove and determines that only tea will work here. The first time he offers the tea Stella takes a good pull, then she spits it out all over him and curses. He takes her hand and gives it a good whack, as if she were a naughty child. This infuriates her. She leaps for his throat. He dodges her. She goes sprawling across the floor.

Ned picks her up and sits her down.

"You're strong enough to want to whale on Jim, then you're strong enough to tell us what happened to your child."

Stella takes a slow look around the room and wonders where her child is. Her mind grabs fogged-up pictures of pokers, a man, her mother trying to strangle her, and some force that keeps grabbing at her ferocious mother and stopping her. The pictures waltz around her mind, disordered and deranged. She cannot seem to sort them. The dream of her grandmother flies at her through the fog and she starts recounting it like some crazy woman.

"She said the goat loved us. How can a goat love us? She was sitting with me on that rock. We could see that goat. High up on the mountain ..."

Ned looks at Jim, whose head is tilted with his left ear to her.

"That your gramma sitting on the rock with you?"

"Yes," she says slowly. "The water felt so good and my feet were so small. Gramma, she said that mountain goat climbed down and then up because he loved us. She said he was like us. How come I am not like us, Gramma?" Stella sinks into the chair and drifts back into her gramma's night world.

Ned stares at her.

"You nap, Pop. I'll wake you when she comes out of it," Jim offers. "I'll catch some winks myself then."

Ned takes a look around and decides to nap in his car. He can't bear sleeping in this hellhole. "How did she get to this?" he asks no one as he staggers out the door.

Jim shrugs and settles into looking out the window toward the hills. He never wonders about anything. He remembers when he has moments like this; he remembers things that take his mind off worrying about the present.

HIS MIND WANDERS ACROSS the old yard. He hears Stacey's bare feet scampering in his direction. Must be suppertime, he tells himself, and gathers up his tools to put them away before going in to wash up. She looks at the neat little piles of nuts, bolts, and gears and asks him what he's doing. "Putting my hub back together, the gear inside is stripped. Got to replace it." He shows her the piece he is talking about and puts it back on the paper in the same place he picked it up from.

"Why is it stripped?" she asks.

"Don't know," he answers simply. At dinner, she pushes her fish around on her plate, looking quizzically at him. When she asks him why he never wonders about anything, he answers, "Doesn't help. Something breaks, you fix it. You don't need to know why anything happens. You only need to know what to do is all."

"You got that right," his grandpa says.

"But if you know the why of things, couldn't you prevent them from happening?" she asks.

"For a while," Jim answers without any concern for the paradox in his point of view. "But someone else more curious will have to figure that out." He laughs in that self-satisfied kind of way that marks who he is and will always be. Stacey looks disconcerted, so Gramma explains to her that Jim is a man. She says it under her breath, so Jim cannot hear her. It appeases Stacey's misgivings enough for her to accept Jim's response. Jim looks at the picture of his family, sees Grandpa's diminishing mind, Gramma's diminishing health, and Momma's increasing fatigue; he wonders about none of it. In his mind, if Grandpa gets stupid, someone will act as his guide; if Gramma dies, Momma will rise to the occasion; if she gets too tired, she won't. The sun will rise and set, chores will need to be done, things will break, and he will have to fix them.

He and Stacey are on the stoop later that night, his bike is fixed and Jim is fed and content. She asks him where he found the part. He tells her he rummaged around the dump for it.

"Doesn't it bother you?" she asks.

"Not if I don't wonder about it. You going to make me wonder about it?"

"I don't understand how you can go rummaging around in the

dump and not wonder how come Mom and Pop work so hard and still can't afford to buy you a bike part."

"Wouldn't help to wonder," he says flatly. "It wouldn't get them any more money. It would hurt like hell to let myself go there. If I wondered about it, instead of going to get it, I may not want to rummage around in the dump and then all I would be left with is a broken bike and a bruised ego."

"And you need your bike," she finishes for him, unconvinced but resigned to Jim's way of seeing things.

Jim knows she will never stop wondering about things. Wondering is a gamble. So is climbing that mountain. Stacey gambles on wondering and Jim decides to gamble on that mountain. "No sense wondering" is an instruction for himself, not Stacey. He is going to fix what he can and let the rest take care of itself. He likes that Stacey wonders, but the danger is that she might never figure it out, might never solve the riddle. If she does figure it out, the next generation may not have to rummage around in the dump. That would be all right too.

He told her so on that stoop so long ago.

STELLA SLEEPS FITFULLY, CURSING in her sleep. Jim looks at her when she stirs. Jim has spent his life translating the words of others into action. He has always seemed to be able to figure out what to do to make something work, how to get people to back up, back off, or turn around. The trick is to get Stella going in a different direction, away from this hovel and the men who have demeaned her and tortured her child. He does not need to know the why of how she got to this low point. He's sure he doesn't want to know, it will anger him and he'll be fired up about what she did or didn't do or what happened to her or didn't happen. Jim knows he can't do anything about that. The past is over; the present is already dying. His knowing what happened to her in the past will not help her stay away from the road she's travelling. The future is what counts.

Humans are going somewhere all the time. Every act, every moment, is leading them somewhere whether they know it or not. The trick is to make sure their actions help them to go in a good direction. Jim knows this. Everyone leaves behind tracks showing the way that led them to wherever they are; "breadcrumb trails," he calls them. Stella will wake up eventually and show him her breadcrumb trail, and it will mark the way out. All he has to do is recognize that first little crumb, get her talking, and get her to follow the next crumb and the next crumb until she finds her way out.

Stella stirs again. Jim sits up, ready for another round of cursing, crawling, fighting, and shaking. He decides to deal with it before waking Ned up. The smell of the place is starting to bite his nerves. Stella must not have ever completely cleaned the place up. He decides to make her clean it up as soon as she is fully awake. Might help her to sober up. Meanwhile he grabs a branch of cedar from outside, builds a fire in the stove, and tosses the branch on top of the hot stove. It masks the stench.

Stella's eyes open. She thinks she recognizes this man.

"Jim?" she asks.

"Right here," he answers.

She almost brightens for a minute at the thought that she has dragged his name up from some clear place of memory. Something about her is right. Then she looks around.

"Shit."

"That's right, Stella, and now you have to clean it." He calls her by her name. The men who cross her path rarely call her by her name. She waits for him to plead with her, to prod her or threaten her, but he doesn't. He leans against the windowsill and stares at her. The hard edge in his eyes commits her to cleaning. She waits for him to help. Her mother always helps. Standing motionless, Jim's eyes bore holes in her. In front of him is that damn beer they will only let her have in tormenting little sips before they pull it away. She saunters over, sultry and coy. His eyes narrow. He grabs the neck of the bottle without taking his eyes off her. She stops. He looks capable of murder. The anger of the other men wasn't wilful; it had no decision attached to it like this man's anger does. Jim has decided she is going to clean up the place. He pushes anger into his decision. She sees it and relents.

The sunlight shakes the shadows out of shadowland, it transforms wet moss into dry tinder and opens up wounds to filth. Right now the light Jim has fired up shines on the mess Stella's home has become. She can't think of a way to contemplate it. The light burns her eyes and frightens her. It wakes something up in her she cannot name. Jim is neat and trim in the shadow, wearing this smug I-know-what-I'm-doing kind of look. It comes at her from the half-light just beyond the lamp's range. She wants to hide. She tries to bolt. Her body will not move. His eyes hold her, will not let go of her. She can see his eyes pinning her to this place, this moment, this spot. She gives up the idea of bolting. This frees her to move. Best just to clean up like he wants.

Stella moves gingerly at first, trying to figure out what cleaning up is all about. She picks up bits and pieces of something in her rubble-filled home and stares at each item, confounded. The need to decide what to do with each piece floods her addled brain and taxes it to distraction. She looks about. There are so many things all over the place, on the floor, on the sorry excuse for a table, on the bed. Each one screams for her to decide where it should go. There are so many decisions to make. What is this? Where was it before it was on the floor? Who owns it? Where does it go? Where does it live? She picks up a sock, tries to recognize it, tries to trace its origin, some foot belonging to somebody whose name should roll easily off the tongue, but which refuses. She cannot remember. She looks around the room, trying to find some place for it, her head shaking from side to side like an old blind bear. Unable to find a place, she puts the sock back on the floor where she found it. Item after item, the process repeats itself.

Jim watches. After an hour or so, he hands her something to drink. It isn't what she wants, but she has no fight left. She drinks it in one pull. It's hot. She doesn't seem to feel the heat sufficiently to register pain or to slow the pull she took from the cup until it is too late. It burns her lips, tongue, and throat. She goes back to the rubble and tries to put it in some kind of context that will tell her how to order it. She looks at herself. Her dress is filthy. She looks for something clean. There is not a clean garment in the place. She looks at Jim, and says she's sorry. She sits down and cries. Her voice is so loud it wakes Ned. He stumbles in.

"My dress is so dirty."

Ned wants to slap her. Jim sees this and puts up his hand. The dress is the first breadcrumb. He does not want Ned to pull it out of her path, hooked as it is to the journey away from this mud hole. Ned knows what Jim's hand means and backs off.

"What do you want to do about it?" Jim asks.

"I have to clean it," she says in the small voice of a child.

"Go ahead," he says. "Clean it."

She looks at them both. "Could you ...?"

Jim turns around. Ned wants to spit. It's ludicrous, this sudden modesty coming from someone who has lived worse than an animal. But he turns too. They hear her fill a bucket with water and wash the dress. She dumps the dirty water and replaces it with clean. She examines the dress and puts it back in the bucket.

"I have no soap," she weeps.

"I'll get you some." Ned is fighting for civility.

She kneels, staring at the dirty dress in the bucket for a long time, like she's trying to remember how it got this dirty.

Ned returns with soap. He hands it to her, careful to avert his eyes; but by now the notion of modesty has vanished in the woman. She washes her dress and wrings it out. She puts it on still wet.

"Do you want us to dry that next door?" Ned asks.

"No. It will keep me cool. I'm so warm," she sighs. She goes about the room, discovering things again. She decides to clean every dirty thing she finds. She finds a little shirt-and-skirt covered in blood and puts it in the bucket of soapy water. She picks up socks and finds another empty bucket to put them in.

"I have a lot of empty buckets." She gives a half-embarrassed laugh.

"That you do," Jim answers, smiling back at her as if she were the most delightful company he'd stumbled across in a long time. Ned wonders how Jim got to be this way. How could he look at all this, see that child, then warm up to the woman who set in motion her terrible suffering? "You get it washed and I will fix you up a clothesline outside."

This is the first connection she has made with her cousin in a long time.

"Okay," she says. She scampers, collecting up the laundry as if traipsing off into the fields to pick flowers. She picks each filthy item up like they are small jewels. She finds a washboard and kneels on the floor, scrubbing the shirt-and-skirt until clean. She puts a sheet in the bucket and scrubs it as well, then the other things. She tries to drag the bucket of dirty water outside, but her arms fail her. Ned moves to help her. Jim puts up his hand and says, "She has to climb this mountain on her own. Wait till she asks."

They wait. Stella wrestles one more time with the bucket. The bucket moves. She walks it toward the door, rocking it and moving it forward, sweating and grunting, finally dumping half of it over the side of the porch. She hauls the bucket farther away before she dumps the rest.

Ned and Jim stand in the doorway in case Stella bolts for freedom.

From the fringe of the overgrown lawn, she looks up and says, "I don't want the bloody water near my door." Her standards are changing; she has a principle to hold on to. It takes hours, but finally she has washed and hung every dirty thing in the house. She flops onto the uncovered bed and sleeps.

While she sleeps, the two men plan out the restoration of her house. There is a lot of second-hand wood in various people's yards. Ned will fetch it and bring some tools. When she wakes up to clean out her house, they will build cupboards wherever she wants. Ned still harbours ill will toward this woman, but he swings in behind Jim and feels a little easier about it.

XVII

JACOB REACHES THE TOP of the mountain as the sun sets on the flatlands in front of her seven peaks. He looks about him. There are mountains to the east, south, and north as far as his eye can see. Before him is the valley floor. He sees the twinkling lights of the white man's towns and identifies them in the growing dark. The moon changes places with the sun shortly after he arrives. He marvels at the view, like everything is right with the world. He reaches into his pocket and pulls out a packet of smokes, takes one from the box, and lowers himself onto a log. Just as he lights up, a voice jumps up from beside him.

"Them is all your relatives." Jacob turns around to see an old woman sitting on the log with him. She grabs his lit cigarette, helping herself to a good long pull on it before handing it back.

"Who are you?" Jacob asks.

"They called me Alice. I'm your gramma's gramma." This piece of information makes Jacob dizzy. First he'd seen living people who weren't really there, doing what he saw somewhere at some other time. Now he is seeing dead people who aren't really there. He's climbed the mountain without anything to eat. It took him all day. He had witnessed the worst thing he could imagine happen to his small relative. He'd seen it before it happened. He watched it shape itself into a movie. Now this dead woman is sitting next to him, sucking on his cigarette. This cannot be good. He feels sickness coming up again. She disappears.

"Oh Christ, I am too goddamned sane for this," he declares. He curls into a tight ball and prepares to sleep. Jacob does not dream. The forest wraps him in its sounds, its smells, its feel; he drifts in its dark cool world until the cold wakes him up. The sound of birds meets his ears and soothes the dark. It will be light soon. He has never seen the sunrise, the mountains have always blocked his view of it from the village. He wonders if from up this high he'll be able to see it. He sees the moon pale and stands up. It worries him to stand. He isn't sure his memory serves him very well in the dark. Where is the edge? He decides not to think about it, just to stay there, not moving, praying he is facing in the direction of the sun.

A golden hue bleeds into the western skyline, painting the edge of the sky with the promise of light. In the growing dawn, Jacob sees he does not need to stand. He is about to sit when the fireball of the sun meets the valley between the two mountains he is staring at. It seems rude to sit now with the sun entering the territory. He stands. The sun pushes hard against the golden-hued black edges of dwindling night. The pale blue under gold fires the sky. The sun rises to a bright gold, no red, no orange, no other colour to taint its gold. The purity of its light bathes the mountains. Jacob breathes in the sight of the sun fighting with the overwhelming dark of night.

Jacob ponders what his uncle did up here for four days. There does not seem to be much to do. He remembers he hasn't eaten. "Pick the berries; they like it," he hears his gramma say. He wanders about. There are berries everywhere, different ones on different bushes. Some of the bushes have no thorns and some do. Some of the berries grow on vines, others hang from what look like small trees. There are berries of all sorts of hues and shades from white and blue to red and purple to black. Which ones should he pick?

"Be wary of shiny things," pops into his mind. He picks the dullest purple berries he can find from a laurel bush. He holds them in his hand, hesitates, then pops one into his mouth. Its sweet flavour bursts, and he waits to see if it is toxic. Nothing happens, so he gathers a handful more and sits down to breakfast.

After he's filled himself up, he sits on his stone again. High above the valley, he sees its size; it stretches between two sets of mountains, in the middle of which the river winds lazily through it. It is sixty miles across, north to south. Jacob remembers the stories old Alice told about how the land was underwater until the Dutch drained it and put up windmills and canals. He wishes he had been around to see the mills chugging excess water. The valley has flooded twice since the mills were removed; it is probably not a good idea to live below the water table without windmills. It doesn't take long for his belly to begin rumbling dangerously. He has to relieve himself. Those berries are doing their duty. He hadn't thought about that. Where? He takes a look around and decides it had better be far from this stone. He walks through the bush to an old log, grabs a stick, and digs himself a small hole. What to do about toilet paper? An old vine maple hangs over his head, the answer to his question.

Agitated, he strides about for a while, carefully marking where he had just been, which direction he had walked in, trying not to lose sight of his stone. He stands still for a minute, trying to think. Rivers begin as creeks in these mountains. He listens. He hears the sound of water and heads for it. He approaches the creek politely. No one there. Just as he is bending to wash his hands, a doe comes by for a drink. She drinks, sniffs the air, smells him, and bounds off. He is stunned by her grace and closeness. In place of soap he uses sand. It feels good. It satisfies him to know that he could eat, wash and clean himself, and watch the whole of his known world without help from anyone.

He walks back to his stone to study the colour of the world he knows. In the distance, he sees a discoloured chunk of sky heading toward the valley near his home. There is something wrong with it. It is huge. It takes up a good portion of the blue as it floats ominously toward the valley. It is moving steadily and, as it does, he sees that it is picking up clouds and discolouring them too. It must be smog from Vancouver. He sits down on the rock to consider what smog could do to the valley. He lights another cigarette and Alice reappears.

"You must really like smoking," he teases.

She takes a drag from his smoke. "Before ceremony there was madness. It isn't new, this business of killing children. There was a war. Blood was let. Humans love ritual. They cannot escape from it. They need it just like they need air. Love is a ritual. Hate too. We are busy loving or killing depending on the direction we choose to move in. Life is an experience, but our movement through it is a ritual." She crushes out the last of her smoke and walks straight off the edge of the mountain. The image of her fades through an opening in the clouds.

Is that what had happened? The snake had gone to war. He had killed. The ritual of killing, day after day and year after year, became his life's direction. He could not stop killing, destroying his family, raping his own mind and sharing that with his daughters and Madeline. The ritual of inflicting pain, watching men squirm under the bullets he was raining down on them, never went away. The snake killed men for six years, men he did not know, men who were also killing other men, the killing was sanctioned and revered by everyone. It became normal. Jacob searches for the words that these men must have used to justify the ritual killing. Maybe murder was just a direction that men sometimes travelled toward, as old

Alice said. Once you start you can't stop, unless somebody turns you around. At some point in all that killing, life itself becomes worthless in the mind of the killer. The devaluing of all those lives gave the snake permission. Maybe choosing that direction is the permission we give or do not give ourselves to value life. No one had known how to turn the snake back in his original direction.

Ceremony must be a conscious use of our natural need for ritual. "Thou shalt not kill," the Christians say, but the pope himself had blessed that war and the blessing of murder was the ceremony that altered the snake's direction. Too bad they had not given him some ceremony to restore him.

Jacob beds down and animals come, surround his sleeping body, whisper, "You have a ceremony to restore your path," then are gone. Jacob in his sleep is aware that he is dreaming and determines not to remember his dream when he awakes.

BY THE TIME STACEY comes home, Jacob has already left and the dark is folding over the house, sweet and comfortable. She does not expect him to be home; since becoming a teenager he has roamed freely from her house to his grandpa's or his cousins, but usually he leaves a note or calls. This time there is no indication of where he is. Still, she is relieved. Guilt twinges her as she wonders when his absence had become a relief. She had loved fussing over him, when he was a small child, playing with him, comforting him; every part of him seemed so enjoyable. Then, as his body stretched, his face changed, and his bones arranged themselves into the shape of the affair with a man she had never meant to keep, she distanced herself from Jacob. During his grade school days she felt crowded by him; he reminded her that she couldn't dress up on Friday and walk into some dimly lit, crowded bar and pick out a little comfort for the weekend. It had nothing to do with her looking old or acquiring morals; it had more to do with her feeling that motherhood felt too dignified to just squander her body on one night stands. Jacob was about twelve when she bumped into Steve in the mall. She told him to call her, he did, and, on a weekend when Jacob was with his grandpa, Steve had come over. The affair seemed easy, but now she realized it had all sorts of constraints. Jacob should never be an inconvenience. Her freedom was up, left somewhere in the run of diapers and dishes.

She finds herself a candle, lights it, and sits down. In the fire of the candle an old memory burns. She was thirty-five. The tables were full of people. Her attention was drawn to a handsome-looking woman of about fifty. The woman sat with a group of men who all looked like they wanted to be the one who got lucky. She smoked a cigarette, sitting wide open and laughing hard at something one of them had said. There was a hint of crying in the way she laughed. Her movements were subtle and jerky. Some smell of fear pervaded her perfume. She was a little too made-up, a little too dressed-up, a little too everything. Stacey turned around and walked out. She wanted more than another romp. She wanted some piece of that mountain in her life.

When she got home, she turned on all the lights in her house. Then she remembered Steve. He had made a point of telling her he was single again. He kidded her about it being her fault. They both had laughed, but he had had that you-look-yummy-enough-to-eat kind of look. She had asked him if he'd like to visit sometime. "I make a nice cup of coffee and a passable piece of fry bread," she'd said. "You call me when you want to make more than one piece," he'd answered, "and I'll bring the coffee." He'd given her his number. After seeing that woman in the bar, she dialled Steve.

Jacob was thirteen. Steve understood her rule and never violated it. She figured she was safe to invite him over and her son would not be the wiser. She told Steve that she needed him to be discreet. He understood. At first she only rang him when things got trying or something confounded her; but, as Jacob wandered off more frequently, she found herself dialling Steve for no reason at all.

She doesn't, even now, believe she loves him; it's more that she finds him comfortable. She has an easygoing romance with Steve, so comfortable she doesn't feel she can possibly end it. She has never gotten up the passion to get angry and argue and test the relationship; she figures it will never get any better. It will always be comfortable; she isn't sure she can be satisfied with that. And then her phone rings.

"Hello." It's Steve.

"I was just thinking about you," she says.

"I was just sniffing around for a nice piece of bannock and a good cup of coffee," he says. She hears something different in his voice, like the sound is being scraped as it runs by his vocal cords.

"Are you all right, Steve?"

There's a pause. "No. I'd really rather talk about it in person."

She wants to tell him about the child, about the fight for her life, about the chance they are all taking, but she doesn't think he would understand. Nervousness sets in. This might be the end of her and Steve and, although she isn't sure she loves him, she's beginning to suspect this is only because she doesn't dare let herself. Loving him brings expectations, and expectations require common ground; she has no common rock for both of them to stand on. He would never understand this family. "Love is not enough," she whispers to herself. It takes a lot of elbow grease to accept someone else's way of being.

"I would really rather talk about it in person." She recognizes the intent behind these words. Five years is about to be flushed down the toilet by an ultimatum from him; she has no way to brace herself. Although she has not dared to love him, she has not ever wanted to let him go. She wonders if she could. For some reason this wondering brings her back to her nephew.

She looks up at her kitchen wall where the photographs of family smile down at her. A black and white of two boys, Jacob and Jimmy, blowing bubbles from those little stems with a round hoop at the end. There is a wire fence behind them. She loves that picture of her nephews; there was such beauty in them, confidence and innocence. After the funeral, Jacob went to remove the picture and she had panicked. "No ... please ... no." She couldn't let Jimmy go; he was tied so tight to her memories of Jacob that she couldn't separate them. Taking down the picture would somehow have removed Jacob too, but she hadn't said that to him. They had gone through the rest of the day without talking. Now, she looks up at the wall again and thinks she catches a glimmer of sadness peering through Jimmy's smile. She cringes. Why had she not seen it before?

The knock comes too soon. She opens the door. Her voice softens, and she is humbled by the picture of his frame, backlit by a full moon. Damn if it doesn't loosen the tide of tears lurking behind her eyes. Steve holds Stacey. Her sobs are so deep, so long, and so hard they worry him. He wants to ask what's bothering her, but he knows better. Stacey's great aunt Ella had told him that Salish women believe the less a man knows the better.

He waltzes her through the door when he hears the sobs calm into ordinary weeping, and sits her down on her couch. He isn't sure what he can do for her when the sobs end, but Stacey reaches for a cigarette and solves this for him. After a pull on it, and a few chuckles about how old that need to cry had been, Stacey recovers and relieves him of having to do anything.

"I think you came here to hurt me, Steve. You better do it and go on home."

"Actually, I think I came here to get hurt. But you're right, I ought to do it and go on home. I want more, Stacey. Don't interrupt." He puts his hand up to warn her not to respond before she starts. Most white men in their fifties don't have much hair, but Steve still has a full head and the yellow light works magic on the blond. She wants to touch his hair, to pull him down next to her, to ask him to love her just one more time before he hurts her.

"Stacey. I got married and it didn't last. I couldn't stop think-ing about you and I think my wife had some kind of sixth sense because when she asked for a divorce she mentioned you. Not in any kind of a nice way. She was right. I saw you in the mall that day and it all came back just like I was still standing on the bridge watching fish swim upstream all over again. In the mall, you asked for my number. I never said anything about the kind of relationship you wanted because my daughter was young and I hadn't finished paying for the house. It's been ten years, ten years of making double house payments and socking away money for my daughter's educa-tion. My ex-wife phoned me yesterday and said she just made the last mortgage payment. I'm free. Suzy has a job. She starts college in the fall. Today I took her to the bank and gave her what I had. I don't have much saved up for my retirement, but I still have my medical practice. I have no debts and no obligations besides my daughter's future wedding — if she has one."

The candle flickers. Stacey remembers their last day on the bridge. She feels the same hurt she had felt in her room that night after she left him there. The dark had settled in and the pain had scraped away at her. She remembers that she knew the decision she had made was the right one. He was so young and so white and she knew he would insist she move to white town, where she would get lost. She would be swallowed by her own lostness, be-come unrecognizable to him, and then he would divorce her. She was not like his ex-wife. She could not take him to court, insist on child support and that she keep his house and child and make a new life for herself. She would have withered away.

"It's been five years of waiting for you to call, Stacey. I want … I want to see you every day, bent over the stove frying bread and fixing coffee. I want to see you troop off to Momma's and come back all tight and strained and tired looking. I want to hold you until it all melts away. I believe you want that too."

The chair gives in to her body and his voice settles some unasked question deep inside. She does want it. She wants to see the back side of him retreat into the early morning light and head for some place in white town, and to have him return to this side of the bridge, day after day. She wants to hold him when his shoulders get rounded from whatever weighs on him. She wants to get excited about some small dumb thing and jump up and down telling him about it. She just isn't sure if he wants to be here with her. She never wanted to live on the other side of that river — where no one gives a shit about her, Stella, or that child — and he would not risk his career over some relative of hers he hardly knows. At least not willingly.

In the silence of her absence, if she didn't tell him where she was going and what she was doing, he would grow weary or suspicious and leave her; she would be left here in this house, feeling lonelier than she feels right now. She would never again have this easygoing kind of love from him. He had never said anything about wanting more of her before and she had not thought about where their secret affair was going before now. Now it is out there, playing with her skin, dancing in her belly, teasing her in that deep down forever kind of way that wakes up hope, pulls up promise — the promise of them sitting on a rocking chair sharing one last breath, one last handclasp, one last look before their eyes close forever.

"Why did you have to go and do that?" The tears roll out as she laughs, her voice so gentle. He smiles at her. "Look at me."

"I am. I like what I see." And he winks, takes both her hands in his and finishes what he started. "This is a promissory ring. You get to keep it no matter what you answer. It means that I promise to get you an engagement ring and then I will marry you. If you can see your way to saying yes then I will get you the biggest gawdamned engagement ring white town has to offer."

"You people get to take everything so lightly."

"Don't call me 'you people,' Stacey. You know I don't like it." His voice tightens as his body stiffens.

"You know what I'm talking about, Steve." He does not. He cannot. He sighs.

"I just don't want to be called 'you people.' The name is Steve." His earnestness makes her laugh.

"Okay, Steve," she says, mimicking his tones.

"Okay you won't call me 'you people,' or okay you'll put this ring on your finger?" He means to push the envelope right here and right now. The memories that had no pressure attached to them slip away. He is telling her he's always loved her and had married someone else because she'd turned him down. He's set his daughter and wife up with a house and investments. He's coming to her penniless, but still productive. She plays cynically with his words; she doubts he would set her up as neatly and cleanly if she was the one he was divorcing. He does not wish to be called "you people," but she doubts that he treasures her in the same way he did his ex-wife. On the one hand, she doubts they could go forward as a married couple, but she also knows they cannot go back to that easygoing, come-on-in-stranger, long-time-no-see, take-your-shoes-off-and-stay-a-while arrangement after he's asked her to keep him. She feels an all-or-nothing tone in his voice.

Living with him would require extra care; he's white, different. She has no way to frame that difference without offending him and jeopardizing the future of the relationship. The situation would require carefully measured words. She would have to let him know where she was going and figure out how to get what she needs without saying too much. She would have to figure out what he needs and give it to him and still maintain her private world of family. There would have to be a separate world and a together world, which means life with him would be complicated. He has no idea that it would be this complicated, and she is not sure she can deal with it.

"Steve, you have no idea what you're asking of me."

"Sure I do. I know you don't want to live on my side of town. I'm prepared to live here."

"How mighty white of you," she wants to say, but restrains herself. So arrogant, as though being prepared to live here were so decent and big of him. At best it is shallow and simple. She wants to scream at him and at the same time she wants to sink into some momentary sweetness of slow-burning desire.

"I guess that sounds arrogant. I am prepared to live here, since living there presents a whole different set of problems for you," he catches himself.

He caught himself; maybe this isn't going to be as difficult as she imagines. She feels herself relenting, succumbing, and loving him for catching himself.

Another voice nags: No more. Jump right in here under my covers. Let's just roll around for a while. I'll make you breakfast before you go. No more watching his back receding into the day knowing she didn't give him much. No more waking up and deciding to head over to Madeline's and camp out with her and her quiet girls for a day or two without saying a word to anyone. No more heading to the bank on Friday with Alice's gal and buying all kinds of makeup neither of them needs, then coming home and playing with it all night long. No more you're-welcome-to-visit-anytime with each of you knowing that to visit someone you have to leave. She hadn't had to think about him at all over these past five years. He's offering her a ring that brings with it a terrible tension; she feels too stuck to respond.

She needs to talk to Momma about all this, but she will have to wait until the crisis is over. She doesn't think Steve will wait out a crisis she does not wish to explain. He wouldn't understand and, like Judy, he would insist they call the police. Tears come; they slide over her cheeks and fall to her hands in her lap. Out of the blue, she laughs; she hasn't given one thought to how or what she would do without him. She laughs, because she knows she wants to keep this man without all hell breaking loose and only Momma can help her with that.

"Are you still an Owenite?" she asks.

"I am Steve, the man who loves you and makes his living as a doctor."

Stacey's light goes on.

"Doctors have ethics, don't they?"

"Yeah, but what's that got to do with us?"

"Could you ever see your way to breaking your rules for us, for this sorry-ass village?"

He stops breathing to clear his throat. He wants to ask what regulation he would be expected to break, but thinks better of it. First of all, she would not think it mattered; secondly, she would not likely tell him. He figures she wants to know what he would risk for her and he remembers the epidemic. His father would not risk his medical practice for a bunch of scraggly assed Indians. He tells himself that things are different now, but would he gamble his practice for people that remain a mystery to him?

"If you insisted."

"You do pick the damnedest times to ask me for things, Steve. The last time was long ago, in '54, during that flu epidemic. I hadn't slept for a week and you sat there in class discussing the unfairness of your own people not wanting to help, not thinking of what it meant to us who were staying up all night trying to save the dead from dying. You never once asked me if I was sad, tired, or even if I wanted to fight that flu."

"I was a kid then, Stacey. I was seventeen for Chrissakes."

The words sting.

"You aren't any smarter now, Steve. You don't get smarter as you get older; you know more, but you aren't any smarter about what you know."

There is some loathing in her voice, and he has to look at her hands and wait for the hurt to pass. She sees it, but knows that he had skipped over her hint about the crisis her family is caught in now, so she finds his hurt annoying.

"We are in the middle of a different crisis right now. My nephew killed himself. We don't have near the women left in our family to deal with it. Women leave to marry now. The vice of a hundred years of not being allowed is off, and some people are running around, crazed by the relief. And you're putting ultimatums at me. In the mall that day, you told me you were glad that we were finally having our rights recognized. It didn't occur to you that after a hundred years of no rights maybe our sanity had been twisted just a little. You look at my mom and don't see the forever-tiredness that never leaves her. You have no idea what it's like to grow up and never see your mother anything but tired, dead-dog fucking tired. You don't see the sadness lurking under our smiles. You can't feel the hot tension wire of fear that never leaves me, not even for one second. It isn't fair, Steve. You don't know it. We still don't fully exist for you. So don't tell me you were dumb because you were young. And I don't want to hear any more about you being white."

The sting of her raking slides away. The candle flickers light across her face. Quiet nestles around them. He can't go back to an affair, he wants more, and he can't alter who he is, change his history, and he can't see himself going forward without her.

He knows she's right and he suspects that he will never fully understand her. He's familiar with their history, but can't connect it to a response. He hasn't thought much about the effect that history has had on her or her family. Poverty is a word with no practical application to him. He knows her mother had crawled up and down those mountains, sometimes dodging helicopters with a load on her back, but he did not think about her being chronically fatigued until Stacey said it. He begins to realize that her loving him might be painful for her. He's known that she's been painful to know, but he's never thought about how painful it might be for her to be with him. But he knows he's not been happy with just bits of her.

"I'm not that dumb. I have the good sense to love you."

Stacey laughs. "I also know that I have got us both pretty stuck, haven't I?"

"Yeah." He toys with her hand and remembers what she said about the flu and about the crisis they are in now.

"Don't go taking this the wrong way. I really do want to know the answer to my next question: What has this new crisis got to do with me?"

"It isn't as simple as living on this or that side of the bridge. There are some things on this side that women don't talk about with men, but that doesn't mean the men don't know about them. Maybe we should talk together, but we don't. There are so many compromises both of us will have to make every day. Do you have any idea how trying that will be?"

"No. But we can't go back, and I can't see myself going forward without you."

"Okay, Steve. I am going to tell you that my heart wants this. My body needs it. But my mind needs some clarity and I want to talk to my momma first before I say yes. I don't have a clue how to be with you." She pushes his hand with the ring in it away. "It's the best I can do right now."

He puts the ring on the table. "Keep it. It isn't an engagement ring. It is my promise to engage myself to you. If you don't want it, give it away. If you do want it, call me." Square-shouldered and purposeful, he strides out the door.

"Cokscheam, Steve," she whispers at his back. The sadness sinks into her body, a clear stone swallowed by water and sinking for what seems an eternity. She closes her eyes and watches the sadness sink.

STACEY WAKES UP, REALIZING she's still in the chair that she was sitting in when Steve left. The digital clock from her radio shines the time red: 2:00 a.m. The house feels emptier than it has ever felt. She has to go to sleep or go to Momma's. She opts for the latter.

She can almost smell the fried bread of the day before at Momma's house when she arrives. Judy stares at her bannock and fish, unable to touch it. Momma sits next to her, struggling to eat hers. Both looked dead-dog tired. Celia, too, pauses with every bite. Shelley is moaning softly in the background. Even Rena is having a hard time swallowing her food with Shelley's moaning going on. Stacey joins them.

"You throw out any dirty old herbs from Rena's lately?" Celia asks. The tension breaks. They all laugh, the melancholy falls away and creates a space for them to wander in a different mood.

"Celia. Where did you find so much spunk?" Stacey asks.

"I don't know. It seemed to spring up overnight." She pushes her plate away.

The child must have brought it up in her, Stacey decides. "I need something, Celia." Stacey is searching for a way to bring up Steve, but can't seem to find one. The women wait for her to continue. When she doesn't, they move on. Celia talks about how strong and amazing the child is. She reminisces about the women in this family. Stacey marvels to herself at the clarity and accuracy of Celia's memory. Momma drags out her photo albums and they sit around the table looking at them, while Celia reminds them of what came before and what followed each picture.

"You are such a gift, Celia."

This draws a great laugh from Celia. "Just what I always wanted to be: a present."

AT FIRST LIGHT STACEY wakes up, but does not rise. She lies there watching the sun brighten the landscape outside Momma's window and she thinks about Steve. She cannot define what it is, but not having him in her life would make it desolate and she knows it. It's six a.m., an ungodly hour to call someone. She should wait until tonight. What difference would it make if she said yes now or later? The family is in a crisis. They have been in several over the years. But Stacey has never had the pleasure of adding to the crisis; she has always been steady as a rock. As the sun bathes the grass on her mother's well-mown lawn in bright light, she decides to go ahead and add to it. There hadn't been much of a break between each crisis. If things went on the way they had in previous years, there would never be a good time to marry Steve. There would never be a good time to deal with his whiteness and there would not likely be a good time for him to deal with the absence of whiteness among her fellow villagers. "The hell with it." She dials his number.

Steve recognizes her number and hesitates. It's too early to be good news. She can't have talked to Momma. She's decided to say no before she's even spoken to anyone. "Hello." It comes out tense.

"Were you sleeping?" She speaks softly so as not to wake up any-one in Momma's house.

"No." In fact, he hadn't slept much that night at all.

"I'm not ready, but I don't suppose I ever will be. That's a pretty stone you're offering, Steve. My old fingers could use something pretty."

"What?" He sits up. This is not the answer he's expecting.

"I said I'm not ready, but that's a pretty stone you're offering. My old fingers could use something pretty."

"Is that a yes?"

"Yes. I want you to know I'm mad, though."

"Mad? What about?" He laughs. She could go ahead and be as mad as she wanted to be, as long as she sat next to him.

"You're about the only easy I had in my sorry life and now you've gone and made yourself hard on me."

"I'll be over after work, tonight. Will you be at home?" There is a brief pause, and he adds, "I'll be bringing my clothes and closing up this apartment. Just thought you might want to know."

STACEY ASKS CELIA TO have breakfast with her; they head home to Stacey's to cook. As her feet crunch the gravel and the sun rises, she thinks about how to tell Celia. Celia removes her coat, and before she sits down she tells Stacey that she knows about her secret lover.

"So does Jacob."

Stacey finds this addition of Jacob funny, though she has no idea why. She had thought she would die if anyone knew, but now it's funny. They eat, wash the dishes, and talk about the shock it will be for Momma, who never knows what's going on until it's pretty much over. In the middle of washing the last dish, Stacey asks, "What on earth did I think would be so humiliating about telling you I had a lover?"

"Beats me. Maybe it's because no one ever says that in our family." Celia looks at Stacey, surprised, although it's true. No one has said it before. Said out loud like this it sounds preposterous — why did they never talk about their loves? White girls talked about lovers and their women talked about husbands. Celia doesn't like the implications. Maybe they don't talk about men because their families are in such disarray. She stares at Stacey, studying her.

"Celia, I swear something has got into you. You just go ahead and say anything that comes to mind these days."

"I do, don't I?" Celia says it as if she's surprised to learn this about herself, as if she's not been paying much attention to what she's been saying or doing. "What in the world is making my mouth run on so?"

"It doesn't matter," Stacey says, taking off her apron. "I love you this way. I mean, I loved you before. Maybe I never said it. But I always felt it. You know that. But now, why, you're downright lovable and so ... so ... likeable. Gawd that sounds stupid."

"Don't worry about it. Emotions have no brains, they move you to say pretty brainless things. That's why they're called emotions."

Dishes put away, they leave for Momma's without thinking any more about it.

STACEY IS ON THE couch reading an old magazine when she hears Steve's car pull into her gravel drive. She closes it and waits. After spending time with Celia she feels ready. "Every relationship takes work," Celia had said. "Each one takes different work. What you need to decide is whether or not you want to put the kind of effort into this one that is required." Celia makes things seem so simple and so profoundly straightforward. And it feels true to Stacey. It settles her.

She remembers working with the rest of the women until four in the morning and it strikes her how close she feels to them. That closeness took a great deal of effort, but it was an effort she was familiar with and willing to put in. She wonders how each of them will receive the news about her and Steve. His family might forsake him the way Stella's husband's family had him. Her family might forsake her the way Martha had forsaken Stella. Stacey would get stuck in the marriage. Steve would not love her for that. Celia helped her to see that love was a birthright, and no one had the right to intervene in the deciding of with whom you enjoyed that birthright. You can't care for yourself without someone there to witness it with you, Celia had said. Stacey decides to tell Steve she will never forsake her family or the village and that he has to take her, her family, and their sorry-ass village lock stock and barrel, just as they are.

She holds her hand out. He reaches for his wallet and hands her everything in it. She smiles and slaps it gently, putting his wallet back on the table.

"What am I going to do with all that whiteness, mister? I want your hand. When I want money, I will ask for it."

He looks at his wallet, then at her. She takes his hand. "Don't you pout on me, Steve." She smiles. He can't retreat from her smile. He pulls her into his arms.

"What are you going to do with all this whiteness?"

"Get used to it, I guess. I don't mind it most of the time."

"Where's Jacob?" he asks.

"I don't know. He doesn't spend much time here anymore." She lets go of his hand and looks out at the mountains. She's beginning to plan her day. She whispers, "Help me out here," as she looks up at the peaks. "Help me get through today without busting the sweet mood this man is putting me in."

"Was he your little mistake, Stace?"

"First, it is Stacey, not Stace. Second, a mistake is what you make when you add two and two and get five. No child is an error. Children are a critical part of the process known as procreation." Her voice has a sharp edge.

"Breathe a little softer on me, Miss Stacey."

"Don't ask questions like you half-know the answer, Mr. Steve. You may not want to know how I felt about Jacob's dad, or you may want to know if he's still in the picture, or whether or not I planned to have him. You can ask any of those questions without prefacing the remark with a value judgment, specifically referring to my son as a mistake. He was not an error." She leans toward Steve like she is leaning into a windstorm. "Do you understand me?"

"I don't know if I can do that."

"If you're telling me that this is too hard, or that at some point in the future this question may divide us, I am warning you, sir, that you get just one chance to say you're going to leave."

"Why, Miss Scarlett, I believe you're threatening me."

"Scarlett O'Hara was a white woman, and not half as wilful as you'll find me, mister."

"I have no intention of leaving. I worry, though, that I am ever going to get it right."

"You need something from me?"

"Yeah. Some patience." Steve sits in her easy chair.

"Last night put me in a sweet mood. I want you to let me replay it this morning, while I plan my day out. We've got the rest of our lives to negotiate the maze this relationship is going to be."

XVIII

JACOB DECIDES TO STUDY the colours of the plant life around him. He recognizes hundreds of shades of green leaves. No two are alike. Under the green are hints of gold and brown, sliding into red. He picks up stones flecked with blue and shaded with grey. Some have shiny black flecks and bits of crystal and pink in them. So much colour to hold his attention that he forgets about eating until late afternoon.

He cannot face another round of berries. He slips over to the creek and drinks the water. The sun falls below the horizon and he sees the moon. She is blue and bright, spilling light around him. He goes back to his stone to consider his world in the growing dark.

Alice steps up to him.

"What do you want with me?"

"Your company. Seems like I've been waiting for you for a long time."

"Did you know my cousin Jimmy?"

"Of course, you silly boy. He is my grandson too." She jabs Jacob's rib and grabs another cigarette off him.

"He killed himself."

"He gave up before that. And before that, he made decisions about how everyone else felt but himself. Righteous little bastard." Alice giggles.

"It isn't good to talk about the dead like that," Jacob cautions.

"You mean it isn't good for the living to talk about the dead like that."

This quiets Jacob. He would not have thought of this on his own. He wishes Alice wouldn't answer him with statements he himself could not have said. He does not want to believe he is actually seeing a dead person. She is making it difficult to believe he's imagining her.

"Okay. I give up. You're real. What do you want with me?"

"Your company," Alice repeats. "What is wrong with you? You deaf? Or don't you listen?"

"I guess I don't believe you."

Gramma Alice laughs, and then she tells him what she wants from him.

CELIA FALLS INTO THE rhythm of the women trying to save the child. She is quieter than usual, but when Stacey saunters through the curtain to the child's room, wearing a big smile on her face, Celia rolls her eyes.

"Must have got some last night," she says through her teeth.

"HI, BABY. IT'S ME, Stacey." She leans over the child.

"Yep. She must have got lucky last night," Rena says, winking at Celia. Celia relaxes.

"I did," Stacey responds. "I truly did."

"You going to tell us this story or just tease us?" Momma asks.

Stacey decides to tell her story. The women move about the room, cleaning and attending to the child while listening to it.

"I have me this doctor. He used to come by when Jacob took to wandering. Every time he came, he seemed to take the edge off this dusty, hard-edged living. He lifted the veil of disappointment that comes with children, you know, he made me want to pick up that dust and just sweep it out the door. He would come whenever I called. It was all so easy — easy loving. You know?"

The women responded with deep acknowledgement. Except Celia, who isn't sure if she should laugh or be horrified. She wonders what kind of people think about sex while tending a dying child. She looks about the room. The women have relaxed into Stacey's story. They seem to need to be relaxed to keep up the madness of tending Shelley, so Celia decides to help Stacey along.

"Kind of makes you yearn for something more?" Another round of "mm-mm" comes from the rest of the women. Celia opens a window. The air lightens and hope spills in.

Stacey leans toward the little girl's face. "You know what I am saying, baby?" Stacey's voice is so soft it draws a thin smile from the child. "Look, Shelley smiled right through the pain."

"Then what happened?" Rena pulls at Stacey's skirt, the way Jacob used to.

"Jacob is just like you. He used to tug at my skirt like that trying to make me finish a story."

"Don't you change the subject, girl."

"Last night he said, 'Miss Stacey, either you keep me or let me go.'"

This stills their breath with wonderful anticipation. The light goes on in Celia's mind and she prays Stacey told him to stay.

"He left for work this morning. I took the money he gave me and bought me some new cloth, fixed me up some curtains, fixed him some head soup, and left him a note saying I would be late, eat the soup and hang the curtains."

"I hope you wrote please at the end of that," Momma says. The women cheer and tease Stacey. Celia remains quiet.

"Stacey has a man," Rena says.

"I heard she has a doctor." Celia's emphasis on "doctor" stops the women in their tracks.

"Did you say you had a doctor?" Judy asks.

"Yeah. I asked him if he would risk breaking his rules for me, for my sorry-ass village. He said only if I insisted. Do you want me to insist?" She turns to the child. "You want me to insist, baby?"

STEVE LEANS AGAINST MOMMA'S porch railing, telling Stacey that she is going to make him crazy. He accuses her of manipulating him into agreeing to risk his career for her, all the time knowing what she was going to ask of him. It was manipulative. She gives him that. He paces back and forth. She stands still and watches him, then she turns to head back into the house. He follows. He wants her to promise never to manipulate him like this again. She stops in the hallway and reminds him that he had had his chance to name the conditions of the relationship. He had said there were none. He can't go adding them now just because he doesn't like what she's done. Besides, she wouldn't make those kinds of promises.

"Why not?"

"Because you aren't one of us." It comes out flat, sounding dangerously final.

"Don't bring up that 'you're a white man' shit," he hollers.

She shoves him out the door and onto the porch.

"First, that child does not need to hear a man bellowing. Second, my momma does not deserve to have you upset the spirit of her house. Last, I didn't say you were a white man. I said you aren't a Sto:lo."

"What the hell is the difference?"

"If you were a Sto:lo I would just say 'I have to go to Momma's' and you would answer 'Okay' and come with me. Breaking some white man's rules would not ever be a question. Nor would it require a moment of consideration, because they aren't our rules. But you are not Sto:lo, so you can't be counted on to just come along."

"If I was a Sto:lo, I wouldn't be a doctor." He is sorry for saying it even as it comes out of his mouth.

She slaps him.

"How the hell did I get to be this white?"

This makes her laugh. He does not get the joke. She confounds him.

"I believe what you're saying is that if I can't be like you, I have to let you manipulate me for the rest of my days. I don't know if I can do that."

She holds up her hand and repeats what she said: "You don't get a second chance." He sighs and says that he wasn't thinking of that. It is going to drive him insane to do what she is asking, and he is afraid of what she might do if he fails.

"Not a damn thing," she answers. There is nothing to be done about it if he fails. She would try, he would try, but they would not always be successful and that is that.

"Do you need a minute by yourself?" she asks.

"No. I just want to know why you picked that cloth you picked for the curtains."

She smiles. "Because the sun picks up the pink through the cloth and spills onto all that blond in your hair. I like the strawberry hues it brings out."

"You are going to make me crazy, Miss Stacey." He walks into the house to assess Shelley's situation.

WHAT'S THAT STACEY HAD asked her gramma one night as they trundled home in the dark? She had pointed at the skyline, which was jumping all over the edge of the earth with a pale blue light.

"What's wrong with the sky, Gramma?"

"Nothing," Gramma had answered.

"What's it doing?"

"Sometimes our northern relatives get tired of all that snow: shiny diamondback snow; slushy, wet, grey snow; blue-hued snow; icing sugar snow; big, white, flaked snow; house-making snow. They get so many kinds of snow. Even so, sometimes they get to wanting to look on some green; so they come down here and dance at the edge of our world."

Celia finishes repeating this memory to Stacey. "Do you remember telling me that?" she asks. Stacey does.

"Well, it's doing it again. The sky is doing it right now."

The women drop what they are doing; they leave Steve alone with Ned and go outside.

Steve is shaking, he can't get his hand to steady up.

Ned notices. "Sometimes the weasel is the best teacher," he says.

Steve laughs. "Don't you go trying my patience with an Ella riddle now, Ned. This story better be good and plain, because I am still as dumb as when I was young, except now I am older and slower." He settles down to watch the girl. "She needs a lot of vitamin E. I'll pick some up from the pharmacy. I can't believe anyone could make it through all this, but it looks like she might. She should be dead. It's more than the burns, Ned; she's emaciated. Whoever did this was doing it for a long time. I'm surprised she lived long enough to give him the chance to do this much damage."

HE BARELY REMEMBERS WHAT he had been harping about when his aunt Ella told him that weasel story. He told her he had no sympathy for weasels. "You definitely don't," she had said and laughed one of those old people's isn't-that-the-damnedest-thing-you-ever-heard-he-doesn't-like-weasels kind of laughs.

"Do I look like a man whose woman has pulled the wool over on him?" Steve asks Ned.

"You look like a man who's mad his woman has pulled the wool over on him."

He isn't surprised that it shows. He is easy to read; it's one of the things Stacey says she likes about him. He laughs. He cannot remember finding himself funny before, and says so to Ned. Ned finds this funny. The two of them are laughing when the women return, talking about the lights in hushed tones. They tell Ned and Steve to go out and have a look.

"I DIDN'T PARTICULARLY WANT any of my girls to bring a white man home, but if we have to have one you would be my first choice, Steve."

"Not much weasel in you, Ned."

"No. I'm kind of like you, Steve: a little on the dumb side, but I get around. This clutch of women is full of every possible medicine; if you know your light isn't always shining, you just learn to move along with the rhythm they set in motion and wait for the story to unfold — or they will drive you to distraction. They're always interesting, if they're not always sweet."

"You know what's scary, Ned? On the other side of that bridge, I am one of the smartest men I know."

Ned nods. What Ned thinks is even scarier is that they don't think their own women are very smart on the other side of the bridge, and so they cannot imagine the women in this village being smart either.

The lights dance. Ned imagines hearing the hum. Steve thinks he sees faint hints of blue and green in the columns that sway as though reaching for the top of the sky. The light bathes him in some kind of strange calm. He has never felt calm coming from outside of him and getting under his skin like this.

"Is she worth it?" Ned asks.

"Yeah," Steve says without hesitation. This satisfies Ned. They continue watching the lights.

"I have to go back to Stella's," Ned tells him as he butts out a cigarette. Steve helps him load up his truck with scrap lumber and tools, though he's damned if he can figure out why they want to help Stella at all — she belongs in jail.

THE LIGHTS DANCE THEIR way around the belt of the night, glowing blue and green for a couple of hours. The women come out again when Shelley has gone to sleep. Awe silences them as the lights form human shapes. The lights reshape themselves: first into mountains of blue glacial light, then into humans again, ending as abstract shapes in motion.

There doesn't seem to be an adequate way to address the dead staring at you in their numbers. Silence is the only reaction they can call together and still maintain their awe. Each has stood calling out to the ancestors in a holy mass, eyes pointed skyward, bodies still, prayers completely silent. When the lights leave, their eyes turn to one another; this is their communion.

Celia begins the circle by embracing her mother, before moving on to each woman, her mother following, until every woman's heart beats with the other.

Momma begins to sing. "They came to remove that awful tired you-know-the-one that slows the blood, thins the mind, and tortures the memory." After Momma finishes that old sweet song, Celia slips her arm into her mother's and asks if she knows many songs.

"Now I do. I don't know why, but seeing all those people swaying up there all sexy and dead woke up a song in me."

"You still have that drum?" Stella's poppa asks.

"Can you sing for a while?" Celia cuts him off. As Momma leaves the house with her drum, Steve falls in behind her, wiping up his hands.

"I can do anything, child, anything at all." Momma says something to Ned in the language and he fetches a bench from the woodshed and a couple sets of sticks, one for him and one for Steve. He sits on the bench, tells Steve to face him, and Momma picks up the drum. Momma sings. After the first round is finished, the others join in. Judy can't get past her Prussian accent, and Steve can't get past his lyric-less English, but it doesn't matter. They sing until near sun-up, all except Celia. They sing until their voices crack.

"AND THAT IS THE last song I know," Momma says.

"That's all you know?" Steve asks, and they laugh. He takes Stacey's hand. He knows he will sleep now. He will wake up. It will be a new day. He will be too sober and too serious for his own good. He will have grave doubts about what they are doing, but as long as they come together like this he will get through every completely insane and irrational demand Stacey makes of him.

XIX

GRAMMA ALICE SITS AT the end of Momma's bed, saying, "Something has to die before something can be born." Momma floats through her dreams, wondering who will die and what is going to be born. She sees Celia sitting at Alice's house and knows they are up to something. Alice looks like she is reading from a slim sheet of paper. Celia is quiet. Why in the world would Alice still be reading to Celia? Surely Celia can read. What in the world is one grown woman doing reading to the other? What has that to do with Gramma Alice telling her that for something to be born something has to die?

NED IS BACK. JIM is leaning against the same windowsill Ned left him leaning against; the place looks cleaner. Things are arranged in neat piles where Stella intends to put them when the cupboards are built. With clean clothes folded neatly, Ned feels a little safer and more comfortable. She has made a lot of decisions over the past three days. It surprises both men. She still seems strange, not quite all there, as if she is walking through a dream, but they have started to build whatever it is she asks them to. Ned brings a couple of windows with him, old but serviceable. He tells Jim to start putting up shelving while he installs the windows.

The industry of building eases the tension within the men. Stella sings as she puts things away. There is a lot of garbage to be tossed. Ned hands her a pack of garbage bags and tells her to fill them up and load them onto the truck. No one lives close enough to mind the sound of sawing and hammering, so they carry on through the night trying to bring some sort of order to this place Stella calls home. Jimmy does his best to choose pieces of wood that are better on one side; he trims the edges so the shelving looks good.

There is a bucket in the middle of the floor that Stella keeps avoiding. Jim finally asks the obvious: "Does the roof leak?"

"Yes," Stella answers, just as if he were asking "How are you?" and she were answering "Fine." They will have to head up the hill for some cedar to make shingles; a couple of squares is all they'll need. Jim half-smiles thinking about dodging a helicopter one more time.

"Getting too old to dodge the man, Ned, you think?"

"Never too old for a little adrenaline rush, lad. Never too old for that." They kick around stories about the times they poached something that used to be theirs until the magic foot of the white man landed on it and it wasn't theirs anymore.

"I want a pair of white man's boots before I die. I want to be able to step on something and make it mine," Ned says to Jim.

"Ain't they some shit," Stella says like a man, coming out for a smoke. They turn sharply and look at her.

"Yeah. They're some shit all right," Jim says.

Ned decides it's time to talk. "What happened to that little girl of yours?"

Stella looks around. "Where is she?" she asks.

Ned closes his eyes and shakes his head. Jim thinks it's too soon, but he answers her. Stella fights for some kind of grip on what has happened. She bounces words around, letting go bits and pieces of phrases that make no sense. She runs into the house, unable to handle the cacophony of sound that is going on in her mind and not quite coming out of her mouth. Jim and Ned finish their smokes. As he crushes out his cigarette Jim looks at Ned and says, "Too soon." He gets up and goes into the house.

The quiet emptiness is palpable. Jim feels it the moment he steps in the door. She's not here. He looks around. The window in the sole bedroom is broken. There's a pillow outside, on the ground. She broke it and bolted. Jim runs out of the room, nearly knocking Ned over. "She's gone," he tells him. They both head for the truck. They drive straight away from the house, down the main road. "Is anyone home at Martha's?" Ned asks. Jim doesn't answer, just turns the truck in the direction of Martha's house.

The seconds click by hard. They have to reach Martha's house before Stella does something crazy. Crazy is getting to be so common. They pull up to the door and hear a scream. Jim kicks the door in and flips the switch. The gun in her hand, Stella lies in a pool of blood. They grab a blanket and staunch the bullet wound. Sam, Martha's husband, stands by in his underwear, trying to figure out what the hell has just happened.

"What the... What the ... Stella ..."

"Can't even do this right," she says, and passes out.

They haul her into the truck. Sam fetches his pants, he means to go with them. When he gets outside, they are gone. He heads for Momma's house. He's gonna give that girl a piece of his mind. Two of his children died in that damn epidemic in '54. He lost another one to a drunken car accident. And now this, this suicide shit, threatened to take another. No more, he mutters, no more.

Halfway to Momma's, he turns back.

STELLA DREAMS. SHE DREAMS of soft lace curtains, of white counter-tops, of pretty blankets, of dresses. She dreams of a softer life. She imagines that white women have everything she sees on the tele-vision. She pictures them in the malls, fingering everything like it belongs to them, all they have to do is decide what they want and poof there it is. Marry a white man and he will magically soften your life. All she had to do was find one that wanted to keep her.

She offered herself up to one after the other. Which one of you wants to keep me? They took her all the way through high school, taking turns and discarding her. John came along, plain boring John, John who carried the promise of softness, John whose feet were magical. John merely had to step in any direction and he could get much of whatever he wanted. She would do anything for him. She did do anything for him. But the more she did the crazier he got. He wanted a woman, not a doormat. How could she have known that? She wanted softness, not John. How could he know that? They slid into one drunken crazy moment after another because Stella thought that was what John wanted and because he had no other idea how to deal with this woman. Two children surfaced and John changed. Everything became a war, the girls needed this, and why aren't you doing that, the girls, the girls … and Stella began to hate those girls. They consumed her softness. They sucked up every penny she imagined should go toward easing the hardness of her life.

There was no softness. She looked everywhere for it. It slipped through her fingers the moment she turned around. She gave up. She convinced herself she would have hardness then, raw hard-ness, brutal hardness, and she hunted it down. And she found it, around every corner she found it. Her hunt began as a means to forget John and the promise. It helped her to forget those little girls whose own softness made Stella insanely jealous. It became some ordinary demon she had to feed each day, an old mean dog sitting on her porch. She fed it.

What happened? She went mad. "I went mad," she tells herself. I deserve to die. I don't deserve to live. I don't deserve the hammering, the sawing, and the tending to my house. I don't deserve this child, this life, this anything. She had bolted out of the house, headed down the road to her father's house, found his gun, aimed it at her heart, and failed to kill herself. What's that voice? What's it saying? "Get some snarl, girl. You are going to survive. You are going to get through this and you are going to straighten up and live." There is a threat in that voice. Poppa, is that you? "Yes it is. You aren't doing this." Poppa, where are you? "I'm right here, baby." Poppa? Poppa, don't hate me...

She drifts off.

STELLA HAS LOST A lot of blood. "She needs blood," Steve tells them. "We have no way of giving it to her. She needs to go to the hospital."

Martha won't let them take her. "If she is going to die, she will die right here. Maybe she ought to die," she says. "Look at what she did."

No one knows what to say. They stare dumbly at Martha. "Don't talk crazy, Martha," Celia says. Steve figures they can't take Stella to the hospital unless Martha agrees to it. He shudders to think that one generation of women has so much power over the next. He cauterizes the wound and stitches her skin as best he can. He prays Martha will be brought to her senses. Ned and Jim lean into the wall, their minds blank as they wait for the outcome of this mad chatter to emerge.

Sam arrives before it does.

Celia holds Martha. Martha stares at Celia. She is about to relent. Sam, gun in hand, goes to his daughter. He takes her in his arms. "No. If she is to die, she will die here in my arms."

"No, Poppa, we can't do that," Momma tells her uncle. "Keeping the child here is one thing, but not this, not this."

Poppa has the gun. He threatens them. Steve freezes. "This is making me crazy," he tells Stacey. Jim tries to soothe Sam. Not even his voice, buttery and assuring, can change the old man's mind.

"Don't we have some of them rigs the boys stole during that flu epidemic?" Celia asks.

"What rigs?"

"Blood transfusion rigs," Stacey answers.

"You have blood transfusion rigs?"

"They're in the back house," Momma says.

"But we have no idea what blood type Stella is." Judy throws water on the fire of hope sparking itself up in the room.

"Sure we do. Same as mine," says Martha.

"Okay," Steve hears himself bellow. "Let me try then, just let me move around this fucking room without that gawdamned barrel pointing at me."

Ned is out back with Jim, digging around for those rigs. Momma puts more water on to boil. Rena goes home to get more alcohol. Celia fetches bandages. Judy grabs syringes from Steve's bag. Ned and Jim return with the rigs and a box of the intravenous bags. Steve cannot believe what he's seeing. He recalls the theft; he'd read about it in the papers when he was a kid. These women are either insane or have very large brass balls hidden somewhere inside them. Sam backs up, but now aims the barrel at Momma. Steve gasps. Stacey sinks into the wall and slides to the floor. Celia moves toward her mother.

"She dies if anybody moves, Celia." Sam cocks the gun.

"You die right after, if you shoot her," Ned says, straightening up.

"Settle down, Ned." Momma smiles at Sam. Momma nods at him, calm as she can be. She's known him for a long time. Martha was her gramma's youngest. She was younger than Momma by a decade. She had met this man late in life, married him, and given Momma an uncle. She doesn't for a minute think he would kill her.

"Don't fuckin' anybody move." Steve does not know this man; it's the first time he's seen him. It is also the first time he's seen anything like this. So he hollers and gets down to work with Judy.

Ned believes anything could happen, a dish could fall, someone could sneeze or cough and this man would mistake it for traitorous movement. He squares off in the room, teeth grinding and fists clenched. The very moment that gun goes off, he will leap for the man's throat. He slows his breathing so he will be ready.

Jim wonders if the white people in the room will be able to fix this woman. He wonders if the old man is serious. He wonders if he could survive seeing his Momma, his hard-working, all-giving, tired Momma shot right before his eyes. He decides he can't. He decides he will jump in front of her. He stands stock still, aiming his eyes at the old man's trigger finger. As she and Steve are patching Stella up, Judy keeps mumbling, "Ain't this some shit, ain't this some shit."

Momma watches Sam. Celia stares at her fingers as the humming in her mind returns.

The humming takes her to the top of Jacob's mountain.

Rena is close enough to move the barrel, but something keeps her locked still; it's familiar, she knows this stillness better than she knows anything else.

Celia sees Jacob sitting next to Alice. They are planning something for the parched man.

Momma recognizes the tired in the old man's eyes.

The snake is running loose. He needs water. No water, there cannot be any water.

He's tired of losing.

The snake will consume us all. Only a pure-hearted man can kill him. She can too. Clean out your mind, your body, and your heart; the ceremony will clean your spirit.

He has fought so many battles and lost. He is aiming the gun at losing.

This is not about anger, vengeance, or retaliation, Jacob. It is about the snake. It is about ritual, about ceremony, and about restoring our original direction. It isn't about her at all. It is not about finding yourself, Jacob. It is about finding your own song, the song that will move you through life. We are not lost. We are travelling in the wrong direction. Song moves us toward our humanity and right now we are moving away from it.

Knowing why Sam stands there with his gun pointed at her soothes Momma. Celia's humming stops. The picture of Jacob grows still. Celia is back in the room, her eyes focused on Momma. Momma seems so calm — too calm. She is looking at the old man with a small smile on her lips. Celia thinks she is enjoying his rage. Sam's gun-toting piece of insanity looks like it's bringing up some kind of pride in Momma. Momma must think that Sam's gun is motivated by his love for Stella. Celia doubts that. The whole scene is perverse. Momma decides to tell Stella how much her daddy loved her when she comes round. Sam is the first man who has dared to threaten her.

MOMMA'S POPPA COMES INTO view, she sees him standing on a cliff edge, tying her off, complaining about her. She insists on trying to dip into the river to catch a fish. He complains about how precious she has become to him. He complains about seeing her being born, coming through that sweetness of her momma, squealing before her body was all the way through. He saw her tiny face; her small hands all covered in blood and knew his love for her could kill him. Sam is cut from the same cloth.

MOMMA'S FATIGUE NEVER LEFT her after that damn epidemic. She looks over at Celia. As the tired in her dies and her strength returns, she comes to see that she had betrayed her father's love. She had not bothered to bring Celia home. "Poppa spoiled me," she says out loud. "He loved me like you love Stella, Sam."

Sam winces. "Don't you try weaselin' me, Momma."

"I'm not trying to weasel you, Sam. I am just remembering my own poppa."

Celia keeps her eyes on her mother. She sees the lines around her eyes disappear. Her shoulders, always so slender and sloped, square and drop gently in a nearly sexy posture. The skin on her face loosens and looks brighter. Celia tries to remember the last time her mother looked this good. "You look good, Momma." Stacey and Rena share a confused look, and then they both shrug.

"SHUT UP!" Steve hollers.

"Relax," says Judy.

This night will change them all. Momma has no idea how, but she knows it will. Sam has found himself a way to win. She wants to find a way to win too. She will pick her battle more carefully than Sam has. He has been dropped into this battle against his will. She will choose a battle, calmly and coolly, then she will plot her victory. Sam's battle made him a victim of his love and that renders his attempt a loss. She vows that she will never be a victim; her win will be a triumph.

Her calmness agitates Sam. Sweat appears on his brow. The sweat beads. The old man shifts and a little river of sweat slides from the top of his forehead toward his brow, just above his good eye. Jim sees it; just leak down into that one good eye, he prays, his fingers twitching. Jim gets ready. The sweat slides down and lands in Sam's good eye, blinding him for just a second. The old man blinks and shakes off the sweat obstructing his vision. The gun in his hand shifts and loses its focus on Momma. Jim leaps. The sight of Jim coming at him through this moving blur confuses the old man. He shifts the gun back and forth, not sure if he wants to re-aim it at Momma or aim it at the blur, but it's too late. Jim whacks the barrel upward, the gun goes off and, for just a second, the room freezes. Momma is still standing when the screams erupt. The child cries. Ned's leap followed Jim's by a half second.

They rise. Jim has the gun in hand. Ned is about to hit Sam, but Momma smiles. "Don't, Ned. He didn't mean me any harm. He's just tired of losing."

Everyone stares at Momma; she has lost her mind. Judy starts to say, "Ain't this some shit." Rena shouts, "Shut up with that shit business." Steve looks like he feels he must be the one who is out of his mind committing himself to these people, this family, and this village. Stacey faints. Rena catches her. Celia clears the room of everyone but Steve, herself, and Judy.

Stacey's faint shocks me; I have not realized how like Momma she is. I lick my paws and pray.

Without song wind cannot play inside our bodies. The spirit of our co-creators cannot adore us unless we sing. We cannot feel foreverness without passing air over carefully controlled impassioned vocal cords, uttering sounds that are so beautiful they articulate the soul. Songs are about light. They teach our children to adore the light inside. They tantalize the musculature and restore cellular movement in that easy way that the breath of the four winds has of tantalizing the earth, dragging sound through trees, and haunting the world with the beauty of breath's power. Breath on vocal cords, rendered melodic and rhythmic, can inspire humans to resist the most terrible tyranny. Breath across vocal cords, uttered softly, can settle the fears of a child. Song's breath across vocal cords can excite the love of a woman for a man. Song's breath across vocal cords can restore the peace of the body after the agony of divorce. Song's breath across vocal cords can urge men to rise to fight, to kill for vague concepts like freedom, nationhood, or revolution, but they can't always live for them. Song's breath across vocal cords can heal the sick, raise the dead, and encourage the living to go on in the face of terror.

Without song, the body cannot rest, cannot rise again, cannot face tyranny, cannot look at itself, cannot see, think, or feel. Without song, the body cannot grieve the dead, send them off to another dimension, cannot work or love. Without song, the body cannot recover from loss, from divorce, cannot express its yearning, and cannot dream. Four generations of men and women have not been allowed to sing. Without song, all that is left is the thinnest sense of survival. This spiderweb of survival has snapped from whatever mooring it attached itself to and the silk threads lie all withered and tangled in a heap on the floor of a burned-down longhouse that has not been rebuilt.

Jacob sees the longhouse on that mountain, the one that had fallen face forward, exposing the moulded blankets and the bones — so many of them. He sees a tangled spider's web and in each silk strand he sees some aspect of the crisis everyone in this village is bound to. He intends to pull at this silk and unravel the whole damned mess. The mountain has brought him a song and the dream of rebuilding the longhouse. This longhouse appeared as the old man who fired a useless shot into the house where Stella lies wounded by the same gun. Suicide is a beast, Jacob decides, and it must be laid to rest. It is one head of sea serpent consuming the other. He means to kill the beast inside him as well, the one that drew him toward the old snake's shack. He will find the people he needs to make this dream come true. This longhouse will be born again.

From the mountain, Jacob belts out a song. He eats some more, finishes the last of his tobacco, and heads down. Alice and Jacob had sat on that mountain, plotting a response to the snake running rampant through the village. Alice cautions Jacob on the state of cleanliness he has to achieve before he can do this. "You have to be awake, Jacob. So awake that you need only hear this once. You know?" He does. She walks him around the mountain, pointing out the foods he needs to eat. She talks about the medicines too. With every instruction, Jacob swallows. He floats behind Alice, glad to be there on that mountain at that moment.

He smiles as he makes his way down the mountain.

THEY ARE FINISHING HOOKING Stella up to the IV. Martha lies on a cot drained of a pint of blood and fatigued by her vigil. Sam and Momma are outside on the porch. Jim has gone outside with them; he is not about to leave his mother's side. Stacey has come round and is sitting next to Steve, who is standing in the corner, rubbing his chin and doubting himself and his sanity as well as the sanity of everyone in the room. Rena and Judy are resting. They have had enough for one night. Shelley is awake and moaning. Celia changes the bandages. The child quivers every time Celia touches her body; Celia murmurs, "I am not fit for this child," her voice full of apology. "I don't know how to do this without feeling like I am your torturer. I hardly know any encouraging words at all. I spend most of my time imagining life, instead of living it. I am just a very large child."

The little girl's lips move. Celia bends down to hear her say it's all right. She thinks her knees are going to give out and then she hears it, clear as a bell. It's Jacob, singing his own song.

"You hear that, Shelley?" Celia smiles. Her fingers deftly dress the open wound. Of course, she does not, Celia chuckles; I am the only one who hears things. I hear things. Celia looks at the little girl and tells her, "I hear things." The little girl smiles and Celia accepts that the simple truth is that she hears things. Steve comes in to examine Shelley before finishing up for the night.

Out on the porch, Momma sings. Stacey goes out to join her. Shortly after, Rena and Judy follow the sound of the singing. Sam moves over, next to Momma. He curls his pudgy fingers into hers and sings as the water rolls from his eyes. Momma places her other hand over the one he's holding on to. Jim shrugs and joins the singers. They continue to sing while Steve and Celia finish ministering to Shelley. Finished, Steve joins the family on the porch. Celia stays with Shelley. "You hear that, baby? When everyone sings like that it sounds to me like the voice of divinity itself." Celia is humming what the others are singing. Shelley stops quivering and goes to sleep.

SO MUCH OF THIS night has brought back memories of the epidemic of 1954. The healing circle Celia belongs to are all convinced that suicide and violence were part of a new epidemic. "We just won't come out of our house," an old woman visiting from Vancouver Island had said years ago. Celia remembers the days following the battle with the flu. The fatigue on her momma's face scared her when she was a child. She remembers how she lay awake at night picturing the tall ships, Momma's fatigue, her gramma's unrelenting sense of panic, and how she wished she were born in some other time, to some other family.

She and her gramma visited Momma almost daily. Stacey was gone, Jim was busy with Ned, and the house had grown bigger. New windows and curtains had appeared like magic. The driveway was paved, the house painted. Momma had a garden. It was pretty, but so empty that Celia couldn't be there unless she escaped into her dream world. Momma didn't seem to see her. Celia would come and go from the house without Momma saying much to her. When the pavers were working on the driveway, Celia had asked her momma if they could build her a swing.

"Honey, don't sit on Momma's new cloth. That's going to pretty up my new windows soon." Celia had gone outside and plunked herself down on one of the stones edging the new garden, where she watched the men. Her body warmed the stone underneath her. She slipped into hearing an old song full of punch and vigour. After the song ended, she asked the men if they knew how to build a swing.

"I'd build a pretty little girl like you anything," one of the men said. The other laughed. They scared her. She wanted something cleaner than that. She wanted them to build her a swing because she wanted it, not because they thought she was pretty. She stopped interacting with people after that. She coasted from dream space to dream space until her son was born. She made him her anchor and now she wanted to cut him adrift, not so she could return to her dream world but so she could enter the world of humans again. But she needed something and she could not figure out what it was. Shelley inspired her re-entry, but she does not want Shelley to become a new reason for her to be.

On her way home, Celia stops at Alice's.

"Did you see the lights?" Alice pours her a familiar cup of tea.

"Yeah. Did you write something?"

"Yeah." Alice swings into her chair and begins to read:

Gramma Alice hums a berry-picking song,
Drumming up pictures of white snow, blue snow,
Diamond-backed, glinting, hard, house-building snow
powder snowshoeing snow.
From across the berry bush
while her blue scarf and green-pink-purple-blue paisley dress
bobs up and down, looking like northern relatives dancing
filling the sky with their sound, as Gramma Alice makes love
to sky, to night, to day, to berries, to us.
Memories stretch out over hot days
Of picking at bushes whose fruit becomes a berry pie
declaring Gramma's love.

"Momma sang too, Alice. Write one about Momma singing."

"I can't, Celia. I didn't hear it. You did. You could. Let me show you." Alice draws a circle, writes "Momma sang" in the middle, and draws spokes out from the circle. She asks Celia to close her eyes and tell her what she saw when she heard Momma sing.

Dark lines on Momma's face melt into song
Filtered through her daughters'
nighttime reverence for Northern Lights,
Momma's song a power breath.
Gathering the weight of the women into a purple ball

that floats on the back of Momma's song
Rising to the ceiling to be swallowed by the beams.

"Lovely," Alice says. "That is so lovely."

"How do you know it's poetry?" Celia asks, staring in awe at the words her voice made.

"'Cause it's written on the page different from a story." Alice leans back and laughs. "I don't know. Stacey told me that's how poetry is written." Alice, still laughing, reaches out to tap Celia's hand.

"Then how do you know that what I wrote is poetry?"

"'Cause you did it the same way as me." She pauses. "You remember Stacey talking to us little ones after the epidemic?"

Celia admits to her cousin that she didn't much listen to Stacey in those days. Stacey made her feel tired then. Mostly she daydreamed her way through the conversations. Alice thinks this is funny, but she goes on to remind Celia: "The night was pale. You know how it gets when the clouds stretch themselves into a dull see-through sheet dimming the sky, dulling the moon and the stars but not quite making them disappear, until you aren't sure you really see them or not. Stacey told us then that not singing made her feel tired."

Celia wakes up. "Yes. I remember that. I remember it just like I am feeling it right now." Stacey must have known the songs Momma sang. That's why she slipped into them so easily. "She is an old skunk," Celia decides. "Why didn't I know those songs?" Her blood starts to run hot.

"Fish," Alice answers. "Fish."

"Fish?"

"Yeah; someone cast a net and Stacey got caught and you didn't." Celia looks at Alice, goes blank, and pushes out a chuckle, holds it in, then laughs and cries all at the same time. When Celia is done, Alice shoves a plate of berry pie forward. Politely, Celia tastes the pie, shakes her head, and pushes it back. Alice thinks this is different, but she lets it go. They sit together, remembering one thing after another until dawn's light accuses them of wanting to sleep in. Then they part.

Alice watches Celia trundle down the drive, still trying to figure out why Celia ate just a small bite of that pie then left it. That's when she thinks she sees it: Celia's hips aren't taking up so much space. She wonders if Celia is trying to lose weight.

On the way home, Celia remembers the pie, the song, the lights, and the memories she and Alice had played with. She smiles at the rising of the sun. Alice had looked at her funny when she didn't finish the pie. Likely thinks I am on a diet or chasing some man, she thinks, and laughs. It wasn't either of those things. After seeing that child's hunger, she cannot bear to eat so much anymore. It just feels wrong.

XX

CELIA MISSES JACOB. SHE wants to show him her poem. She has reworked it in calligraphy, trimmed the edges of the paper with flowers, and hung it on the wall. She has cleaned the house and is waiting for him to come back. She had heard Jim tell Ned he believed Jacob was up on the mountain, trying to figure out something about something. Jim found that amusing, like wanting to know something about something was the damnedest, most ridiculously wonderful thing a man could want. She recalls Jim hiking up the mountain and being gone for days. She had asked Gramma if she could too.

"Of course you can. That's why you don't have to," was all she'd said.

Celia looks at her poem and thinks she understands what Gramma meant. She runs around the house, tossing chocolates into the garbage. If that child could fight so hard for life on an empty stomach Celia figures she can go on living without all this chocolate. She makes plans to tell Jacob all that has happened to her as soon as she's cleaned her house and found just the right words. Then the phone rings.

"Miss Celia James?"

"Yes?"

"You don't remember me, do you?" Yes, she does. She remembers his voice and everything about him. She could not forget, but she does not want to admit it, not yet. She wants him to work for it. "Who is this?"

"It's Alex. Do you remember me now?"

"Alex who?" Celia teases her words out slow and easy, hoping they urge him to stay on the line; at the same time, she purses her lips together and thinks, How dare he imagine that I would have forgotten him?

"Ah. You're breaking my heart, girl. Twenty years ago, I was at the North American Indian Brotherhood Conference and you were there with your sister Stacey and your dad."

How could he possibly imagine that she does not remember? Alfred Hope Junior had been on the agenda of the Conference. She had gone with Stacey and Ned. Alfred was some sort of distant relative and he was about to take his case to the BC Supreme Court. They went to raise money for him. Alex had been one of the young organizers for the Brotherhood. He talked her into staying in his room with him. He was smooth as glass and his voice was buttery sweet and full of promise. She had no way of knowing that he didn't mean much of anything he said.

"Oh, right. You were sent to torment me. I remember now." They exchange silences, and then he tells her he is organizing a women's conference.

"That makes sense, the women organized the chief's conference, the least you men could do is organize one for us. But isn't that some kind of an oxymoron — organized men?"

Celia still has a good bite to her sense of humour, he thinks. He remembers that he had promised her he would call her and hadn't.

"You must think I'm a lying sonofabitch."

"No." She pauses to let it sink in. "To call you a sonofabitch, I would have to call your mother a dog. I have no ill thoughts about your mother at all. I wouldn't have called her a bitch for all the berries on our entire mountain range. I blamed you."

He stays quiet for a minute. "Celia. I was walking down the street yesterday, watching the flowers bloom, and I thought about you."

"Why are you really calling me?" She suddenly wants off the phone. Not enough to hang up, just enough to hurry him along.

He considers saying it is his job to call every woman he knows. It is the sort of honest little fact that cowards rely on to cover the truth. He doesn't wish to be a coward anymore, so he tells her the truth. He had been completely taken with her, but he hadn't been ready for a family. He busied himself with a career. When he was ready to talk to her, he told himself it had been too long. Celia was likely married. So he married. It had taken ten years for the woman to realize she was doing all the loving in the relationship. She had asked for a divorce. He acknowledged that if he had not been asked to call every woman he knew, he would not be on the phone admitting to Celia that he had been a cad two decades ago.

"I realize that I've missed you all these years." Even to him it sounds false. How could he miss her after spending one weekend with her? But he has. He'd searched for something more intelligent and persuasive to say, but couldn't find the words. He hated this language. There were so many ways to say "pass the peas" and no believable way to express his missing Celia and his not calling.

"How am I supposed to tell the difference between this story and the other one?"

"You won't know unless you try me out."

"You give me your number and I will roll this around for a while, then I'll call you."

"You're a tough woman, Celia."

"Men like you force me to be."

Now what? He doesn't know that she had had a son for nineteen years; that his son was raised by a stepfather who left when he was six years old. She had made the stepfather come back to build the coffin. This stepfather, this husband who had never bothered to divorce her, who had withheld his own feelings, had buried this man's son. He had called her, twenty years ago, before the Conference. She hadn't turned him down, but she wasn't convinced she wanted to spend her life with him. They were dating. The Conference interrupted. After it became clear to Celia that Alex was not going to call, she had taken up with him again. When she realized she was pregnant, she told Jimmy's stepfather. He wanted to do the right thing.

When Jimmy reached three years of age, it became clear that he looked neither like Celia nor her husband. Her husband stayed as long as he could bear the humiliation and until Celia's assurances that Jimmy was his son wore thin. Finally, she told him the truth. He met someone new and left. He came back to bury her boy because he felt guilty about leaving his wife and his stepson, but not because he loved them. Now this man she had loved so instantly, so completely, was back.

She hadn't told anyone but her husband about the child's real father. She had been dating this man both before and after the Conference, so there was no reason for them to doubt the parentage of the child. They would not have said anything anyway. It didn't matter. Jimmy was Celia's son and that made him Momma's grandson and Stacey's nephew. He had his own place in the life of the family, free of his parents' identity.

Celia lights a candle. She watches it burn and then she goes to her bedroom and leafs through an old box of papers. She finds an instant photo of herself and Alex at the bus depot right after that first night. In the picture, she is smiling bigger than that damn mountain. She holds the picture and her tears roll out. Where were you all this time? I was so fucking young. I needed your love then. I needed the kind of attention that belongs to youth. I wanted to feel so pretty, so sweet, and so treasured. I wanted us to be there together, holding our child, walking him, rocking him, and then loving one another the way we did that first time. Damn you. You have no idea how much I have tried to hate you. The hum begins. It fills her ears, the room, the house. It is a magnificent hum. It licks at her skin, warms it as it makes its way to her softening lips. It crackles and burns as it travels down her throat; it warms her belly.

HE WAS STANDING THERE, legs apart, so handsome and so male; his body angled slightly, one hand adjusting blue jeans, the other stroking hair like he was getting ready for her. He was elegant, graceful, and light-footed. He was talking to someone else. He turned to look and saw her. He touched the arm of the man he was speaking to, wrapped up the conversation. He headed Celia's way. His eyes wandered subtly across the litheness of her body as he walked toward her. The room came alive. He put out his hand and introduced himself as the primary organizer of the Conference.

I do not want to remember you, she thinks. I never wanted to remember this and now I will never be permitted to forget. You bastard. I feel myself opening up, skin screaming for your touch. She sinks into her bed and pleads for sanity.

The phone rings. What disaster now? Celia rolls off her bed.

"It's me again."

"Who's 'me'?" Her voice is curt.

"Come on. I called you not an hour ago. Your memory can't be that bad."

"What can I do for you?"

"I'd like to visit."

"On Saturday?" she asks.

He feigns a laugh.

Celia does not respond.

"Come on, Celia, please. I want to apologize in person."

Celia looks at the picture of her son on the wall. Their son.

"You come on by. Wear a nice black suit. I have something special to show you."

She commits herself to walking down a dark hallway with Jacob, even before she hears Alex's grateful goodbye. She hatches a terrible, awesome plan. She thinks it will mean brightening Alex's path when she first says it to herself; but now she realizes it will mean sharing her darkness with him. It would be cheating not to. He may be the only who can help her.

Celia bites into the cold northern end of her breath. She thinks it might be nice in a serves-him-right kind of way to introduce him to his son. She gets her things ready and trots over to Momma's house. It's high time she tell her family the truth. Before she leaves her house, Celia calls the old man from up Boston Bar way, who will do a proper burning for her boy now that his father is coming home.

HER FAMILY GATHERS AND listens to Celia's story. She leaves nothing out. She had slept with Alex. She had become pregnant. He did not come by. She phoned him twice on someone else's phone using her savings from berry picking to pay for the call.

"He promised to come, but he didn't. All those years my son wondered why his daddy didn't like him — his stepdaddy, really. In the beginning he was too young to know Melvin was not his daddy. In the end, I didn't have the courage to tell him. Melvin told him in a drunken fit one night. He told me in the last month he was alive that Melvin had told him about his father. Then he killed himself. I so wanted to kill Melvin. Now his daddy calls and wants to see me like nothing happened." She looks at Momma and says,

"That's when I stopped drawing, Momma. When Alex didn't come by. It had nothing to do with you."

She hands her mother the folder of her childhood paintings. Momma gasps. She picks up the folder, then drops it as if it is too heavy with paintings. She fondles the outside of the folder. Finally, she opens it. Inside is a record of Celia's view of many significant moments of this family's life. On one page, there are wisps of paint suspended, two human shapes wrapped around one another. In the background are fire colours. Only the face of the woman seems real. Momma sees herself. The faceless man is Ned — she can tell by the body. Their love is a rainbow of pastel against fire colours. She likes it. The next painting is of Stacey and Momma standing on the bridge, arms locked together. The sun lights up every detail of the shrubs, the aging wood of the bridge, and their skirts. The last picture is from the point of view of the window in Gramma's house. It's of Momma and Celia strolling toward it, arm in arm. Celia looks so lonely through Gramma's window.

Momma weeps. She sees what she has not been able to see until now. Celia has always yearned for her, for Stacey, for the family that had forsaken her.

"You were lonely, lonely for your momma. Sometimes a child lonely for her momma grows up too soon; she thinks giving her momma a gift like Jimmy will close the gap between them. It wasn't your fault, baby."

Celia does not want to think about this right now; the emotions circling her mother's words might deter her from carrying out the decision she made this morning. She is considering telling her this when Momma hands the pictures to Stacey, jumps up, and runs into the kitchen. She comes back with clear plastic shelving paper, sticky on one side, and a pair of scissors. Stacey runs for another pair as soon as she sees the first painting. They let Celia go on while they cut up the shelf paper and laminate the paintings so they will keep forever.

Celia has kept the grisly pictures of her dead son; she keeps them in a box and now she holds that box on her lap. She wants to weep, she says, not for the loss of her son, but because this man could take her, promise himself to her, and then just walk away, not even calling to see if there was a child.

Now he wants to look her up as if twenty years haven't elapsed.

Celia tells them she called an old man from up the river to do a burning for her boy. She means to burn these pictures, but not until his father has seen them. She passes the photo album around. They are full of police photos of Jimmy's suicide. Jimmy, blue and breathless, rope marks circling his neck, face twisted. A closeup of Jimmy's face as he hangs from the rope. Another, taken from a distance, the shed behind looking sombre, nearly evil. Jimmy looks like he is being swallowed by the shed instead of hanging from the rafters.

Underneath these photos are his baby pictures, toddler pictures, and school pictures, all happy and sweet. Under these pictures are pictures of Momma and Jim holding Jimmy. Beneath that is Ned, Jim, and Jimmy with Stacey holding Jacob. There are pictures of Celia's son waving to his aunt Stacey as Celia pushes him on the swings Ned had built in the yard for his grandsons. There are pictures of his first bike ride, his first baseball game, his first soccer game; pictures of him trying out his hand at pulling a dugout. Birthday party pictures. Momma weeps as she views the life of her grandson.

"You want to burn all this?" Ned asks, as if Celia is insane.

"Only after his daddy sees what he missed."

No one likes her plan. Momma thinks about the torment of Stella's daughter and how she and Celia had said that they thought they could kill the man who did this.

"Because you're angry?" Ned's question sounds like an accusation.

"What has anger got to do with this? This hungry boy, who this man refused to feed, hung himself. His father needs to feel that."

"But he didn't know Jimmy was born."

"Don't talk shit, Ned." Celia surprises herself. She has no idea she has so much steel inside, nor that it could enter her voice so easily. "Every man knows how babies are made. No woman would call a man and tell him she needed to see him sixty days after a romp unless there was a child. He had to know there was a child, and he didn't come. It's been twenty years. He can add. The child is grown up."

Momma caresses each picture as though she knows Celia will have her way and burn them. She passes them along to the other women, one at a time, and each woman does the same thing.

"It will be done. The old man agreed," Celia finishes. "You can participate or not, but it will be done."

"Does he know the story?" Momma whispers.

"I told him exactly what I just told you. He didn't ask the questions you are asking me now."

Jim slaps his knee and looks around, signalling the men to leave the room. They head outside and begin to light up when Jacob walks into the yard. He looks older, more grounded, and a couple shades darker. They invite him into their circle, telling him what they could remember of Celia's story, each filling in the other's blanks and then letting him know what she wanted them to do.

"Sounds good to me. I want to talk to that old man anyway."

Jim is stunned. Jacob always waited until everyone had pretty much made the decision for him before he committed himself to anything. He wonders if Jacob understands what he is saying yes to. They look at him. Jacob carries on. "You don't go visiting empty-handed, isn't that the rule? You don't go calling on a man who's building his house without bringing your tools. You said that more than once in my life, Grandpa. That means to me that everything is about fair exchange. He honoured her with an offer. She honoured his offer. Twenty years of pain and suffering is what has to be paid up. He owes her something. She just means to make him pay up."

"That's a chilly point of view. Did that mountain freeze your blood, boy?" Ned stomps out his cigarette.

"As a matter of fact she warmed me, Grandpa. She warmed me."

"These women seem to mean to do this." Steve lets the words go, careful not to be too arrogant. "Maybe we ought to be figuring out what our responsibility is here?"

"To figure out how we are to live with it," Ned answers. "But I don't believe we have ever done a burning to scorch the insides of a boy's father before." He spits. He does not like the direction this conversation is travelling in.

"I don't believe we ever had a father in this family who refused to face fatherhood before. For sure we never had a suicide because of it." Jacob drops this plain and simple, as if it's the morning news.

Ned shakes his head. What happened on that mountain? Ned takes a good look. Jacob looks settled in the manner of a man who has made a decision that has settled the direction his life will take. It makes Ned suspicious and just a bit nervous, because it includes burning pictures of his cousin. Jim shrugs when he sees that the die has been cast, and that all that is left is for him to get in line. He adds, "I think we ought to have both dads at the funeral then. The one Jimmy thought was his dad is just as responsible as the one who wouldn't claim him."

"How is our little girl?" Jacob asks.

"She's all right, but her mom shot herself. She's still in there. She'll live. Probably her arm will work fine too. Damn if this isn't the craziest time to live."

INSIDE JIM'S HOUSE, ESTHER tries to persuade Celia that *vengeance is mine, saith the Lord.*

"Esther, honey," Celia says in the warmest tones her voice can muster, "we love you. Your God knows my brother loves you, but I am not up to your Christ or your God today. I need to hear something old. I need to know that the way my poppa looks at my momma is still my birthright. I need to know that the men here are not going to get all twisted up into the hungry side of that old serpent and eat us alive, tormenting us every step of the way. I need to know that someplace deep inside them they really don't want to do this. The only way I can know that is to do this burning in this way."

LATE THAT NIGHT, STACEY repeats her sister's words to Steve. He believes he understands and says so to Stacey.

"Explain to me this vengeance of Celia's," she barks.

"It isn't about revenge. You can't love your son unless you know how to love a woman; unless you truly love a woman, you can't truly love your children. I think I know, because I was relieved when my daughter finally grew up — maybe too relieved. I didn't desert her, but I'm not sure my staying was much more than duty."

"Now I feel like I'm standing on the white side of the bridge," Stacey says.

"It's about consequences. Every society has rules; you break them, and there are consequences. My side of the bridge has one set of rules and the consequences match. This side has another. You can't have it both ways. If you aren't going to call the cops on whoever did that to that child and make him endure our consequences, white town consequences, then you have to live with yours. Celia means to bring the consequences to bear on the man who deserted her son. If she is wrong, then someone in this village better figure out what the old consequences would be and tell her that. Meantime, I was told that I had to come here and live your way. Ned told me that the responsibility of men is to figure out how to live with decisions made by women and that's what I am going to do."

"Well, I don't have to go along with it, unless Momma says I do."

"Up to you." Steve gathers her up in his arms to sleep.

NED, JACOB, AND JIM appear at Melvin's house early, dressed in their best black suits. Jim is the one who asks him to get dressed up in a suit and come to the cemetery. The looks of the men tell him they are not giving him any choice, so he finds his funeral clothes, gets dressed, and follows them out the door.

IN BOSTON BAR, AN old man makes ready to build a longhouse. He knows he has to do this burning. But this isn't the main reason he is heading for Celia's village. He heard the longhouse calling him. That longhouse wants to be built and he is curious to know how she will shape herself.

JACOB SITS IN THE car, singing songs Ned recognizes as belonging to Momma. When had she found the time to sing to this boy? Jim sings along. They sing every song Jacob and Jim know on the trip back home. Ned isn't up to singing with them at first, but the sound of the songs catches him and pretty soon they are all singing and tapping. As he sings, Ned begins to realize that he doesn't agree much with his wife or her family, but he goes along with her because he doesn't know any other way to be. She is his personal hurricane, stirring up the dust inside him, whirling him this way and that. The boys don't seem bothered by what they are doing; they seem to be a whole lot happier than he is.

What is it that has me twisted this way while these guys just shrug, roll up their sleeves, and get busy doing whatever's necessary to make it happen? He pulls into his wife's village and looks toward the mountains behind. They seem to be smiling at him. Above the peak closest to the village, an eagle glides. She's moulting. Damned if he doesn't see a feather drop. He stops the car just over the bridge and gets out. The feather continues drifting toward the ground. Ned watches it as it lands a few metres from his feet. He runs over to where it has landed and puts out his hand to his son. Jim scrambles for some tobacco. Ned picks up the feather. They all circle around it; even little Jimmy's stepfather is standing in the circle. Ned looks at him, half-surprised. Melvin gives him a half shrug.

THE WOMEN ARE GETTING ready for the burning, cooking food that the dead like to eat, when Jacob corners his gramma and tells her that he needs to talk to her. She follows him to the living room.

"I'm going to ask that old man to build a longhouse."

"You want to dance?"

"Mm-mm, I want to dance someone else in there too. I know who did this to her." He shifts his look to the little girl who seems to be waking up for longer periods now.

I am excited, probably too excited, but I can't help it. Rebuilding the longhouse means restoring the position of the serpent as protector.

"You want to make a winter dancer out of him?"

Jacob raises his eyebrows. "This can never happen here again, Gramma."

She smiles and touches his shoulder; she knows what he is up to and approves. These are my children: my Celia, my Jim, my Stacey, and my Jacob. She smiles. The tired melts as she dreams up an old song that she had heard Gramma Alice sing just once. It was so pretty.

Momma takes special care of the food. Stacey thinks she is stepping rather lightly for a woman about to fry a pair of men. Jacob looks different too. Jacob saw Steve step out of the shower and he watched him turn into Stacey's bedroom without saying a word to either her or to Steve. Steve's things were everywhere. Jacob saw his razors in the bathroom, his jacket hanging in the closet; he looked at it all and decided they had moved from keeping company to something more permanent. He took a moment to shake Steve's hand and say, "Welcome home, Pop," and laugh.

STACEY IS RESTING ON the porch, and Jacob comes out to join her. He fingers the little stone on her finger and raises his eyebrow.

"Too many changes for me to swim in," she tells him, and begins to explain.

He holds up his hand.

"Don't you hold up your hand when I am trying to tell you something." She grabs his hand as she speaks. "Jacob, do you worry who your daddy is the way Jimmy did? Funny, you can't feel the love for your son unless some man loves you like Steve does me, like I do him. I am not like Celia. I couldn't just go on without you."

"I worry about it constantly, Mom. I even saw him once. I wanted to walk up to him and say 'Hey, Pop,' but some lead got stuck in my butt and I just stood there gaping at him, looking and wishing. I'm not Jimmy, though. I never worried about anything quite like Jimmy did. I wanted a dad like everybody else had across the river. I didn't want to be some orphan like half the kids on this side. I can't have that right now. I'm too old, and he won't have me. Unlike Jimmy, I have to find some way to make my life fine with that piece of information." He grabs his mother's hand. "In the middle of all that craziness with that little girl, I told Uncle Jim I couldn't watch them work with her. He told me that he had climbed the mountains near the village and that I would be able to watch if I climbed them, so I did. Jimmy had the same piece of information, Mom. He chose not to. I don't know why he took his life. I do know I can't bring him back. I miss him more than I've ever missed anyone, but I can't just up and leave. I have to find some way to live with all this."

"Now you sound like your gramma."

"Who's talking about me?" Momma stands behind Stacey with Celia. "I swear I have seen more water leaking out of this family's eyes in the last week than all my days before." Momma takes off her apron and hands it to Stacey.

"Yes, but you know where your family is," Jim says from behind her.

"Amen," Esther says from behind him, completely missing the point. Jim turns, wraps his arms around her waist, and rocks her back and forth.

The serpent is hungry. He is bestial. He crawls around looking for food. He wants to be swallowed. He lurks in the shadows behind bushes wherever he hears the shrieking sound of rage or desperation. He knows there will be a meal. Once swallowed, he will consume courage; in the night, when the mouth of the beholder hangs slack and open expelling toxic breath, the serpent will escape with whatever he manages to eat. He is crazed. There is so much food here and it makes his blood pump into a frenzy to imagine the banquet that the doubt that corrodes the minds of the villagers presents.

"What? ... Are you sassing me? ... What'd you say? ... C'mere ..." *The belt rises along with the desperate screams of the children. The serpent has found a meal. The child whimpers from a closet in the dark and the serpent wraps himself round the child. The child is lonely when he feels the serpent; it feels like someone trying to comfort him. His mouth hangs open, letting whimpers drop. The serpent enters. Tomorrow the child will find a cat, tie a rope to its tail, and hang it over the bridge, smiling as the cat wriggles itself loose of its own tail and plunges to the icy raging water below. The serpent lies in the meadow, satisfied for a while. At night he will awaken and hunt another meal.*

The serpent fears boys with courage. He must swallow them before their first song. He must partner with them before their first dance. He remembers. He wants to find the boy with so much cokscheam. That boy who swallowed the soul of the mountain is his enemy. He hunts for a way to make him let go of that mountain, let go of Cheam. Blowing himself up and stretching himself out, he wraps himself around the house the boy lives in. If he can just find a way to open the door to their dreams, find someone sleeping, their jaw slack; he will loosen those tongues, get their words going in the wrong direction, and slip inside that boy before they burn that cedar and the boy will be all right.

XXI

CELIA TAKES GREAT CARE in preparing for the burning. She fusses over her hair, even paints her lips and nails. She fusses in lieu of waiting.

Alex arrives well before the appointed time. She invites him in with a wickedly nice hello. They exchange niceties. He did not have the good sense to stop bragging about what he had been up to all these years for even five minutes. Celia had left one photograph on the wall: Jimmy looking almost the same as his father, twenty years earlier. Alex is so full of himself that there is no room left in his mind to see that the picture bears so much resemblance to him. She wonders what in the world she had seen in this man. After a while, she asks him if he would like to take a walk. He says he would.

Celia likes the way the cottonwood line the road, making a pretty, sweet-smelling hallway. Their leafy green dresses fill the space between the trunks, making a nice wind break. Today the green leaves face their silver side up. It's going to rain, the leaves say. Celia secretly hopes that it will be a good rain — a violent rain. Booming thunder and lightning would be nice.

Alex walks with his hands in his pockets, prattling on about his life. Halfway to the graveyard, he tells her he wants to see her, and Celia says it would be all right — if he still felt that way at the end of the day. She cautions him not to be in too much of a hurry. He mistakes her meaning. A lone purple iris grows in the ditch on the side of the road. He pulls out a small pocket knife and clips it. Celia wants to laugh. How appropriate: he offers her a ditch-plucked flower and thinks it's romantic. He can put it on his son's grave. He hands it to her. She tells him to hang on to it. He is disconcerted, but he hangs on to it, twirling it as they stroll.

A single mass of grey-black cloud scoots in the direction of the sun. Alex checks his watch. Just like a white man, Celia thinks. Alex looks up and points at the cloud. "Just rain," Celia says and laughs. He says he's not dressed for it. She assures him he'll be all right. "No one drowns from rain," she teases. She feels his resistance. The hand holding the iris wants to be in his pocket. He plays with the coins in his pocket. He casts a sidelong glance at the coming storm and, just as they turn the corner to the graveyard, there's lightning across the sky. He sees the crowd of people standing under a canopy, by the grave.

"What's going on?" He stops dead in his tracks.

Celia slips her arm through his and grabs his wrist with her other hand. She holds the sensitive part of his wrist and urges him forward.

Alex wants to run now. He isn't as dense as Celia thought. Some feeling of empathy for Alex comes up in Celia, but she shoves it aside and tells her dead son, "This is for you, Jimmy." In her mind she says to Alex, "This is for your son," and to Jimmy, "Your daddy is here, here at last."

"I want you to meet someone."

The singing starts. Alex resists, but Celia has a good grip on him. The more he resists, the more she digs her fingers into his flesh.

"Hey, girl. You're hurting me."

"We'll all hurt you, if you don't keep moving."

"What's going on?"

"You'll see when we get there."

"I think you ought to let me walk on my own," he says. "Let go of my wrist."

"I don't think so."

He stops resisting and walks with Celia to the grave. In front of it, the men in black funeral suits circle him without saying any kind of hello. The old man starts to talk. The thunder booms out a halloo between the old man's words and the lightning flashes. Alex figures out what's going on. There are pictures of a boy surrounding the grave. Some are under glass in frames, others are loose. Alex's legs weaken. As each family member takes turns talking to Jimmy, unravelling the story of this fatherless boy, Alex realizes this Jimmy was his son. He leans on Celia, his head shifting from side to side.

As the last man in Celia's family finishes, a car pulls up and a group of people from Mission step out. In between a middle-aged couple is a young girl, also dressed in black.

The men look at Melvin.

"I'm not asking for forgiveness, Jimmy. I just want you to know I am so sorry."

He huffs, then carries on. "I couldn't let you know that through it all I did love you. You were hard not to love, but some crazy jealousy had a hold of me and pushed my love aside." He stops.

The young girl walks over to the photo stack and takes one. Everyone but Alex stares at her, but no one moves to stop her. Celia clenches her fists, not wanting to know that Jimmy had been loved by this girl, but it was obvious who she is. Alex falls to his knees and looks at the photos of the boy who so looked like him. It overwhelms him that he has a son he will never know. He tries to tell himself he that hadn't known about him — and then he remembers the phone calls, his suspicion and his conscious decision not to return the calls. He had known. He tries to assuage his guilt by saying he was young, but nothing worked. He falls to his knees, unable to satisfy himself with lies.

The family takes the photos to a fire not far from the gravesite — all but the one the young woman still holds. Celia stands in front of her with a menacing look on her face. The young woman clutches the photo, the middle-aged couple move closer to the girl, and Celia backs off. Alex lunges, attempting to stop them from throwing the photos into the fire. He screams, "WAIT!" He is too late; the photos curl at the edges as they are consumed by the fire. As the last photo burns, he utters a pathetic "No!" Celia walks away from him and the fire. She glares at the young woman and swings out, onto the road, back straight, legs strong, her teeth fixed in a wide smile.

The old man falls in step with Celia and the family follows him. The middle-aged couple join the procession, determined to be a part of what the family is doing to set things right. They leave Alex behind, alone in the rain by the grave of his son.

The storytellers are at it, pumping up the laughter about Jimmy's antics. The family is feeling freer than it has for a long time. Steve wraps his arms around Stacey's waist and whispers, "I think I was wrong about me. I can do this." She rocks him. "I think so too." She leans up to kiss him. The young woman with the photo walks toward Celia when the storytelling is in full voice. Jacob is going on about a memory of Jimmy; he ends it with a delicious laugh, which is interrupted by a knock at the door. Jacob, still laughing, opens the door.

Alex stands there, looking like a crazy man who after months of spending time in a trapper's cabin has lost his sense of reality. No one expected to see him again, least of all Jacob; seeing him now stops his laughter and he just stares at him. The old man walks to the door and ushers Alex in. He takes Alex's arm and whispers something to him that covers the crazed look on his face with one of desperation and fear. The young woman whispers in Celia's ear and she freezes. Alex starts to speak, takes a look at Celia, and decides against it. He fills himself a feast bowl and stands in the corner instead.

"There was this woman," the old man says. "Two men were fighting over her." He struggles a little with the English he is using to tell this story. "She kept telling them not to fight over her. It was up to her anyway which one she gave herself to. They carried on fighting. She went to the lake near where she lived. That time. Lake, humans, animals all spoke the same language. She told Lake how sad it made her feel to see these two boys fighting over her like that. Challenge them to a canoe race, Lake told her. She did. They did. Out in the middle of the lake they were. Lake swallowed them. 'What did you do that for?' she said. 'Now they are both dead.' Sometimes to move ahead, you have to go back to the beginning." The old man laughs. Momma, Celia, and Jacob join him, but the others just smile and wonder what the story was about. "Sounds funnier in the language," the old man says and laughs some more.

XXII

UNCLE JIM WAS RIGHT. Four days on that mountain make Jacob feel like he can do anything. This is what the old man's story is about, he thinks. He swallows the tea Momma gives him. The old man is at his elbow, gently urging him outside. Ned and Jim fall in behind. He hears Celia asking young Alice to read a poem as the door closes behind him.

> *I'm not sleeping, Momma*
> *And I can't quite seem to die yet*
> *I float trapped between the endless pages*
> *Of confusion my death seems to represent.*
> *This floating is light*
> *And strangely slow.*
> *Clouds appear and disappear.*

The sun rises and sets, but I'm not dead yet.
There is this wisp of thread
Tying me to the world below,
Each time I move in the direction of the other side
The thread tenses and I return to the sky above your head.
But my feet can never again touch the ground
I can see you hanging on to the other end, Momma
And I am asking you now to let me go.

The thread in Celia's hand feels sticky, spider-web sticky. She lets go, but it's stuck. The spider weaves its sticky web with slow deliberation; she means to entrap the small world in the design of her murderous home.

"I'm pregnant with your son's child," rings in her ear, over and over. Celia feels small. She had brought her son and his father together, thinking it would end her yearning. This was not what Jimmy wanted. He wanted to be let go. Now here he is, showing himself again in this woman. She had thought him too young to know who his father was when she refused to tell him, but he was never too young. Jimmy had beaten a retreat, exited, and freed himself of becoming a negligent father by hanging himself. Celia had held her son too close and too tight, strangling the life out of him. Momma is right. She is lonely. She had this child, hoping to close the door on her yearning for her momma. Alex had closed the door on his son, yearning for success. Her son had closed the door on his progeny, yearning for freedom from this terrible neglect. All this time she thought it was about Alex and how he had cast her adrift. The serpent was off the house front and each and every one of them had grabbed some terrible thread of bitterness from the restless head that stopped them from becoming who they needed to be. As long as each of them holds onto some bitter thread, they cannot really give life.

Momma watches Celia for a while. She moves over to her, wraps her arms around her, and whispers, "You take your time, child. You take as long as you want."

Celia has to let her mother go. She can't embrace her without letting that thread go, and yet she so needs her momma now. The thread of bitterness is in her hand, the young woman stands squarely in front of her, challenging and certain. Celia's eyes drop to the woman's belly. She opens her fist, holds up her arms. "Haitchka *siem*," the song rolls out.

"Jimmy. Say hello to the first Alice when you see her." The thread breaks.

JACOB MAKES HIS WAY to the front of the bar. He sits next to Amos who is already half lit up. The bartender asks him what his pleasure is. "Coffee. Yeah, give me a cup of that java." Amos turns to face him; "Wuss," he says. "Think so?" Jacob says and serves him up a winning smile. "Difference is, in a minute I can order a beer, drink it and leave, you can't." The smile makes Amos squirm. It makes him feel like Jacob sat next to him on purpose, that he wants something from him. He says as much. Jacob says he does want something. He wants to know why Amos keeps his hair long. Amos thinks this is an odd question and looks back at Jacob.

"I know why I grow mine." Jacob tells Amos the story of Cultus and asks Amos if he knows that story. He finishes his coffee and orders a beer. Amos does not feel like admitting he doesn't know the story. Jacob pulls his own hair. "My hair is about truth, about beginning and about never ending. What's yours about?"

"If that's the case, what are you doing in this bar?"

"Talking to you, Amos. I came here to tell you I am going to the longhouse. We are building a longhouse. First one erected in decades. Your hair will get in, but the dance will likely kill you." He points at the beer. Then he drains what is left of the beer he'd ordered.

"Fuck you."

"I don't think so." Jacob gives him another smile, tosses change at the counter and swings off the barstool. He walks out the door, smiling back at Amos. It unnerves Amos, who drinks more than he intended, much more, so much that the bartender has to throw him out.

ON HIS COT IN his rooming house, drunken pictures of other binges whirl. He leans over the side of his cot and vomits. Traces of his empty stomach lace the bed. Images of Jacob's smile, the little girl's whimpers, the crazy woman he beat half to death drive his sleep to distraction. He wakes up, cussing as he realizes he had slept in his vomit. He lies there, no sense in moving. He looks around. Besides this cot, there is nothing much in this room. He has an old shirt and a single pair of pants hanging over the back of the cot. Both reek from want of washing. No dresser, no sink, no stove, nothing to make this stinking place look like anything but what it is, a stinking hole.

Amos looks up at the ceiling. Jacob's face comes into view. He is telling that story about the lake that swallowed two men. "Lakes don't talk, fool." Amos says it out loud as if Jacob is standing in the room. He rolls over, to go back to sleep, and his face hits a streak of last night's sickness. "Shit." He wipes his cheek and gets off the bed. In the corner of the room is a rat. Well, that about sums it up. I'm sleeping in my own puke and my only company is a rat.

Amos grabs his hair. It's one massive rat's nest. This makes him laugh. It makes some kind of crazy sense. He reaches into his torn pocket and pulls out the rest of his money — two twenties. He can't remember the last time he had a good cup of coffee or decent company. They've all been rats of one stripe or another for years. Amos starts to realize how absurd this sounds. He's fifty-nine and he's been drunk and keeping company with filthy rats for years, decades.

What did that sonofabitch want? He fingers his money and decides to hit the Sally Ann for some new threads and maybe get himself a coffee. He cusses Jacob out as he does so. How did that sonofabitch know his name?

JACOB IS STANDING ACROSS the street from the rooming house. Amos can't believe his eyes. Great, now I got the fuckin' DTs. Jacob saunters over.

"Say, Amos. What you up to?" Just like they were old friends.

Amos fakes, "Not a lot, bro. Thought I would head to the Sally Ann for some new threads."

"I'm heading that way myself. Mind if I join you?"

Amos isn't sure if he minds. He hasn't been asked that for a long time. He tries to think, but the only words that keep popping up are that Jacob could drink a beer or a coffee and he couldn't. He thrusts his hands in his pockets to hide the shaking and decides to tell Jacob about the puke and the rat. It's a story. Indians can't seem to stop telling stories and they love hearing them. He puts it out there, like it's a damned happy piece of shit, only Jacob doesn't laugh.

At the Sally Ann, Jacob turns and gives Amos that smile again. "You know, my old auntie Celia says black slacks and a white shirt are sexy. Must be because she's nearly forty, huh?" Amos laughs. Jacob has him; it's just a matter of time. He watches Amos stew over the price of every shirt and jean he fingers, finally settling on a couple of shirts and two pairs of jeans. It comes in under ten dollars.

On the way out the door, Jacob says he's heading back home. "Got things to do and people to see."

Amos is about to invite him for a drink, but doesn't think he can handle another talking lake story, so he says, "Sure man. Later."

THERE IS A WOMAN in the bar. She looks like an old she-cat from any local rez; older maybe, but still looking good. She's sitting at the bar alone. In front of her is a book; she's scribbling on its blank pages. There's a cup of steaming coffee in front of her. Amos decides to begin with coffee and end with beer and this woman.

"Writing love letters?"

"Poems." Celia smiles. Amos thinks he recognizes the smile. Celia keeps him entertained all afternoon. She orders coffee and declines beer with "It's too early."

"Yeah," Amos agrees, stupidly, he thinks right after he's said it. Now he feels like he has to stick with it. The bartender is surprised. Amos is a regular here, but he rarely drinks coffee. Matter of fact, the bartender has never seen him drink coffee. Man will just about do anything to get laid, he thinks, and keeps the coffee coming. About four o'clock, Celia swings off her stool and says she has to go.

"You going to give me a phone number or something?" Amos asks. "Or you just going to eat and run?"

"That would be 'drink and run.'" She scribbles her number onto a page, tears it out of her book, and slides on out of the bar. Jacob is waiting for her. She smiles.

"He's ours."

The serpent is desperate. The air is cooling off. Fall is being pushed back by winter's tide. The snake can't slither so easily, but he is so hungry his eyes bulge. He must make one last foray out into the village to find something he can swallow, some piece of madness to satiate the cannibal spirit consuming him. His skin tightens. Each head threatens to eat the other, he is so hungry. All summer long he chased Jacob, but Jacob wouldn't budge. That mountain is inside him. He is too big. On the bridge, just before white town, a boy stands. He holds a rope. At the other end is a cat, his tail tied to the rope. The boy hangs it over the bridge. The cat screams, and his squirming loosens his tail from his body. He falls to the stone below. The little boy opens his mouth to laugh. The snake enters and fills himself up. The snake returns to his pit.

He can barely move. He hasn't much time before the air will be too cold for him to move.

The old bones have managed to sing the new ones into hopeful cooperation — the longhouse will see that they are buried properly in time. They begin to sing the old songs.

XXIII

THE OLD MAN HAD been here all summer and into late fall. He sat with these men, unloading the basket of knowledge he carried until he thought they were ready to build the longhouse. Jim and Jacob enter her first. Ned isn't ready. The old man doesn't think Ned will ever be ready. He doesn't mind. Ned remembers what the old man said and he will stay long enough to remind them of his words after he is gone. The boys listen to Ned. The old man feels Ned's inability to walk through the door of that house, and the melancholy coming over him, but he just can't muster the sincerity of those boys.

AMOS SAT WITH THE boys from late summer through the fall. The old man knew who he was. Jacob admitted it one day when the old man asked him. The old man was glad that Jacob told him the truth, the whole of it. When Jacob told him he meant to dance him — really dance him into his comeuppance, the old man shrugged. "It's your house," was all he said. "Does that one know?" And he nodded in Ned's direction. "No, but my auntie and my gramma do." He shrugged again. "It's your house."

THE OLD MAN TELLS the story of the last war the humans in this area had engaged themselves in. "That's when clubbing came into being," he said softly. "They got so bloodthirsty, they had started to war on one another. Pitch woman gave that boy a club, that one who couldn't kill. It was like the war drained all the blood lust out of that boy and he knew he had to end the war. The boy was so drained of any desire to kill that he could hardly get up the motivation to kill something to feed himself."

"Pretty bad, huh, Amos?"

Amos agrees.

The old man laughs. Amos has no idea what the old man is talking about; the old man knows this and finds it amusing.

That night, Celia and Jacob decide to club Amos's old friend — the other one.

Jacob smiles at his aunt. "We got them both. We're ready to dance."

ON HIS WAY TO the edge of the village, the old man signals Ned to join him. The other boys start to come. The old man shakes his head. At the ramparts to the bridge, the old man speaks: "Those fish are swimming upstream. Let's watch them for a bit." They are standing at the arc. The old man points to a dead fish on the bank, its mate atop the falls, waiting for him.

"They all jump. Not everyone makes it, but all those guys jump. The dead one there, he inspires the others to try. They won't necessarily make it either, and that woman there, she waits. Doesn't matter how long to her, she waits, she won't swallow anything else until he comes or she dies. It goes that way sometimes."

"I'm too old to leap."

"No," the old man said. "You're too old to make it, but you're young enough to remember. You remember what I said for them boys. We're both too old to do much besides remember, but it's enough. It has to be."

When the doors to the smokehouse open, a scraggly group of villagers not related to any of the family walk through too. This surprises Ned. Momma looks prettier than she had ever looked and that worries Ned some. It means she is keeping a secret that pleases her. He doesn't much care for the notion that she keeps secrets from him. Jimmy's baby is due any moment now and Momma can hardly wait. Martha's Stella has recovered. She lives at the old Snake's end, but now no one would recognize the place. She had a fair hand at a hammer and saw and had fixed the place up pretty good with what she scavenged from the other broken down homes in the village. She is going to college now and her little girl is at school.

Alex comes back to visit every now and then. He stands at his son's gravesite longer than is comfortable. Celia is kind to him now, but she will never again call up that old feeling. Ned told Alex about the opening of the longhouse, so he is here too. Celia and Jacob spend a lot of time together, talking about this thing called culture. It brings Momma into their private world. Ned listens, but something makes him want to wait and see.

Steve is excited. The last smokehouse had been burned in the twenties. He had listened to old Ella recount its story when he asked her how come they don't just cross the bridge and join the world of the others. They were free to do so, he ended his question. "You are not free, you are not free to cross the bridge and come into my smokehouse, so you are not in a position to determine how free I am," she had begun the story. She had ended it with, "You are never free if you have only one choice." Steve feels the freedom this house represents to him. Stacey wasn't sure about building a smokehouse, but she likes excitement coming from this man — it's infectious.

There are six men and two women about to be initiated into the house. The snake wakes up. He manages to slither to the outside of the house. Soon it will be too late. He slithers in different directions. His skin shed too soon. His eyes dried. His tongue is beginning to dry. He has to swallow Jacob or acquiesce to losing this battle before it's too late and winter freezes his blood. He tried. He slithers through the middle of the village, cold stilling his back. He weaves his way through, hunting for something.

There is something on the bridge. That solitary boy is dangling another small cat. The serpent circles the boy. The boy feels him and panics. The boy starts to pull the screaming cat up. His mouth hangs open; the snake leaps inside, squirming as he does so. The boy feels it, and jerks the rope taut. The jerk cuts the cat loose of his tail with a terrifying shriek. The cat splatters over the stones below, its blood thin as the water that sends the cat cascading over the rocks. It pales from red to pink and finally runs clear just as it runs under the bridge and out of the boy's sight.

The boy leans back, into the echo of the serpent's laugh as it goes off inside. He leans as far back as he dares over the rail. "More," the snake hisses. "More." The boy leans some more. The water pushes up on the cat's squirming body. It is still alive. It shrieks as the water's push ends its life. The boy leans one more time and falls over the side, crashing his head on the stone next to the cat. The serpent leaves the boy's body at the same time that the cat breathes its last.

In the meadow near the stone the restless head of the serpent smiles. There are plenty of victims where that one came from. He sleeps. Restless dreams he ate the sense of choice from everybody in the village. He dreams of snaking his way across thousands of miles of forest, field, and desert, swallowing this newly born joy before it grows too big for him to threaten. Gramma Alice watches him with a wicked grin. It won't be long, she smiles; you'll be back under the ground where you belong.

She floats back to the feast hall. Momma is stirring fish-head soup. She mutters the whole time she cooks. Stacey thinks she is getting old, talking to herself like that, until she listens to what her mother is saying. The words make some kind of crazy sense. She wants to know what Momma is doing, and then she remembers: she's talking to the food. Stacey's language is rusty, but she joins her mother's quiet muttering to each thing she cuts and cooks. Celia breaks into English, uttering whatever good thoughts and gratitude come to mind.

They dance in that house. They dance day and night. The sticks clack against hollow logs and the benches all day and night for four days running and then Jacob sings. After that comes Jim. But that one, the clubbed one, that one can't get the rhythm, can't seem to stop complaining; his voice won't come. The men keep him dancing. During one of the trips, when the three women bring food for the helpers and the villagers, Stacey thinks she might have seen Jacob taunting the clubbed one. The clubbed one looks so dry and so tired, she thinks; she steals a glance at Steve to see if he looks concerned. He is singing along with the rest of the people, engrossed in tapping his stick on the log. His eyes appear to be on the clubbed one, but no concern registers on his face. He must be all right, Stacey mutters to herself. Steve is a doctor; he will know when enough is enough.

Amos's feet touch the ground, each time his step is lighter than the one before, until he feels like he could fly, like he could dance forever. As he dances, the horror stories his body collected float in his belly and leave his body through his song. He sees them floating in front of him and he tries to make some sense of them. The first story to leave is of the flashlight coming into the dorms when he was away at that school; the lay brother carrying it, sidling up to his cot, taking his hand, leading him down that dark hallway to the basement, the basement where the lay brother tore at his child-hood sex. Amos wretches, then his step lightens as this old memory exits his body; it lightens his heart too. The hunger of never having enough to eat leaves next. His little skinny body that never seemed to grow relaxes. The bullying by the older boys leaves too, and then the stories of his bullying smaller boys and the mask of joy their whimpering brought leaves along with the shame he feels.

His feet tap out the rhythm of the exiting stories, the song comes and he feels like he can feel his grandma entering that house as his voice belts out the song. He is sweating — years of toxic memories sweating out through his pores, years of alcohol, putre-fied by never having given his poor body a break. He reeks of the deep toxicity of the memory of hate, of hurt. He dances faster and harder. Finally, here she is, his grandma; behind her are hundreds of people, some old, some young; they are floating in the rafters of the house. He raises his face to his long-gone family and deter-mines to dance himself into their arms, to dance his way to the other side. He begs them to take him home, away from his toxic insane life and he dances some more. Redemption comes as his ancestors reach for his dancing body. His spirit struggles to extri-cate itself from the living world.

Round about midnight silence falls. It drops like a lead weight. Momma wipes her hands and holds one up to stop the women from saying anything. She motions them to follow her; she picks her way with grace across little stones between the house and the kitchen, trying not to disturb their sleep. The moon is up, round and full. Celia wants to tell the other two that she can see the moon smiling, but some little voice whispers, "Not now. Not yet." She tosses her head and keeps walking. They arrive about the time Steve pronounces the clubbed one dead. It breaks the spell of death coming from the longhouse.

One of the Christians shrieks. Maybe it is Esther, no one sees who screamed. In any case, Esther is the one who runs to fetch the chief. He comes. By the time he arrives, the whole house is singing again. Everyone seems to recognize this one now. "He was the one. The one who lived with that Stella woman down near the old snake's? Stella looks particularly pretty tonight, doesn't she? Odd, isn't it?" They look at the man lying dead on the floor and shrug; a small clutch of young men stand about, chatting while the chief looks at him. They take him out of the smokehouse and over to the chief's house. He dials 911.

The baby is born at the moment Amos dies. The nurse who announces it to the girl is in awe. "Wendy," the nurse says to the baby's mother. "She is the most beautiful child I have ever seen." Wendy babbles thank you to the doctor, the anaesthetist, the nurse, and to Jimmy who gave her this beautiful girl. She weeps and laughs with joy as the nurse hands her her daughter.

XXIV

THE SERGEANT AT THE RCMP station has a bad feeling about this. One of the cops has heard a story about something like this happening before. "It was back in the thirties. An old woman and her four sons sang outside a little station in some isolated village in the interior. The cops inside died that night. Coroner couldn't figure out what killed them. Witchcraft." He lays down the letter opener he'd been toying with. "It took seven years, but they hung them boys. Had to try them in secret. Some old woman claiming she was their grandma kept singing outside the courthouse, so they moved the venue to a larger town without telling anyone where the trial was being held." The old cop is sure this is the work of the same kind of sorceress.

He sits behind his desk, staring at the case file. All this sorcery is legal; "culture," everyone calls it. But he knows better. They will have to dig for a charge now. Someone has to pay. This was murder.

They set the ears in the village that belong to them to listening, but their informants kept saying they never heard anything. Truth is no one wanted to mess with the old man or the smokehouse — they might get clubbed too. A year passes.

ANOTHER ONE DIES. "ISN'T that the friend of the one that used to be with that Stella woman?" the sergeant asks his men. The one who told the story of the sorceress nods. The village is being ripped in two now. The Christians dig in. The smokehouse people took to preaching about culture, about law and song and belief. The Christians took to bellowing about Satan and his work. The ones in between, the fragile and the meek, just took to drinking. Everyone ignored the serpent, who continued to crawl about swallowing this one and that, dividing the fractured village into more parts.

Witchcraft, mumbo jumbo, voodoo, cultism were being whispered throughout the town. White town was terrified at the power that house seemed to have. The RCMP kept up a dialogue with the judge. Someone had to be charged. But who and with what? It took some time before they could conjure up the right wording, but they finally settled on a charge of criminal negligence causing death. This implicated Steve, who was the only doctor present. Stacey worried about it, but held her tongue; she prayed that the racism inherent in the charge would be thorough. She prayed the RCMP would be satisfied with the incarceration of a few dancers. Steve did not hear the rumours flying about the village. He didn't understand why the RCMP were questioning each of those who had been to the dance. None of the dancers told the RCMP Steve was there; not even the Christian villagers felt compelled to say Steve was there. They had a doctor who lived in their village. They weren't about to give him up. Steve had no idea what the RCMP were up to. He knew enough to maintain his allegiance to the ceremony.

Shortly after the charge was laid against the old man and the head dancers, Steve drove into the RCMP parking lot.

"Sonofabitch," the old RCMP sergeant muttered after Steve left. "That crazy Doc Williams is going to testify on behalf of the longhouse." His desk sergeant urged him to dig up some anthropology evidence against the longhouse.

The deaths of the two men had been good for the village, Celia believes. It signified the birth of their beautiful smokehouse and its feasting ways, as well as the end of their sickness. Momma's step lightened and the lines on her face fell away. She looked like she was a young woman always getting ready to go somewhere. Babies were named in that smokehouse, marriages happened in there. How could anyone think this was wrong?

STACEY'S SCHOOL OPENED ON the day they came for Ned, Jacob, Jim, and the old man. The old man said if they intended to lock him up, he was leaving. The cops took his belt and searched for something the old man might use to kill himself. The old man just smiled and said goodbye as they loaded him into the car. He was dead on arrival. Just before he went, he turned to Jim and Jacob and grabbed hold of one of each of their legs and smiled. The old man was out of his cuffs.

The town came alive with the fear of sorcery and witchcraft. No one said it, but it could be heard in the hushed terror of the tone used when they said "criminal negligence causing death." This dancing and singing stuff was a way to kill people. "Bad medicine" was being whispered everywhere through the village and the town. "That hall, that one, is where they killed those boys," they warned their children. The prosecutor swore Dr. Williams in and Steve became the defence's expert witness. He testified on the medical value of the dance. It sobered people up, healed them in a way Western medicine could not. The clubbing was symbolic, the dancers could stop anytime, no one was forced to dance. They all went through the same rigours. They were assigned caretakers. There was no proof of any negligence of any sort. "Just the opposite," the judge said, "the dance seems to help more than it hurts. It was clear, however, that these two men were in no shape for the rigours of the dance. The head men and the dancers had no way of knowing that. I am dismissing the charges, contingent upon insisting that all initiates be given a physical prior to initiation into the longhouse."

Steve's practice dwindled as the town people stopped seeing him. He represented a betrayal they could not name. He reduced his hours to part-time, but eventually his patients returned, assured that he had testified as a white professional and not as someone who believed in sorcery. The talk inside the family changed in that smokehouse. The women from the healing circle joined the longhouse and Momma heard stories she never wanted to hear. Terrible things happened to her granddaughters and her grandsons. Judy and Rena seemed to be good at getting these stories out in the open, getting the girls and boys past their nightmare existence.

Momma has been swimming in a pool of negligence that began to fill up in the time of the epidemic. Each swab of a patient was followed by a "What's the use, it is never going to end." Once she said it out loud, while trying to save Ella. "Be careful what you pray for," old Ella had managed to say before a coughing fit wracked her thin, frail body. This apathy, this red-boned, stone-hard defeat settled in, despite the warning. It raked her soul. When the raking scraped away her laughter, her enthusiasm, and her appreciation for her life such as it was, she took to talking to Dominic at night while Ned slept well. The death of Amos seems to have lightened her load and enlivened her sense of caring. Her fussiness returned. Her laughter filled the house. She teased her daughters into hope and thinking of the future. Ned's footsteps altered. He shuffled after that bout of flu. He spent more time listening to the talk of children, but it tired him some to wake up remembering the stories the next day.

The laughter of his wife brings back his old enthusiasm. He picks up the old language, listens to the old man giving him instructions about the longhouse and by some miracle he remembers just about everything the old man told him. Laughter sings out in the valley and the pall of fatigue lifts. Youth stay in school, play with computers, and song fills the winter air.

JACOB HAD SPENT EVERY spare moment with that old man from Boston Bar. Stacey knows he is slipping away on her. She supported the longhouse reconstruction with a fairly big dose of doubt, and now she watches as her son becomes more and more devoted to "our ways," as he calls them. She wonders what is to become of him. To her surprise, he enrolls in college. How does all this longhouse stuff fit into his desire to be Western educated? Her husband seems to have an explanation for it. "I'm a doctor, we are persuaded that nothing outside of science exists, but belief is not about science, provability, logic, or reasonability. It is belief. Jacob believes in the longhouse, others are Christian — you just may be an agnostic." Stacey knows it's the best she'll get, so she lets it go.

One night, Momma told the old man from Boston Bar that she did not want Ned to beat her to the other side. "I'm just not built the way Stacey and Celia are, I can't find peace without a man."

"Okay," he said.

THE YOUNG WOMAN NAMES her child Celia, after Jimmy's mom. Every other weekend, she brings Celia to see her gramma. She had liked the sound of Celia's name whenever Jimmy spoke of her. "When can I meet her?" she'd asked one night.

"My momma is next to impossible to know," he answered flatly. "She is barely there, Wendy." He hesitated. "Celia sees things, she wanders about lost in her own world most of the time."

Celia was watching her five-year-old grandchild the day Momma got sick.

Ned tended her as he would a child. She got no better. Finally, Steve said it was time. She was hospitalized. They took her to the hospital, even though the women all knew it would do no good. Momma acquiesced; she knew there were just a few feet left to her run at this world. When the smokehouse closed for the winter, Steve announced that Momma's life was coming to her end, those who knew and loved her had but a few days to make their peace with her.

Two at a time they went. Jacob and Jim were the last to visit. She visited with them and gave them the last bit of love and light left inside her. She smiled when she said that odd thing to Jacob, Jim recounted later to his sister Celia as he smoked with her on the porch. "I know what you did to Amos, Jacob." Momma paused. Jacob flushed. She took as deep a breath as she could and said, "Good for you, son." She closed her eyelids so slow it hurt to watch.

Celia went inside to peel potatoes for the feast that would follow the funeral after Jim told her about Momma's last moments. Her grandchild was outside digging up her garden with a wooden spoon. Every now and then Celia looked up to enjoy the sight of her. She didn't want to think about what Jim had just told her. She wanted to send her mother off in grand style, participate in the raising of her granddaughter and look far into the future, determined to re-quilt her life with the odd bits of scrap cloth left over from the past that Momma had stitched to their new context. The longhouse had grounded her and the old man had taught her how to deal with her peculiar visions. She would miss Momma, but she was happier than she had ever been; she didn't want to disturb this deep underlying joy inside her. Jim had threatened to disturb what little peace there was to be had in this life. He could be such a pain in the ass, she thought, nodding with every stroke of the paring knife. The peels fell away; the sweet dirt scent from the skin rose with each stroke and made her want to plant some in the spring.

Half a dozen potatoes sat in the pot of cold water when Celia suddenly saw what Jacob had done. "I'll bet she smiled."

"At what?" Stacey asked. Celia was sorry that she had spoken out loud; now she had to recount the story. Stacey thought they should tell someone.

"Who?" Celia asked, the peels falling flatly into the garbage bin. She stooped to pull them out. "If I save these, maybe some of them will germinate. If they don't, they'll still be good compost."

"Celia. What are you talking about? I said, 'We have to tell someone.' We can't just let this sit, squatted inside the fold of family, a dirty little secret."

"Tell them what?" She bagged the peelings and set them aside. "My garden, I am going to plant a garden."

"Stay focused, Celia. What Jacob did. You sound as though this is okay."

"Nothing just now is okay, Stacey. Not the old dirt roads, the old snake violating our children, the war he fought uselessly, the epidemic that slaughtered our opportunity to just be, the vote we traded for houses, the residential schools, and not the silence we are drowning in, giving our children to foreigners because we haven't got the wherewithal to care, not even for one more minute. What's okay? The school you could not teach at, Momma dying before her time, my son killing himself before he aged enough to know that this too shall pass, me burning his history before I realized how much I needed those pictures to remind me I had a son? What exactly is okay, Stacey? Just exactly what about our life is okay?"

"But this …" Stacey couldn't finish. Some part of her knew that Celia was right — nothing was okay, but maybe it would be.

"Stacey. We have no idea what Jacob did, if he did anything. We have a simple line from Momma, nothing more. In any case, this is not about Jacob, it is about you focusing on this small moment because it is manageable and everything else is not. Suicide, early death, fatigue, all our defeats, and the epidemics are all part of the same crazy journey and they are too big, too horrific for us to deal with. None of us had any choice in travelling on this road and none of it could ever be managed by us. This thing, this small moment of Jacob's, is a sliver of terror in a long list of terrors. It's small enough to handle, and so you pick it up and suggest that we punish him for it, and really it is just one small stone in a road full of jagged rocks. We have to do something about all this, but spreading rumours about Jacob or making him pay for this journey isn't it."

"I don't have a clue who you are, or what you're about, Celia." Stacey crossed her arms and stared out the window.

Outside, men were raking the stones and preparing for the asphalt truck behind them. The road was going to be paved. No more dust. No more cars with busted springs and no more scrabbling up the mountain scraping up bits of roots, herbs or berries, hoping they would last the winter. The vice was off. Some crazy elastic band had snapped. The whip from the rubber had lashed them all. They were scarred. Half the village ran amok, blind with pain; the other half struggled to rebuild their lives and their sense of themselves without really seeing the journey that had carried them here to this moment of truth about Jacob and the old snake.

Jim was out there in the yard with his too many children putting up a swing set he'd purchased at Kmart. His eldest daughters were each holding up the upside down Vs that formed each side of the swing, while Jim set the horizontal beam that would join the Vs together. He was the one who had told Celia the story about Momma and Jacob. It sat there with him for the thirty seconds it took him to part with it and then he just let it go, and now Celia was peeling potatoes humming that Christian song Momma loved, "Amazing Grace." Ned was sitting in the rocking chair on the porch, smoking a cigarette and smiling at the little one he had on his lap, not bothering to help his son.

"WE'RE ALL MAD," STACEY said. "We're insane." She slapped the pot full of peeled potatoes onto the stove. "You drop some news that maybe Jacob might have done something to cause those men's deaths and in between talking about murder and suicide you tell me you will save the potato peels for a garden. You're nuts, you are plain crazy, and your brother is too. He tells you this story one minute and the next he is putting up a swing he bought at Kmart."

Celia finished the line of the song that spoke of how we have more trials and fewer days, and then she stopped peeling. Stacey turned her back to Celia and stared out into the yard where Celia's grandchild sang and dug holes in the dirt. She shook her head back and forth. Celia was slightly taller than Stacey. Both faces were cut from the same cloth. But for the ten years between them, they looked nearly identical.

"I don't want to tell you what to do, Stacey, but seems to me, figuring out who we are is our only obligation to those kids out there."

THE ASPHALT TRUCK'S GEARS shifted, the sound of the engine deepened, and the truck rolled onto the flat gravel surface. Under the rollers a black flat ribbon of road appeared like magic. The driver waved to the men and children in the yard. Jacob was driving the truck; he was smiling that broad-toothed grin. His teeth were bright white and even, like his grandma's. He didn't behave like anything was amiss; in fact, Stacey had never seen him quite this happy. She wondered what they had done with people like the old snake and Amos before and asked Celia if that old man had told her.

"Same thing Jacob did." The water in the pot of potatoes began to boil.

Stacey did not like the answer, but knew she would have to live with it. She felt like Steve, so foreign.

"Damn, if your boy isn't just handsome," Celia finally said and she slipped her arm about her sister's waist.

"Damn." Stacey clutched her sister's folded arms close to her body. "I should never have come back. Maybe now I would be living in Chilliwack, a doctor's wife who had no idea what was going on this dusty little village."

"Stacey. What do we really have to tell? Momma was all hyped up on morphine, seeing angels, seeing Great Grandma Alice, Dominic, and failing to recognize any of us half the time. What is there to tell but the drug-induced hallucinations of an old woman? What is the matter with you?" Celia felt compelled to blindfold her sister. Everything she said was true. Momma was out of her mind at the end, babbling to her son as though he were her first husband, whispering "my Jim" to Ned as though they had never had a life together, speaking the language intermittently. At the same time, Celia was desperate to quiet Stacey's judgment of her nephew; after all, implicating Jacob would uncover her complicity. "Do you really think Jacob could set about to murder Amos or anyone else? Do you really think that sweet old man would have let him?" What is wrong with me, I am lying to the only relative that is close to me?

Nothing. Absolutely nothing.

I am a responsible grandmother even if I wasn't much of a responsive mother. I plan to carry on being one; despite everything there is nothing wrong with me, or anyone else in this family. There never was.

Madeline sauntered in, eyes red and puffy, hips still swivelling as she walked. She had a big brown bag in her arms. "Fruit." She put the bag on the counter. Celia grabbed a metal spoon from the drawer and stared at it for a moment. "What the hell?" she said. "Come on, Madeline, we are going to plant potato peels outside."

"Don't plant too many in a pile," Madeline instructed as the three women left. "Not too deep, either. Better space them a foot and a half apart."

"Where did you learn so much about planting potatoes?"

"You have never been to my house," Madeline said. "Had a garden for years." Both sisters nodded. It was true; they had no idea what Madeline did in her home, the women all met at Momma's and they rarely went to each other's homes. They dug a dozen holes, loosened the dirt in their hands, and buried the peels. Stacey wasn't enjoying herself a bit until the kids showed up asking what they were doing. "Starting a garden, sugar," Madeline answered as if it was her idea.

"How did you learn about planting before you grew your own garden?" Stacey asked, fighting for some kind of mundane civility that would push back the terrible truth about Jacob that Celia had revealed.

"First farmer in La Pas was a Saulteaux-Ojibwa woman back in 1756. White men bumped her granddaughter out of the commercial end of farming, but none of her descendants ever gave it up except me — until a few years ago, after the longhouse was built." She laughed. They stared at the little mounds they'd made, as though expecting them to sprout any minute, hands on spread middle-aged hips, bellies slightly protruding, and shoulders beginning to round. Jacob swung into the yard, jacket over one shoulder, slightly dirty, hair a little dishevelled, and behind him was Celia's mom waving at them. He picked Celia up, swung her about like an airplane. Her laughter broke the reverie over the garden they had begun. Stacey turned to look at him. Celia was right, there was nothing in this young man of hers that was either menacing or evil and she let go of Momma's last words.

That night, as Ned spoke, Judy, Rena, Stacey, and Celia flanked his sides. All four of them were afraid. With Momma and the old man gone and Ned barely standing, they were the elders here. They had begun grandmotherhood so young and so tragically and they knew so little. Now they were being forced to become elders too soon. They gathered the bits and scraps of their knowledge together in their minds.

They were aware it was all just scattered scraps, like the little bits of cloth left over after Momma made a blanket. They had choices Momma never had. Scraps made good blankets, Celia decided. Scraps for blankets and they were all Momma had and she had managed to patch together a pretty good life in the end. They had a choice: join the Christians or be who they were and always should be. Under the hum of an old song, Celia could hear Momma say there was always more than one choice.

NED LAY IN HIS bed many years later, when the sun shone fireball red, dew glistening on the grass and the light of the sun painting the world with a faint ashbury hue. Madeline, Rena, Judy, Stacey, and Celia were already outside hoeing the sprouted potatoes and digging the weeds from carrots, cabbage, lettuce, and camas. They had decided to plant camas root. Ned had helped them find it, transplant it; he had shown them how to tend it. None of them remembered eating it. It was an old plant, but they decided to try it out, see if they liked it. The children were still sleeping. Wendy was inside whipping up a breakfast of oatmeal and eggs and bacon. She went to bring Ned his coffee. He refused to get up. Wendy mumbled okay. She stood on the porch and looked at the women and hesitated. Celia saw her. "Damn," she cussed and the others looked up. They dropped their hoes and shovels and headed toward Wendy. "He won't get up." Her eyes welled up, but the tears did not swell enough for her to let them go.

"Damn," they all murmured softly and went into the house.

"Madeline, call Steve." Stacey and Celia entered his room. "Ned. What's wrong?" Stacey sucked her breath in. Celia touched his forehead. He barely moved; his body was cold. "We are taking you to the hospital. Help me, Stacey."

"No," Ned answered flatly. "Just bring Steve." The sun was peeking through the curtains Momma had sewn up the day Ned arrived. The children were stirring and Ned could hear Wendy and

Madeline tending to them. He could see out on the mountains that cradled the valley like a bowl and Ned thought he caught a faint glimpse of his grandson, Jim, perched on a log next to his beloved wife and he sighed. Steve's feet hit the porch running but it was already too late.

He had given them all enough time to grieve Momma's departure and begin to live again. He was tired and wanted to leave. They knew it, they had felt it, but they didn't want it. Madeline had called Martha, Alice, Rena, and Judy right after she called Steve. They arrived within seconds of Steve. Steve had called Jim. Jim collected Jacob and they appeared just as the women looked at one another in shock. "He was fine just last night," Stacey muttered.

"Damn," Celia said out loud. "You're leaving us with one hell of a mountain to climb."

"Oh, I think Raphen had a hand in it, if Ella's right about him bringing me and all the others here," Judy said aloud.

"Her," Rena corrected Judy.

"Her?" Judy looked at Rena, confused.

"Raven is a she." Rena stifled a laugh.

"I am never going to get it right."

I am done here. This is all I committed to tell. You know what to do with the story now. I skitter up the hill, away from the humans, and under the moon's light I lie down to sleep.

ACKNOWLEDGEMENTS

I wish to thank Peter Jones for the many insightful discussions that made the writing of this work bearable and possible, Tania Carter for her literary and oratorical insights, Smaro Kamboureli for reading it and discussing it with me, and Gerry Ambers, traditional healer and counselor, for her reading and cultural response.

ABOUT THE AUTHOR

Lee Maracle is a member of the Sto:lo nation. She was born in Vancouver and grew up on the North Shore. She is the author of the critically acclaimed novels *Ravensong* and *Daughters Are Forever.* Her novel for young adults, *Will's Garden,* was well-received and is taught in schools. She has also published one book of poetry, *Bent Box,* and three works of creative non-fiction, including *I Am Woman.* She is the co-editor of a number of anthologies, including the award-winning anthology *My Home As I Remember,* and *Telling It: Women and Language Across Cultures.* Her work has been published in anthologies and scholarly journals worldwide. The mother of four and grandmother of seven, Maracle is currently an instructor at the University of Toronto, the Traditional Teacher for First Nations House, and an instructor with the Centre for Indigenous Theatre and the S.A.G.E. (Support for Aboriginal Graduate Education). She is also a writing instructor at the Banff Centre for the Arts.

In 2009, Maracle received an Honorary Doctor of Letters from St. Thomas University. Maracle recently received the Queen's Diamond Jubilee Medal for her work promoting writing among Aboriginal youth, and was the winner of the Ontario Premier's Award for Excellence in the Arts.

Maracle has served as Distinguished Visiting Scholar at the University of Toronto, University of Waterloo, and the University of Western Washington.

This book was designed using Sabon Text, which was
originally designed by Jan Tschichold in 1964.
The design roots of this typeface go back as far as 1592
and because of its history with Jakob Sabon — whom
the typeface is named for — it is often referred to
as a graceful and legible variation of Garamond.